The Judgement

A Breakbattle Academy Novel

Ruby Vincent

Published by Ruby Vincent, 2020.

Prologue

I burst through the Elite door. "Derek! Derek, please! I can explain!"

Derek's door was closed. He made it inside.

I stumbled to it as a door across from me opened.

"Isn't this lucky?"

I spun around. Cameron smiled at me as he, Heath, Santiago, and the other Elite boys poured out of the room.

"Nice of you to come to us."

I knew what was coming even before the final boy walked out of the room carrying a black cloth and sack.

"Derek! Hel—"

He shoved the cloth in my mouth. Dozens of hands grabbed me and held me still as my muffled cries reached no one. The last thing I saw before the cloth went over my head was Cameron's smile.

Chapter One

I strained against my bindings, pulling and yanking until my fingers and toes went numb. They didn't budge. Whoever bound me did a great job.

I screamed and wailed through my gag, but no sounds met my ears. I didn't hear the taunting of my captors, or the hum of a busy school. I didn't hear anyone. Did that mean no one could hear me?

I shook my head violently, attempting to dislodge the sack. Tears dripped down my face as panic overwhelmed me. Why had they taken me? What were they going to do?

Calm down, Zela. A rational voice sought me through the chaos. *Calm down and think. Figure out where you are. They didn't carry you far. Where could you be?*

It took a minute for the thoughts to penetrate far enough for me to move. I scooted forward and my knees bumped into something cool. It had the same feel as the smooth surface beneath me.

I'm in a bathtub, I thought.

Of course, I was. That made sense. They took me into one of their bedrooms and stashed me in the bathroom. But why? What were they waiting for? What would they do when the time arrived?

I rocked back and fell against the back of the tub. There was no point shouting and pulling my limbs out of joint when the only ones who might hear me were people that would never help. I needed to conserve my strength for when they set me free.

If they set me free...

I beat back against the thought as a thread of fear wrapped around my spine. I couldn't think like that. If they wanted to hurt me or worse, they would have done it already. Eventually, they would have to let me go and I'd make every last one of them pay for this.

I don't know how much time passed as I sat in my dark, porcelain prison. At one point, the door opened and I sprang up.

"Hey," I said through my gag. "Let me out! Untie me!"

The sound of a zipper was my reply. A few seconds later, the noise of running water filled the room.

No, not water.

The person finished up their whizz without a care to me being in the room. They must have heard me calling them but they didn't give a care to that either. The pissing stopped and then the toilet flushed. I heard the door open and the murmur of voices reached my ears.

They were out there—talking, planning, waiting.

Hours must have passed as I sat alone in that bathroom. The screams and struggling stopped, but the tears didn't. How had things gone so wrong?

One minute I was celebrating with my friends and then the next Derek was confessing his love for me. I never wanted the truth to come out like this. That first day in the cafeteria, I sat at his table intending to tell him everything.

He had been my obsession since I typed Jonathan Grayson in the search engine and discovered he was the owner of the major film studio that produced the majority of Naomi Grayson movies. My father was alive. He was only an hour away from me, and he had a son. My brother.

I didn't lie and trick my way into Breakbattle Academy because I wanted to trick Derek too. I would have told him, but he chased me away. He labeled me another predatory, stalking fan and if I said I was his sister, he probably would have added insane to the list.

Jordan and I agreed the best thing to do from that point was to make him trust me. See me as a friend and know that I wanted nothing more from him.

Instead, I made him fall in love with me.

My head fell back against the tiled wall. My stomach twisted and writhed as that sank in.

I tried to get closer to my brother and he fell in love with me. He kissed me. How in the fucking hell did that happen? More importantly, how do we come back from this?

"—late enough."

I stiffened as a voice spoke clearly on the other side of the door.

"We'll bring Zeke there now." The door creaked open. "No one will see."

I didn't bother to scream as hands lifted me under the shoulders. Somewhere among my worries over Derek, I realized what their plan was. I knew where they were going to take me.

Warm, fresh air touched my skin as I was carried outside. The sun did not seek me through the threads of the sack. Night had fallen, giving cover to their kidnapping.

It was a near silent trek across the grounds. The only things I could hear were the stomps of their shoes and the snap of twigs.

After a while, my captors stopped and set me on the ground. I wasn't surprised to see the boulder when the sack was ripped off my head. Nor was I shocked to see Cameron sitting upon it.

"Hello again, Zeke." He put two fingers to his head and saluted. "Sorry about the wait."

The other Elite boys moved away from me. They fanned out before Cameron, staring me down in stiff silence. I didn't care about them. My eyes were locked on Cameron and that loathsome smile.

"We planned on taking you from your bed like last time," he continued conversationally. "But Santi pointed out that you're rarely in your own bed these days. We were coming up with something else when you barreled into our hallway, always where you don't belong. Couldn't pass up that chance."

I said nothing. I couldn't. They hadn't unbound or ungagged me. All I could do was kneel there.

"You know why you're here, of course," he continued. "You and I have a problem. We both know the chances that Fields beat you on the academic tests are slim. The guy is smart, but he was never as smart as you. That's why I wanted you in the first place. You're going to become Elite."

Cameron looked so regal perched on his makeshift throne. He knew he was destined to lead and everyone else was meant to follow. As if to prove it, he snapped his fingers and Heath sprang forward. The boy removed my gag and tossed it aside in one smooth move.

It took me no time to find my voice. "I will be Elite," I rasped. My throat was severely raw. My mouth dry. It made my speech sound sinister in strange contrast to the pleasant tone of Cameron. "Nothing you do to me here will stop that."

He laughed. "Do to you? What exactly do you think we're going to do?"

I looked at the boys standing ready and willing to do his bidding. "You can beat me, but I survived the first one and the second won't stop me."

I stiffened as he laughed louder. "No one is going to beat you, dumbass. With that stupid disguise of yours, people would think it was some kind of hate crime. I don't need the heat and the school doesn't need that kind of attention."

I blinked, genuinely surprised. "If you're not threatening me, what am I doing here?"

"It's simple," he stated. "We're making you an offer—the same offer."

My jaw slackened as I realized what that meant. "You can't be serious?" I whispered.

"I am serious." Cameron's grin melted away. "We've gone way off track and I finally understand why. Everything went wrong at orientation and it set off a chain of events that made you believe the Network is your enemy. It's not.

"You think you have to go on this crusade to bring us down and destroy our plans for the expansion, but you don't. We're not a threat to anyone and we're not a threat to you."

I gaped at him. "Are you kidding me? You tried to get me expelled! You framed me and turned my friends against me!"

Cameron's expression didn't twitch. "Exactly, *I* did. I was pissed and I used my authority to act against you. I had permission to teach you a lesson, but not to take it as far as I did. I lost my position because of it. Now that I've got it back, I'm expected to behave," he said. "The Network isn't interested in hurting anyone or you. To prove it, we're offering what should have been yours all along. A place with us. What do you say?"

I looked him straight in the eyes. "No."

If I thought he'd snarl or yell at my rejection, I was disappointed. "Why not?" he asked calmly.

"How can you ask me that? Do you think I'm stupid? I overheard you talking to your father about the millions he'd make if this twisted system spread to other schools. I won't have any part of that."

He shook his head. "You see? You're just proving how ignorant you are. You don't understand what we're trying to do, but you're deciding it's bad because I'm involved."

"No," I replied. "I'm deciding it's bad because Dominick Dupre is involved. I've heard all about your dad, Cameron. Plus, I've had the displeasure of meeting him. I'm not so *ignorant* that I can't see he's not a good guy."

Now, his expression changed. Anger flashed across his face, twisting his lips. "Careful."

"Why? Did I strike a nerve?"

Cameron got to his feet, towering even higher over me. "You're repeating bullshit you've heard from Moon and Derek no doubt, but tell me this. If my dad is so shady, why are both Gray Studios and Shea Industries clients of Dupre Financial Holdings? They've all got something to say about my dad until they want him to make them money. They're a bunch of fucking hypocrites!" he spat. "They don't like him because he came up from nothing. Dragged himself off the streets, became a self-made man, and built a home among the Evergreen old money.

"Don't believe the stuff they've said about him. They have their own reasons for being uptight, bitter fucks." He pointed at me. "Just like you shouldn't believe the expansion or Network is bad. Ask yourself this: if what we're doing is wrong, why are your boyfriends a part of it?"

I pressed my lips together, breathing roughly through my nose. Cameron used my silence as a cue to go on.

"Why do the people that join, stay and go on to recruit more members? Do you think we're some worldwide evil organization plotting to take over the world one high school boy at a time?" He lifted his hands. "Or maybe we're exactly what I told you that night years ago. We find the excellent among the shit and we make sure they get where they were meant to go. We'll make sure Landon, Michael, Cole... and you get where you were meant to go."

Cameron cocked his head. "Why would you want to be responsible for destroying that and getting in the way of your friends' dreams? Do you think they'll thank you for it?"

My hands shook in their bindings. Cameron was good. He was playing my emotions like a harp, plucking all the right strings.

"They don't need the Network to achieve their dreams," I said.

"Is that what you're telling yourself to justify your revenge plot?"

Cameron snapped his fingers again. Heath and Santiago peeled themselves out of the pack and reached for me. The two untied my hands and legs and put me on my feet. I stumbled and Santiago caught me. His hands were surprisingly gentle as he put me upright.

The two of them moved to my back as Cameron climbed off the boulder. I tensed as he closed the distance between us.

"Look, it's this simple. The Network wants to help the Coles and Michaels of the world. The more students they can reach, the better they can do that. If the leaders want to get paid on the way, why shouldn't they? The money won't come from the members and it won't involve anything illegal. There is no reason for you to fight against us, so you might as well join us. What do you say?'"

"You must not have heard me the first time," I stated. "I'm not joining you."

He heaved a sigh like I was being unnecessarily difficult. "I told them you would say that. I guess it's time for plan B."

I took a step back and bumped into a hard wall of muscle. Spinning around, I looked up into the hard eyes of Santiago and Heath. I didn't see the need to test them. They weren't going to let me go until Cameron was done with me.

"What does plan B mean?" I asked without looking away from Santiago.

"I told you that I finally figured out what went wrong at orientation," he replied. "Derek."

A hand gripped my shoulder and turned me around. Cameron's eyes swept over my face. "That's what all of this has been about. You're not a boy. You're a girl pretending to be a boy but the only thing you get out of it is going to school on this campus. I couldn't figure out why that mattered. The only difference between our side and theirs is this is where the Network recruits, but you ditched your chance of joining... for Derek."

He shook his head, smiling wryly. "Once I figured that out, it all made sense. The reason you wouldn't leave him in this clearing. The reason you came to this school. The reason every time I turn around, I find you attached to his ass. All of this is because of him."

Cameron leaned in closer. The intensity in his eyes was like a physical force. It bore down on me, pressing me to the spot. "Why? I don't know. I'm guessing Derek was right the first time when he called you out for being a stalker. You managed to charm him anyway, but the guy was never a good judge of character. His last friends posted his mom's tits all over the internet. You must be trying to get close to him for another payday."

Anger roared up in me fierce and fast. The shout was out of my mouth before I could stop it. "You're wrong! I'd never do anything to hurt him!"

Cameron's smile widened. "So, I was right. You do care about him."

I snapped my mouth shut.

"I guess I was also right about you pretending to be a boy so you could get close to him?" he continued. "Did it work?"

Derek echoed through my mind unbidden. *That's not true! It can't be true! Why didn't you tell me?*

"Apparently not."

I jerked. Cameron read my expression clearly.

"You need to stay," he went on, "to finish whatever you came here to do to him."

"I don't want to do anything to him," I said. "Yes, I became Zeke to get into the boys' academy and get to know him, but that's it. There is nothing wrong about what I'm doing."

"I'm not buying it. You didn't go through all of this"—he waved a hand at my clothes and wig—"for nothing. You must have a damn good reason and it's important enough that you've put up with all of this bullshit for the last two years. You need to be here for Derek and I need you to stay out of Network business." Cameron stepped back. "So this is how it's going to work. You'll come back next year, keep your head down, be a good little Elite, and the administration doesn't find out that you're a girl."

I wish I could say I was surprised to hear that threat, but I'd been expecting it ever since that day in the F Wing when he said my real name. This was his ace card and he picked the perfect time to use it.

Does it even matter now? I thought. *Derek knows the truth and he ran away from me. I thought I lost his trust before, but there's no doubt I lost it this time. What could I say that would make him understand this? How could I get him to hear it in the first place?*

I lowered my head. I didn't want Cameron to see my eyes fill with tears. *I lost him. My brother. I loved him so much, and after everything I've done to be with him, I've lost him.*

I opened my mouth to tell Cameron to do his worst. None of it mattered now.

No. I halted. *Derek was upset, but anyone would be after discovering the girl he fell for was his sister. I just need to give him time and eventually he'll forgive me. Underneath that hard exterior was always a good guy. If I give him a chance, he will come back to me, but I have to be close. It'll be too easy for him to push me out of his life if I'm not in it.*

"Okay," I said. I think the word surprised me as much as it did Cameron. "I'll stay out of your way, and you'll keep my secret."

"Good. That just leaves one more thing"—he snapped his fingers—"insurance."

I didn't have a chance to ask what he meant before Heath and Santiago seized me.

"What are you doing?!" I tried to rip out of their hold but they held me fast. The next thing I knew the other boys were on me. I realized instantly what was happening when Heath grabbed the hem of my jersey. "No! Stop!"

Screaming, I fought harder as they tore the jersey over my head. *Not again. They couldn't do this to me again!*

Heath began unraveling my bindings. I yanked my arm free of Santiago and slapped him across the face. "Get off of me!"

The victory of seeing his head snap almost all the way around was short-lived. Another guy grabbed my wrist and held me in a grip like iron as my shorts were pulled down. My screams reached ear-shattering levels. The Elites stripped me down to my bra and panties.

Heath snatched the wig off my head none-too-gently. I cried out as strands of my hair went with it. They finally dropped me in the dirt as Cameron stood over me, holding his phone on me.

I glared at him through my tears. "Why are you doing this?! I said I'd leave you alone!"

"This will make sure of it," he replied easily. "Just in case you were thinking all you'd have to do is deny it if I spilled your secret, I'll have this video to send to Whittaker, Argyle, and Miss Val. The real Zeke Manning. Although..." I could hear the smirk creep into his voice. "They may find out all on their own. That body is shaping up and your tits are growing nicely."

I hugged myself tighter. My skin crawled under his appreciative gaze.

"It's going to get tougher to pretend you're a boy."

My lips peeled back from my teeth. "You need to worry about how tough it'll be for you," I hissed. "You've made it fucking personal."

The corner of his mouth quirked up. "Don't be like that. Not after we've settled things." He shook the phone at me. "The expansion goes through without a problem. The attacks against the Elites stop. And that stupid For All crap ends. No one sees this as long as you keep up your end."

"I don't know who the new For All is," I cried. "I can't make them stop!"

"Ah." He smiled. "But now you have an incentive to try. You're a smart *girl*. I'm sure you'll figure something out."

Cameron snapped his fingers once more and I winced.

The guys didn't touch me. One by one, they filed out of the clearing until it was only me—kneeling alone in the dirt.

Four Weeks Later

"WHY DON'T YOU LOOK happy?"

I tossed the letter on the nightstand and flopped onto my bed. I didn't need to read it again. I read the letter five times by now and the words hadn't changed.

Congratulations, Zeke Manning. You've won the tournament and your place as a member of the Elite Class. Attached is information about your new class and the privileges you're entitled...

Jordan sat next to me. "What's up? Isn't this what you wanted?"

I leaned in and put my head on her shoulder. "Yes," I admitted. "This is what I wanted but I'm tired, Jordan."

"Tired of what?"

"Tired of everything I do going wrong. I got into the Elite Class, but now Derek won't speak to me. He wouldn't even look at me the last week of school. Every time I got near him, he walked away." I squeezed my eyes shut. "Then, there's Cameron."

She pressed her cheek to my head. "You don't think he'll really show anyone that video, do you?"

"Cameron has always underestimated me, but I don't underestimate him. He'll release that video. He might even do worse if something interferes with their plans for the expansion."

"What are you going to do? Are you going to keep your head down like he asked?"

"No," I said, and as it left my lips, I knew it was true. I hadn't been sure until that moment. "No matter what he says. There is something off about all of this. What money-making opportunity did the top leaders discover and why did they bring in Dominick Dupre of all people to do it? Someone they had kept out of their group for all of this time.

"But even if I put aside the Network, this system is not good for students no matter what Whittaker thinks. There are kids that might have been friends if not for a school that told them they were better or worse than the person sitting next to them. If it didn't teach them to look at each other and only see what they can get."

I lifted my head and faced her. "The battle system can't spread to other schools. Someone has to stop it and I'm happy for that someone to be me. I just have to be smart about how I go about it. Cameron can't know I'm behind it."

Jordan sighed. "You know I agree with you. I'm not questioning that the expansion shouldn't happen, but I am wondering why you can't fight it from the girls' side." She grabbed my hands. "The only power Cameron Dupre has over you is your secret, but Derek knows the truth now. Take that power away from him and reveal it yourself."

I shook my head. "I can't do that. Not yet. Not until Derek forgives me. He was unapproachable even when I was a few feet away. I've only been able to get close to him because I kept pushing. I tried to join the Network. I sat next to him at meals. I banged on his door almost every night. I didn't make it easy for him to push me away, but if I'm reduced to only seeing him at breakfast and dinner, that's exactly what he'll do."

Jordan's expression was sad as she squeezed my hand. "All this for a guy who wanted nothing to do with you."

I looked away.

"No, Zela." She took my chin and forced me to meet her eyes. "You've avoided this talk for too long. Pretending like this was all about Derek, but you and I both know there is no way you'd be able to get close to Jonathan Grayson on your own. They'd never let some strange kid walk through the studio gates or the family manor, and saying you're his daughter might get the door slammed in your face that much quicker. You wanted Derek because you hoped he'd bring you to your father."

"That's not the only reason," I protested. "He's my family. My mom won't have more kids. I thought for fifteen years that you would be the closest thing I'd have to a sibling, but all the time, there was Derek. He's mine," I stated with conviction that wouldn't be shaken. "They kept us apart but that is over now. He will forgive me. I will get him back."

Jordan leaned forward and pressed our foreheads together. "What if that's not the best thing for him?" she whispered. "You get that you turned his world upside down, right? He just found out the girl he was crushing on is his sister. That's got to mess a guy up." She raised a brow. "What were you doing with him anyway that he couldn't resist your charms?"

I warmed. "I didn't do anything!"

"Mm-hmm. What's the rule on seducing your brother? Isn't that taboo in *every* country you've been to?"

I grabbed her shoulder and promptly shoved her away. "That's not funny!"

Jordan fell to the floor howling. Apparently, my pain was incredibly funny.

"Jordan! Zela!" Mom's voice floated up the stairs. "Are you ready? Beverly is here."

My cousin picked herself up and dropped a kiss on my nose. "It'll work out, Zee. Whatever is meant to happen. Now, we're celebrating you getting out of that class even if you don't want to. Then tomorrow, we're celebrating some more."

I shouldered my purse and then took one last look in the mirror. Mom was ecstatic that I won the tournament. Ecstatic for Mom anyway. She was taking us out to dinner at a nice restaurant and letting me pick whatever I wanted off the menu. Even the stuff dripping with oil.

"We might not be celebrating tomorrow," I said as I fixed my hair. "Adam hasn't told me yet if he's gotten into the Elite Class."

"He has." Jordan held up her phone in the mirror's reflection. "He texted me earlier and said he got the letter."

I goggled at her. "How exactly did you hear from my best friend before me?"

She giggled. "Don't worry about it. Just worry about how much fun we're going to have when we go up to Evergreen tomorrow. Adam is super excited that we're spending the summer with him again."

"Again. How do you know that?" I called as she bolted from the room. All I got in response was her laugh.

THE RIDE TO EVERGREEN was short, but fun. Adam sent us another car and we goofed off in the back, singing to the radio, and planning how we were going to tackle the next two weeks.

"Only one week for me," Jordan whined. "I couldn't get Mom to budge. She won't let me stay with you the whole time."

"Two weeks is a long time for her to let you stay with people she doesn't know," I said. "Besides, after you leave, I'll finally have my best friend to myself."

She laughed. "You can't fool me. I know you're not stressing about alone time with Adam. It's *Landon* you want all to yourself."

"Jo, shush!" My eyes flicked to the back of the driver's head.

"What?" She caught my look. "Do you think he's going to rat on you? He wants you to get some just as much as I do."

"I swear I'm going to kill you," I said under my breath.

She just laughed at me. "You're planning to see him, aren't you?"

"He asked me out on a date yesterday," I admitted. I don't know why saying that made my face hot, but there it was. "People might recognize me if I go to the Promenade as Zela, so we're going to his house. That's it."

Jordan eyed me, smiling knowingly. "Is that really it?"

My hand closed over the bag at my feet. I was highly aware of the pills lying within them as though they were whispering to me, asking if I was ready to need them. Mom took me to get the pill a week after I came back from school.

I didn't ask her to. She just piled me into the car, lecturing the whole way about carrying life being a gift bestowed upon women, but it was a gift I would not be *bestowing* until I was years removed from my PhD.

"Yes, that's really it," I said, "but if it turns out to be something else... that's okay too."

Jordan bumped my shoulder. "Don't be nervous. When you're with the right guy, everything makes sense."

I snuggled into her, loving her more than I did a second ago. She had experience in this area. I couldn't have this conversation with Mom or Aunt Bev or Adam, but I could always talk to Jordan and feel her support even if it came with teasing.

We changed the subject from sex but spent the rest of the ride talking about what I hoped my date with Landon would be like.

"He swears I'm going to like it," I said as I scooted closer to the window. The gates of Adam's home loomed. "It'll put all my future dates to shame."

"Did he add that in because he thinks you'll be hooking up with Michael and Cole next?"

I laughed. "I wouldn't be surprised, but Michael, Cole, and I have just been talking—getting to know each other. It's easier now that we're not trying to take the other down."

The car stopped in front of the grand entrance and the doors opened as we stepped out. Adam threw out his arms and I ran at them full speed. We laughed as he spun me around.

"We did it," he said. "We're finally Elite. Nothing against the F Class though," he added.

I kissed his cheek. "Nothing is going to change. Tanner and Nico are still our friends, but now we study on the couches in our rooms surrounded by borrowed library books. I plan on sharing the privileges and making a lot of enemies doing it."

Adam chuckled. "That's my girl."

"Ahem."

We turned and found Jordan staring at us.

"Do I get any love?" she asked.

Adam put me down and gave her the same warm greeting. I tried not to read into their giggling but they were making it pretty difficult.

"Come in, guys." Adam put her down and threw an arm around both of us. "You'll be in your usual rooms. Mom had the chef make your favorite, Zee, and if you're lucky, Jessie will toddle her way into your room at some point today."

I gasped. "Oh my gosh. Is she walking already? Where is she? I want to see."

I ducked out from Adam's arm and raced inside.

"She totally only likes me for my sister," I heard him mumble.

"I like you for you," Jordan replied.

Yep. I definitely need to be worried about those too.

I pushed that aside for later as I searched out the baby. I heard her before I saw her. Jessie's shrieking laughs poured out of her bedroom. Peeking around the corner, I spotted her sitting in the middle of a plush rug. The source of her giggles was Mr. Shea. Adam's serious, silver-eyed, sarcastic dad popped up from behind the toy chest and scrunched up his face at Jessie. She laughed so hard she fell over.

Miss Val watched the adorable scene from the circle of Jaxson's arm. She smiled at them like this was her favorite moment ever.

I backed away and let the family enjoy their time together. Adam and Jordan were waiting for me in the bedroom that had become mine.

"Zee," Adam said, "Olivia is queuing up some movies for us tonight. Any requests?"

I hummed. "I'm feeling something with Bruce Willis."

"Cool. And about this Friday. My mom will be fine with you going out with Landon, but she'll ask if you've gotten permission from your mom first."

I spun around open-mouthed on Jordan. She put her hands up in defense. "It wasn't me. I didn't say anything."

"She didn't tell me. Landon did." Adam stood and tugged my backpack from my fingers. "I have to put his name on the list or the guards won't let him in."

"Oh." I relaxed. "That makes sense."

I loved that Landon was making sure everything was perfect for our first real date. I just couldn't help feeling like there was a huge "I'm going to have sex" sign hanging over my head.

I don't know for sure that's going to happen. My stomach is in knots just thinking about it. The moment might come and I could decide I'm not ready.

Adam put my things away for me as I climbed on the bed next to Jordan. I couldn't think about all of that right now. Friday was five days away. I had until then to focus on having a good time with my best friend, my cousin, and my favorite family.

The next few days were even better than I was hoping for. We watched movies, gorged on the best food I'd ever had, and on Thursday Miss Val threw us in the car and took us to the water park.

"You three have a good time," said Val. She was decked out in a black and gold one-piece, wraparound gold cover-up, and black sandals. Baby Jessie was perched on her hip. She was adorable in a pink swimsuit as she munched on a fistful of her mom's hair. It was almost criminal how amazing Miss Val looked five kids later. It was *definitely* criminal how hot Adam's dads were. Maverick, Ezra, and Ryder opted for trunks and swimshirts that clung to every inch of their body. Jaxson, on the other hand, strolled around in nothing but the trunks.

Miss Val pointed over her shoulder. "We're going to take the kids to the splash area. Meet us there in two hours for lunch."

"Yes, Mom."

She kissed Adam and wandered off with her brood.

"Where do you want to start, ladies?"

"The lazy river," said Jordan. "But first, let's find a place to dump our stuff."

We headed over to the pool chairs and snagged three free ones. Adam and I dragged them over to a shady spot as Jordan took out the park map. She read off the rides while I stripped out of my shirt and jeans.

"After the lazy river, we can do the Lagoon Surf and obstacle— Damn, Zee." She whistled. "Adam, did you know my cousin was packing all of that underneath her uniform?"

I clapped my hands over my chest in a feeble attempt to cover myself. "Jordan!"

Adam ducked his head. I peeked his cheeks reddening as he busied himself putting on sunscreen.

She cackled. "It's going to be hard to pretend you're a boy this year."

That sounded so close to what Cameron told me my stomach turned. "Let's just go, okay." I walked. Jordan caught up with me under the sign for the lazy river.

"I'm sorry. Did I say the wrong thing?"

I hooked my arm through hers. "It's not what you said. It's that I think you're right. I have a bad feeling about junior year."

"You're not going to let those guys win, Zee, and whatever happens, you have people watching your back."

"I wish Aunt Bev would let you transfer to Breakbattle. That school would be one hundred times better if you were in it."

"You are correct."

We laughed and dipped our toes into the lazy river. The water was perfect. Cool enough to satisfy on a hot day, but not so cold to be shivering. Adam caught up to us and our trio claimed tubes. We drifted around the park, laughing, splashing, and flipping each other over.

The river curved around a bend. Hanging over our heads was a sign for the Lagoon Surf.

"Let's get out here," I said.

The three of us climbed off our tubes and headed to the wave pool. Dozens of people were in the water, shrieking and jumping as the waves bore down on them. Adam let out a shout. He grabbed Jordan around the legs.

"Adam, put me down," she half screamed/half laughed. She playfully swatted his shoulders as he carried them out to the water.

I hung back, watching them. Adam tossed her in and Jordan came back fast. She tackled him and they both went under. They came up howling.

I came closer, letting the warm water envelop me.

"Jo," I called.

She looked up from dunking Adam's head in the pool. "Yeah?"

"Can you buy us some funnel cake, please? You can take the money from my bag."

"Ooh. Sounds yum." She stopped drowning him and hurried out. "I'll be right back."

When she was safely away, I turned on my best friend. "Adam Moon, I think we should talk."

He reached for me and pulled me to his chest. We jumped to top another wave. "About what?"

"Is there something going on between you and Jordan?" I asked, getting right to the point. "I'd be happy if you got together, but not while you're with someone else. It's been Melody, Melody, Melody since the first day I met you. Don't mess my cousin around if you're in love with another girl."

Adam didn't seem put out by my serious tone. On the contrary, he smiled and hugged me tighter as he lifted us over another wave. "No one is messing anyone around. I told you last year that Melody and I aren't exclusive and that hasn't changed." He sighed. "She doesn't believe in getting too serious, too young. I got the speech on high school re-lationships being doomed to fail. She said we'd most likely be killed by long distance because I want to go to university here and she's going out of state. It's been months and she hasn't changed her mind."

I lost my frown. "Oh. I'm sorry, Adam."

He shook his head. "It's okay. Really, it is. I love Melody for who she is. I love that she has strong opinions about everything from relationships and the best kind of peanut butter. If this is what she wants, I accept it, but..." His eyes flicked over my head. I turned and saw Jordan waving to us from the edge of the pool. "I'm not going to deny what I want anymore. I like Jordan. I can talk to her, you know?"

A smile pulled at my lips. "Yeah. I know."

"She knows all about me and Melody and she's cool with it. I don't know if anything is going to happen between us, but trust me, I would never do anything to hurt her."

I heaved a sigh. "I guess I can trust you, Moon. You've been a perfect gentleman despite living in a hell of tempta-tion the last two years."

He snorted a laugh. "It's been hard. Something about that bowl-cut wig just gets me going."

It was my turn to pounce and shove him under the water. He escaped me and beat it out of the pool. We descended on Jordan and our treat.

The rest of the day passed in a haze of food, fun, and rides. I took Jordan and Adam's flirting in stride. They were cute and having my best friend and favorite cousin get to-gether would not be the worst thing. I told her as much as we got ready for bed that night.

"I'm your only cousin," she pointed out. She was propped up on my pillows, flipping through channels.

"Yes, but that doesn't mean you have to be my favorite," I said from the bathroom. "There was a dark period where we couldn't stand each other."

"When are you going to forgive me for pushing you over in the playpen?"

"It's going to take some more time."

I peeked her eyeroll as I shut off the lights and walked out. I hopped up next to her and relieved her of the remote.

"Are you sure you're okay with it?" she asked. "Me and Adam? If there ever is a me and Adam," she added.

"I'm okay. Adam is a good guy. He'd never treat you like Sean or Malcolm."

"Ugh. Never speak those names." I put my arm around her and she snuggled into my side. "Time for a subject change. What are you wearing for your date tomorrow?"

I shrugged. "Jeans and my purple top."

She tilted her back to give me the full force of her bugged-out eyes. "You can't wear that. This is your first real date, but even you have to know worn jeans and a plain top is as unsexy as it gets."

"I'm not going for sexy." I landed on an old '90s movie I vaguely remembered and I let it stay. "We're going to his house, remember? What if his parents are home? I don't need to be flashing my stuff in front of them."

She sighed. "At least wear skimpy underwear. Something that will be easy for him to take off with his teeth."

A flush crept up my neck. "That's enough about that. Let's watch."

Jordan laughed at me for a full three minutes into the movie.

Chapter Two

That laughter rang in my ears as I paced the front room. My heart beat out of control, rattling my rib cage, and nothing I could do would slow it.

Why are you so nervous? I berated myself. *It's just Landon. You're going to hang out like you've done many times before, and if you don't want to take it further than that, you don't have to.*

I glanced down at my outfit. It certainly looked like I wasn't going to take it further. I would have to cover it up with Zeke's hoodie and sweatpants, but I flew in the face of Jordan's disapproval and put on a pair of jean shorts and a simple, purple shirt with cutouts on the arms. I went a different way with the underwear. My reflection told the story of my tomato-red face as I pulled the thong over my hips.

Am I really going to do this? What if he doesn't want to do it? Am I freaking out for nothing? He might—

Wake up, Zela. In no universe would Landon not drop his pants milliseconds after yours. We've done everything else. He wouldn't object to taking it the final step.

"Zeke?"

I stopped pacing. Val stepped out of the living room. The baby waddled next to her, getting used to the whole walking thing as her mother securely held her hand.

Val smiled at me. "Is Landon late?"

"Uh no. Actually, I'm down early by"—I glanced at my watch—"twenty-eight minutes."

"You're nervous." It wasn't a question.

I laughed. "This is why you're the therapist. You called me out pretty easily."

Val chuckled as she lifted the baby into her arms. Jessie immediately rested her head on her shoulder and closed her eyes. "I was nervous before my first date with Jaxson too." She leaned against the shoe cabinet, settling in. "There were some hiccups, but it was one of the best nights of my life. I realized that he really saw me. I wasn't just another girl he was bringing on a generic date. Being with someone who gets you that deeply is a gift."

I nodded. "And you have that with four someones. You get all the luck, Val."

Val tossed back her head laughing. When I first met her, I wouldn't have felt comfortable saying something like that, but after summers at her house and twice a month in her office for mandatory therapy. We've broken through quite a lot of barriers.

"I have been lucky. My life turned around so sharply, I'm still in shock sometimes," she replied. "But you and I are a lot alike, Zeke."

"We are? How?"

Her smile tinged with a trace of something else. "We were both raised by single moms, our dads ran out on us, and tragedy has shaped our lives."

I lowered my eyes. "Tragedy? For you too?"

"Yes, me too. People can do a lot of damage to us, but they can't take the love we feel for others or what they feel for us. So, have fun tonight, Zeke, and don't be nervous." I looked up as she came over and squeezed my arm. "Okay?"

I nodded. "Yes. I'm okay."

"Good. I'm going to put Jessie down for her nap." She gave me a pointed look. "I'll see you tonight at ten. Earlier is even better."

Chuckling, I waved her and the baby off. The door creaked open as Val rounded the corner.

Adam's butler stepped through the jamb. "Master Zeke, your guest has arrived. Shall I show him in?"

"No, I'm coming out." I took one last breath and stepped through the door as he held it out for me. Landon was at the bottom of the stairs. My breath caught when our eyes met.

He leaned against a blue convertible I assumed was his. Landon went casual too, but on him that meant something else entirely. He wore black jeans, spotless white sneakers, and a hoodie with a cobra printed on the chest. Tying the look together was a tailored, slim-fitting leather jacket that reached to his knees. Landon opened it so I could slide right inside, slipping my arms around his waist and burying my nose in his chest.

"Miss me, baby?"

I hid my smile in his hoodie. "Yes. Like crazy."

He bent his head at the same moment I rose up. We kissed slow and unhurried.

"Whoo! Yeah!"

My eyes popped open mid-kiss.

"Get it, girl!"

We broke apart and tilted our heads up. Leaning out of her bedroom window was Jordan. Over her shoulder, I saw Adam doubled over laughing.

"Who is that?" Landon asked, sounding faintly amused.

"I'm afraid you'll never find out because I'm killing her when I get back."

He laughed. "No bad feelings today." Landon slipped his hand into mine. "First official date. Everything is going to be perfect."

Landon led me around the car and held open the door. I was stuck between smiling or rolling my eyes at the chivalry. Despite almost two decades with my mother, I went with smiling as I slid into the car. Immediately, I took off my Zeke clothes.

"We're going to my place," he said after he got in. "Henrietta and Declan will be there but they promised to stay out of our way."

"Am I going to meet them?"

"Not if I can help it," he said under his breath. The engine roared to life before I could ask what he meant.

"How's it going?" Landon went on. "Have you been having fun with Moon?"

"It's been great. We've gone out almost every day and..."

We chatted as we made the twenty-minute drive to Landon's home. It amazed me how close the guys were to each other. Well, as close as you can be when you have large properties that put dozens of acres between you.

"That's Cole's place." He pointed through the window before turning onto a winding gravel path.

"You mean he's right across from you?" I twisted around to see. I didn't know much about Cole's family or his life except that he breathed swimming and studying. The colonial-style mansion looking back at me didn't offer any more insight.

"Yep. He comes over sometimes to swim in my pool. Ours is indoor and his parents don't let him swim when it's raining."

I shook my head. "He won't take a day off for the rain. That's dedication." I turned back in my seat. "Are your parents... cool with...?" I trailed off.

What in the world?

I blinked. Then I blinked again in case my eyes were on the fritz. I looked away for one moment and we transported centuries in time to the gates of a medieval castle.

Landon's car rattled over the bridge and paused before the portcullis. He stuck a hand out of the window, signaling the guard, and it rose as I watched it ascend open-mouthed. Towers and turrets. Iron windows and a stone wall surrounding the entire thing.

"Is this... real?" I breathed.

He laughed. "A real castle? No. Henrietta had it built. She says every woman should feel like a princess."

"Why not a queen?" I asked, half joking.

"Because queens slave away for subjects who are forced to respect her station, but choosing to ignore her womanhood," he said like someone who heard it more than once. "Princesses have all the power but are cherished and catered to like a woman should be."

"Wow. Your mom and my mom really need to meet." He chuckled as I took in the white stone, expansive gardens, and no less than three fountains. "But you'll definitely feel like royalty living here."

Landon parked in front of stone steps that were split in two by a cascading fountain rising all the way to the top. This feature was hardly medieval, but it was gorgeous. We walked up on either side, holding hands over the water.

"Soooo," I began. "What do you have planned?"

"I was thinking dinner," he said, "and then bowling because it's frankly disturbing that you've never bowled."

"It's not that weird," I mumbled.

"Then, we'll hang out in my room."

I peeked at him out of the corner of my eye. He said that so simply, not bothering to elaborate on what "hanging out" would entail.

"Where are we going bowling?" I asked, changing the subject. I wasn't ready for him to elaborate either.

"Upstairs."

"This place is getting less and less medieval."

Landon let us inside and I saw how true that was. The interior of the Foster Castle was nothing like the outside. Modern—bordering on futuristic—furniture took up the entryway and continued throughout the house. It was all grays and blacks—leather and glass. The only pops of color were the large photographs of incredibly attractive, stylishly dressed people.

"Who are these people?" I asked. "Your family?"

"Models." Landon secured an arm around my waist. "Wearing Henrietta's makeup or Declan's clothes."

I scanned the walls for photos of him and found none. Something inside of me twinged. My mother wasn't the warmest of people, but our home was practically a shrine to me. She had at least two photos of me in every room in the house, three on her desk, and my earlier attempts at art all over the fridge.

"Where are the family photos?" I couldn't resist asking.

"That's not really our thing."

"Oh. Okay." It didn't sound like it bothered him and I didn't want to push something that wasn't my business. I've been to a lot of places and knew by now that there were all kinds of families.

I leaned my head against his shoulder. "There was talk of dinner?"

"Yes." He kissed the top of my head. "Full disclosure. I did not cook this dinner. I'm also not sure what it is. My chef doesn't take requests. When I was in elementary school, he threatened to quit because I asked him to make me grilled cheese like Adam was always packing in his lunch box. He ranted about not being a short-order cook slinging out diner food and Henrietta had to promise never to let me near the kitchen again to calm him down."

I giggled. "I'm sure I'll love whatever he makes."

We climbed two steps and then rounded a corner. "It's always delicious though. He— What are you doing here?!"

Landon jerked us to a stop in the entrance to the kitchen. Three people blinked at us.

I didn't have to ask who they were. A man in a chef's jacket bent over the island, sprinkling parsley on a meal that looked incredible from where I stood. Sitting on a barstool before him was possibly the most beautiful woman I had ever seen. I say possibly because every pore was covered in makeup, her lips in gloss, her brows plucked, and her hair dyed a deep red that couldn't be natural.

She raised one razor-thin brow. "We live here—last I checked."

"You said you'd stay in your offices, Henrietta." Landon released me, went up to his mother, and took hold of her arms. He steered her out. "Go."

Henrietta laughed as she slipped out of his grasp. "We will go when he gets here. When is that, by the way? I thought you were going to pick him up."

"Him is now her." Landon gestured at me. "This is Zela. My date."

I'm certain my cheeks were pinking and not just because Henrietta was looking me up and down. To be fair, it wasn't until we arranged the date that I told Landon he could tell his parents I was Zela. It made sense that he spoke about me as a boy all of this time.

"Him is now her," she repeated. She shrugged. "Well, it's nice to meet you, Zela."

She made to reach for my hand, but Landon took hold of her again. "Now that everyone has been introduced. You can go."

I shook my head at his antics and clasped her hand. "Nice to meet you too, Mrs. Foster."

She stopped shaking. "Oh no. Please, none of that Mrs. Foster. It's Henrietta."

"And I'm Declan." The other man in the room rose from the kitchen table. My eyes widened slightly as he approached me.

I once thought Landon was the most impeccably dressed guy there ever was, but I should have figured his creator would one-up him. Declan Foster was decked out in a tight metallic gray suit covered in bloodred roses, but the pièce de résistance was his hair. Silver wings touched his temples, but they didn't grace raven locks like his son. Declan's hair was dyed a dark, basil green.

He looked moments away from stepping out onto the runway himself. There was no care to the fact that he was in his own home and apparently committed to a night in his office.

"Lovely to meet you," he said.

"Nice to meet you too... uh... Declan. Sorry, I thought Landon called you by your first names to be ironic. I didn't realize you prefer to be called that."

Henrietta sighed as she put an arm around her husband. "People do find it odd, but I ask you, what is odder than society's need to strip us of our identities and put us into familiar boxes? Parent, mother, wife, daughter. Titles shared by so many as to not be unique. We prefer to be known by the names that are ours alone. The one we've had since birth and will have until the day we die."

Behind her back, Landon shook his head, pinching the bridge of his nose.

"You really should meet my mom," I replied. "I think you would get along well."

She beamed. "How nice. I would love to."

"Alright." Landon put his hands on their backs. "Introductions are over. Go—"

"Heaven's sake, Landon. We can enjoy our dinner while we wait for Zela to get ready. Then, we'll get out of your way."

"Wait for me to get ready?" I looked down. "I am ready."

Her brows drew together. "No, I meant ready for your date."

"Um. I did too."

Her smile disappeared in a blink. She and Declan gave me twin looks of shock.

"But you're not dressed," Declan protested.

"You're not wearing any makeup," she said.

I tugged at the hem of my blouse. Usually, I was big on dresses and makeup, but I was going for plain and unsexy tonight—not that I could tell them that.

"I thought I'd keep it simple since we're just hanging around the house."

"No," said Henrietta.

I blinked. "No?"

She turned on her son. "Landon, wait here. We'll be back in half an hour."

"Wha—"

Declan spun me around. "Come along. I have a few pieces from my new line that should fit you."

Henrietta grabbed my face as her husband shuttled me down the hallway. "I can tell you're an autumn. I have a great coral lipstick that will look divine on you."

I strained to find Landon. He stood in the doorway, wide-eyed and helpless. I was on my own.

The two of them got me into a room with bright overhead lights and tile floors. Wall to wall were racks of dresses, pants, skirts, and tops. Declan broke off and pounced on one of the racks.

"Right here." Henrietta led me to a vanity with not one, but five different makeup cases. They were each stamped with the initials H.F.C. "Sweetie, it's safe to say you have my Landon on the hook, but that doesn't mean you should stop trying."

I couldn't reply. She had my chin in a tight hold as she applied the primer.

"Our appearance, like our names, are the few things we own. You must take pride in it."

"Yes, ma'am," I got out.

She looked over my shoulder. "Not that one. Get the dress from the spring collection, love. She's not very chesty. It will give her a lift."

What. Is. Happening?

"And heels," she called. "Light brown pumps to match her eye shadow."

I tugged free. "I can't walk in pumps."

Henrietta's laugh was light and warm. She flicked my nose. "Don't be silly."

It was at that point I gave up.

As promised, I walked—stumbled—into the kitchen half an hour later. Declan and Henrietta were on either side of me, holding on to my shoulders as they showed off their newest masterpiece.

Landon rose from the barstool. His mouth hung open as his eyes traced my body. "Wow..."

Henrietta put her lips to my ear. "You're welcome."

I flushed hot as she patted my back and turned to leave with Declan. Their work here was done.

Landon visibly shook himself. "Now you see why I wanted to hold off on the introductions. Henrietta and Declan have never met a person they didn't believe they could improve." He gently cupped my face and kissed me. "Not that you can be," he said against my lips. "You're perfect."

I smiled. "I don't know. I'm pretty sure they've brought me to my optimal hotness. I will never look as good as I do right now."

I couldn't believe it when Declan spun me to face the mirror. It took one look to know that I had been putting on makeup wrong and dressing myself incorrectly for years.

Henrietta enhanced all of my best features and downplayed my worst. My pores were smaller. My lips were fuller and my eyes sparkled beneath dark brown glittering eye shadow.

Declan hadn't disappointed either. He slipped pumps on my feet with cute, tiny bows decorating the back. To tie it all together, he emerged from the racks carrying a sheer pale yellow dress with a corset top. It did a great job at solving the "not chesty" problem.

Landon's grin turned wicked. "I wouldn't say that. You looked incredible naked in my bed with your legs wrapped around my—"

Someone roughly cleared their throat. We sprang apart like repellant magnets.

"Master Landon," the chef said. He stepped through the sliding glass door on the other end of the room. "Dinner is waiting for you."

"Right, yes. Thanks, Gerard." Landon reached for my hand. "Ready?"

"I'm ready."

Together we passed through the doors. The second I stepped on the mat Gerard flicked the lights on. I gasped.

String lights illuminated a stone path leading to a lone fixture in the middle of their lawn. It was made up of stone columns and a charming thatched roof, but the true draw lit up Landon's grin as he led me up the steps.

The fire crackled in the pit, casting its warmth over the spread set around the stone rim. Black couches with red cushions encircled the walls of the space and we sank into them as I took it all in.

"This is amazing," I said softly.

Landon didn't bother to leave space between us. He pressed himself against my side and reached for my legs. Draping them over his lap, he then rested his hand on my thigh. Landon swept out the other. "We have cheese truffles, strawberry bruschetta, stuffed jalapenos, little quiches, and mini chocolate cupcakes. This is Gerard's attempt at keeping it simple."

I chuckled. "I'd say the man knows what he's doing. The truffles look delicious."

"They taste even better. Here." Landon picked one up and pressed it to my lips. "Try one."

I didn't look away from him as I parted my mouth. Landon placed the yummy treat on my tongue. My lips closed over his fingers as he pulled back. Tingles spread through me at his breath catching.

I told myself I'd keep it chill until I decided how far I wanted to go tonight, but it seemed a part of me would never be able to resist teasing Landon Foster.

Landon tossed his head, looking dazed. "The... uh... chocolate..."

I giggled. "I like you flustered."

"Really? You're into this?" He laughed almost helplessly. "That's good because you've turned me into a complete mess. I've gone from lovesick to jealous freak to raging sex hound."

"Raging sex hound?"

He grinned. "The last one was more me predicting our future."

I shoved his chest and he fell against the chair cracking up.

"I'm serious." Landon pushed himself up on his elbows and peered at me through hooded eyes. "I've never felt this way about anyone." He held out his hand and I took it without hesitation. He drew me on top of him. "Tonight, I want to show you how I feel."

I opened my mouth. I think it was to ask how, but Landon took his chance to claim my lips. We kissed slow and deep and every reason I walked in with for waiting blew out of my mind. If we "hung out" in his room, I was not walking out a virgin.

It felt like hours later that we broke apart, but more likely it was minutes. Landon sat us both up and put me firmly in his lap. We giggled like we were doing something wrong while we fed each other Gerard's creations and talked about everything and anything.

"We leave for Europe at the end of the week," he said. "Declan has a show in Paris and then we'll spend two weeks dropping in on his stores."

I ran my thumb along his chin. I never asked but I had a feeling Landon kept a little bit of stubble growing just because I liked it.

"Can I ask why you model for him? I remember orientation and Cameron saying you had other plans besides taking over for your parents."

Landon sighed. He leaned his head back, directing his gaze to the flickering shadows on the roof. "I wondered when you were going to ask me about that. I haven't really told anyone what I want to do with my life."

"Will you tell me?"

"I'll tell you anything."

I buried my face in his chest, hiding my smile.

"Henrietta taught me as much about cosmetics as I needed to know to work with Declan and the models when she couldn't be there," he began, "but other than that, I don't know much about her business. Can't say that about Declan. I was four when he put the first sketchpad in my hands. The plan has always been for me to take his place. He brings me to every show and makes me the face of his campaigns so that it's clear to everyone—and me—that I'm the future of Declan's."

"Does he know you want something else?"

He shrugged. "Declan never asked and I never said. I don't think it's occurred to him that I could want something else. I travel, meet gorgeous men and women, and I'm good at fashion design. Declan made sure of that." Landon lowered his head. I followed his eyes to my bodice. "I designed this dress."

"You did? Landon, it's beautiful."

He made a noise low in his throat. "It's not what I originally had in mind. The dress I drew was blue and the bodice was covered in sequins." He ran his fingers over the mound of my breasts. He looked at me as he said, "Right here."

"Really?" I rasped. "That would have been pretty."

"I thought so." Landon's fingers continued their journey. "I added this little clasp at the back to make it easy to take off."

I squeaked when a soft pop was followed by the bodice loosening.

"I loved how the design came out," he continued like nothing was happening. "But Declan had other ideas and it became this after he got his hands on it. Even though he praises me and shows me off to other people in the industry, he has changed every single design I've given him. Even the clothes I design for myself get his final approval.

"I've known for a long time that he'll never truly give up control of the business. If I want to work in fashion, my options are to work under his thumb or become his competitor."

"There are... no good choices," I whispered.

"Exactly."

The flames reflected in his bright green eyes. They pulled me in, mesmerizing me as Landon pushed down the corset. The heat from the fire washed over my bare skin, and yet

I shivered as that mischievous finger traced slow circles beneath my bra.

"I'm not destined to be a designer, but working with Declan has shown me what I'm meant to do." He bent and kissed me until my lungs cried out for air. No one could see us. The couch was high-backed and angled toward the woods. We were nothing but writhing shadows to anyone who peeked through the window.

He released me and I ducked my head.

Don't lose all sense, Zela. This isn't going to happen here.

"I want to run nonprofits for kids who weren't as lucky as me. I've modeled with three people who were kicked out after they came out to their parents. They're successful now, but so many others are living a different story. I want to open homes and provide services." His voice rose with his excitement. "I can start in Evergreen, but eventually it'll grow."

I pulled back and smiled into his eyes. "You're amazing, Landon. You're an Elite student with talent dripping from your fingers, but all you want to do is help others."

A rosy tinge touched his cheeks. "It's not a big deal."

"It is." I grasped his chin and placed a light peck on his lips. "It is a big deal."

"You think I can do it?"

"I know you can." I wrapped my arms around his shoulders and pressed my forehead to his. "But how did Cameron know your plans?"

"He must have heard it from his father." Landon dropped a kiss on the tip of my nose. "He advises half the nonprofits in town. I asked him for advice on setting one up and getting funding." His lips brushed over mine to kiss my chin.

"Dominick Dupre works for nonprofits?" I drew slightly back. "Why would he—"

Landon came after me. I yelped when I suddenly found myself on my back.

"Can't be bothered to care right now." He pressed his face to my neck and hummed low in his chest. "I love our talks. They always end like this."

I flushed. That was true enough. Every time Landon and I were alone clothes started coming off.

Landon pushed the hem of the dress over my knees and let it fall to my waist. The kiss he gave me made my toes curl in my heels.

"We should go," he said in between dropping kisses on my lips, cheek, and chin.

I nodded vigorously. "Yes," I breathed. "We should definitely do that."

Landon let me up and I fumbled to do up my dress. We were both a mess. His eyes were glazed and his lips swollen. Seeing him so drunk on me made warmth pool in my core.

"I can't wait," he said.

Three words and that warmth transformed into wetness that soaked my panties. I couldn't wait to do this either.

I made a half-hearted attempt to fix my hair and then grabbed his hand. "Let's go."

"Whoa," he cried.

I dragged him out of the gazebo, down the path, and burst through the sliding glass doors. Gerard looked up from washing the dishes.

"Hold up," Landon said, chuckling. "I have to show you the way."

He put his arm around my waist. We walked out of the kitchen at a more reasonable pace, waving to Gerard on the way out.

My excitement built as we climbed the stairs. Topping the landing revealed another hallway of model photographs and closed doors. There was no way to know what was on the other side but I was disappointed one after the other when the doors we passed weren't Landon's.

We stopped before the final room at the end of the hall. I gripped the knob before he had a chance and flung it open. Rushing inside, my smile vanished in a heartbeat.

"What is this?" I cried.

"What do you mean?"

Landon walked in front of me and spread out his arms. "It's our bowling alley. Don't you like it?"

Did I like it? This room was as amazing as the rest of the house. Two bowling lanes took up one side of the room and before them was a large, comfy couch and a wet bar. The other side boasted a row of arcade games and two big-screen televisions.

I liked it a lot, but that did not matter.

"Landon." I planted my hands on my hips. "Now is *not* the time for bowling."

He cocked his head. "But I told you I was going to teach you how to bowl."

"I thought we were going to your room so you could teach me how to do *something else*."

His expression didn't change as he drew closer and backed me into the door. "Is that what you thought?"

My heart picked up speed again. Landon gripped my ass and lifted me so I could wrap my legs around his waist.

"Yes," I breathed. I closed my eyes. "Let's go."

"We can't go," he whispered. "Not until we do something about this bowling thing. I can't sleep with a girl that doesn't know how."

My eyes bugged. I snapped to Landon's face and finally caught his grin. "What the— Are you messing with me?!"

"Yep," he said, popping the p. The look he was giving me could only be described as devilishly wicked. "Consider it payback for the shit you pulled with Moon."

My mouth literally fell open. It had to be comical, so I didn't blame him for laughing. "You have got to be kidding me. You think now is the time for your revenge? I'm your girlfriend. I don't tease you anymore."

Bright green pools darkened. "Every time you walk into a room wearing fucking clothes when you shouldn't be, you're teasing me."

"Oh?" A smirk spread across my lips. "Well, then you know I can play this game as good as you."

I didn't give him any warning before slipping through his jeans and wrapping my fingers around his length.

He sucked in a sharp breath. His nails dug hard into my thighs, but I only felt a rush of triumph. I drove him just as crazy as he drove me.

I whispered in his ear as I stroked. "Are you sure you want to play this game with me?"

"H-holy fuck, Zela," he groaned. Landon's breath was hot on my neck. "I don't... want to play this game, but I do want to play another one." He tugged my hand out of his pants. "Strip bowling."

"That sounds like fun."

Landon put me back on my feet and kissed me. "Best part is the winner's prize." Suggestion heavily laced his voice. I didn't have to ask what the prize was.

"How do we play?"

Landon took my hand and led me over to the lanes. "It's simple. If I get a strike, you take off something. If you get a strike, I do it."

I looked from the ball to the pins. "But aren't strikes hard to get?"

"For some people." Landon picked up a ball. Holding it up to his face, he winked over the swirly green surface. "Not for me."

Thus began the most unevenly matched game I ever played in my life, and I went to Breakbattle Academy. Twenty-five minutes later, I was down to nothing but my bra and panties while Landon had only removed his jacket and one shoe.

"You hustled me," I deadpanned.

"I did not!" His innocent act might have been more believable if he wasn't eyeing me like a popsicle on a hot day. "I never said I wasn't good."

He rescued his ball, stepped up to the line, and sent it rolling for the pins. I knew before it connected what it was going to be.

Landon whooped at his sixth strike in a row. "So very, very good." He turned on me. His hunger was like a living thing within his gaze. "I'll have that bra."

I unhooked the clasp and gave it to him as requested.

He leaned his head back, speaking to the ceiling. "I love this game."

I used his distraction to snatch my bra back. He gaped at me as I put it on.

"That's cheating," he cried.

I laughed. "You're cheating. At least teach me how to play. Then you'll save your chance to get my bra off again."

"When you offer those terms..."

We giggled as we got my ball and stepped up to the lane. Who knew first dates could be this fun?

I got in position and ball held before my nose. Landon pressed himself against my back. "The trick," he said softly, "isn't to aim for the middle arrow. You want the second one from the right." He nipped my ear. "Think you can do it?"

I nodded rather than speak. Landon was rocking my ass back onto his hard-on and it was making speech difficult.

I drew my arm back and suddenly his hand was there. He clasped my wrist and gently guided me as I shot the ball. That same hand spun me around before the ball reached the arrows.

We stumbled back, mouths attacking each other as we tore at our clothes. I got his hoodie over his head and flung it over my shoulder.

"My room," he got out. My bra followed his hoodie. "Second door on the left."

I slipped out of his arms. Skipping backward, I flashed him a grin. "Race you there."

He dove for me. Shrieking, I raced out of the room in nothing but my panties. I tried to be quiet darting down the hall, but Landon didn't.

A growl behind me made all my hairs stand on end. "I am going to fuck the shit out of you."

I didn't know what other girls wanted to hear before their first time, but that had to be it. I loved this side of Landon. He was all colored contacts, pressed uniforms, and polished shoes in public, but when we were alone, he was wild.

I found his door and threw it open. I skidded to a stop just after the threshold. I pictured Landon's bedroom a few times, but none of them came close to this. It was massive. So big we could probably fit the cafeteria in here. That wasn't as shocking as Landon, Landon, Landon everywhere I looked.

Blown-up shots of him in various poses and clothes—even one in only boxers—covered the walls. They all looked down on a platform square in the middle of his room that housed one thing. His bed.

I had a moment to take this all in.

"There you are." Hands grabbed me around the waist and hoisted me over his shoulder. He carried me across the jet-black carpet. "Are you on the pill?"

"Ye— Ah!" Landon tossed me unceremoniously on the bed.

"Good." He disappeared for a moment but came back just as quickly. "This is for you."

He shoved a sheaf of papers in my hands and then my underwear down my ankles. Half out of it, I tried to make sense of what I was holding as he spread my legs.

A mess of words and numbers gazed back at me.

What is this? It looks like—

Landon put his mouth on me and sucked. The papers crinkled in my fists.

The first moan tore from my lips unbidden. The second one I penned in. I bit my lip so hard I almost drew blood.

The sexual health test shook in my hands. "L-Landon, why—"

He propped himself up and gazed at me over my heaving chest. "I'm not wearing a condom. I've waited too fucking long to be with you. Nothing's coming between us."

"That works for me," I breathed. I threw away the test and opened my arms. Landon fell into them. We rolled and pawed at each other reminiscent of our time on the mat. I pushed down his pants, and then his briefs. Finally, there was truly nothing between us.

I got on top of him but enjoyed my new position for only a moment. He flipped me over and pinned my arms over my head. Every nerve fizzled and came to life just at the look in his eyes.

Landon secured my wrists with one hand. The other traveled down my body, heading for its favorite destination. "Zela? Can I ask you something?"

My back arched off the bed as his fingers slipped inside. "Yes!"

"You're not going to smother me this time, are you?"

I laughed breathlessly. "No promises."

"Damn." His fingers picked up speed and my body contorted until the top of my head touched the comforter. "Just to be safe."

I had the perfect view of him reaching over and knocking all the pillows to the floor. I was mid-giggle when my muscles tensed. Explosions went off in my mind as pleasure ricocheted through my body like those bowling pins off our balls.

I collapsed into the sheets. Landon served up the best orgasms, but this one was ten times better just for what was coming after it.

We kissed, taking our time.

"Ready?" he whispered.

"Not yet." I grabbed his shoulders and shoved. Landon blinked up at me when he suddenly found our positions reversed. "It's my turn."

I placed my hands on his chest, feeling his heart flutter beneath my fingers. I bent my head and dropped kisses down his body.

"Fuck, Zela. I love you."

"I love—"

Knock. Knock.

The door creaked open. "Landon? Zela?"

I yanked my head up so fast the momentum tipped me over. Screaming, I toppled off the bed and landed smack on the mound of pillows.

"Oops."

That light and extremely unrepentant "oops" set off a string of curses.

"Dammit, Henrietta!" Landon scrambled off the bed. He practically fell on top of me in a rush to hide his nakedness. "What are you doing in here?!"

"What do you think I'm doing?" Henrietta leaned against the doorframe. "What kind of mother would I be if I left you alone all night with a girl? I'm much too young for grandchildren."

My face was flaming. I clutched a pillow to my chest, desperately wishing most of my clothes weren't in the other room.

"You chose today of all days to act like a mother?" he snapped.

To my surprise, she chuckled. "I also acted like a mother the day I pushed you out after eighteen hours of labor. It gave me the right to cockblock you, my sweet boy."

I flushed even hotter at her choice of words. *Goodness, this is a weird family.*

"Both of you, get dressed," she stated. "Then, meet us downstairs in five minutes. The four of us will watch a movie for the rest of the evening. I'm thinking a comedy."

Henrietta walked off; her cackles echoed down the hallway.

I dropped my head on the mattress. "This is the most humiliating moment of my life."

"Baby, I'm so sorry."

Landon kept up a steady stream of apologies while we ducked out to the bowling room, dressed, and scurried downstairs.

Henrietta and Declan waited in the living room with twin knowing smiles. My embarrassment was compounded when they made me sit between them on the couch and forced Landon to another. He glared daggers at his parents all through the movie. This was not how I thought my night would end.

At nine thirty, Declan bundled me up and stated he'd drive me to Adam's. Landon had a lot to say about it, but his parents refused his demands.

"I'll go straight there and back," Landon argued. He trailed us to the door while I scurried behind Declan, head down, lips shut. "You can time me."

"Sorry, Landon. You have to pack for the trip anyway."

He let out a frustrated groan. "You know she's never going to come back here again, right?"

Henrietta spoke up from the foot of the stairs. "I'm sure you'll sneak her in the next time we're out of the house."

I squeezed my eyes shut. *Hell, please open up and swallow me now.*

"But you got caught this time and you have to deal, Landon," she continued. "Zela?"

"Yes, Henrietta?"

"I hope we see you soon. You're absolutely adorable and we must hang out again. We'll do a girls' day."

"Um. Okay."

"Perfect." Her smile lit up her already beautiful face. "The dress and the shoes are yours. Good night."

"Night."

She waved and disappeared up the stairs. I honestly wasn't mad at her for busting in. It's not like my mother would have sat quietly in her office while I ran naked through the house with a boy, but I was heady on Landon and at least figured he'd remember to lock the door.

Landon took my hands and gave me a chaste kiss. "I'm sorry about tonight."

"It's okay," I said softly. I was highly aware of his father listening in. "I had a great time."

"I promise I'll see you before I leave. I won't go without saying goodbye properly."

I wanted to believe we'd get to finish what we started, but even if we didn't before he left, we'd see each other at the academy. No one would interrupt us in our dorms.

Jordan and Adam were watching television in my room when I returned.

"Is there a reason you couldn't do this in one of your rooms?"

I locked the door and stripped out of my Zeke clothes. Declan looked at me funny when I redressed in the car, but he didn't ask questions.

"We wanted to hear everything the second you came back," Jordan replied. "How did it go?"

I flopped face-first on the bed. "I will never speak of this night again."

A hand patted my head. "The sex was that bad, huh?"

I swung out and a yelp told me my swat connected.

"There was no sex, and I'm serious, we're never talking about this."

My resolution held for one hour. Their wheedling soon wore me down and I spilled the whole sorry affair. Adam and Jordan both fell off the bed, clutching their sides. So ended the best and equally worst day of my life.

AUNT BEV LEANED OUT of the car window and kissed my cheek.

"I'll be back for you on Saturday, Zee."

"You don't have to. Adam's driver can bring me back."

She gave me a look. "You're settling into this life nicely, aren't you? We're not imposing on Miss Val's hospitality. I have Saturday off. I'm going to pick you up."

Arguing with my aunt would get me as far as arguing with my mother—as in nowhere.

"Okay," I said instead.

She stroked my cheek. "We can stop off on the way back, get lunch, and talk. Just you and me."

"I'd love that." I really would. Aunt Bev was tough, but she was always on my side.

"Bye, Val. Bye, Maverick. Bye, Ezra."

I glanced past Aunt Bev to see Jordan coming out of the mansion, trailed by Val and her family. She rattled off good-byes as she came down the stairs.

"Bye, Esme."

The young girl shot away from the pack and grabbed my cousin in a tight hug. Esme loved Jordan, but then, Jordan took her first kick in stride and spent the rest of the time praising and playing with Esme until she warmed up to her. I tried that but didn't get the same results. Jordan just had the gift.

"I'll see you soon, beautiful," Jordan said to her. "You keep your big brother in line until I come back."

She giggled. "I will."

"Hey," Adam cried. He slipped between his parents, holding Jessie. "Isn't it supposed to be the other way around?"

"Not in your case, Moon."

The two closed the distance between them like a force was pulling them in, but they stopped just short of arm's reach. Aunt Bev watched them like a hawk. Any sign that they were more than friends and these sleepovers would be at an end.

Jordan leaned in and kissed the baby. I couldn't hear what she said, but I caught her lips moving. Adam lifted his hand but stopped just short of touching her. They backed away from each other and she came down the rest of the way, waving goodbye to everyone else.

Jordan and I squeezed each other tight like it would be a year-long separation instead of a week.

"Did you have fun?" Aunt Bev asked.

"So much fun, Mom." Jordan tossed her bags in the back and then ran around to the passenger seat. "They invited me for winter break too, and Miss Val said I'm welcome to come on the weekends when Adam is home from school."

"We'll see," Aunt Bev said simply.

The two stuck their hands out of the window and waved to me one last time as they rumbled toward the gates.

Adam stepped up to my side and handed me Jessie. The baby pressed her face to my cheek.

"It's the original crew once again," he said. "Want to hang by the pool? I need to get some practice in."

"Sure," I said in between snuggling Jessie. "I'm going to have like fifty of these. I swear."

He snorted. "They're not always this sweet and cute, you know. She's peed on me twice while changing her diaper, and yesterday she bit me."

"That can't be true," I cooed at Jessie. "You're always this adorable. You're the sweetest baby ever."

Adam wandered off, rolling his eyes, but we were right behind him.

Val agreed to let Jessie join us. When Esme saw Val putting Jessie in her flowery pink bathing suit, she said she wanted to swim too. Esme came back in the room wearing her two-piece and holding the hands of the twins she dressed herself. Sophia and Samuel cheesed at their mother as she planted her hands on her hips.

"I guess we're having a pool day," she said. "Better go get your daddies."

And that's how we all ended up in their luxurious water playland. Even with his complaining, Adam took his sister from me when we got out to the pool. She shrieked happily as he dipped her in and out of the water, tickling her stomach with his nose on the way up.

I was spoiled for choice between the hot tub, pool, slides, and tubes, but ended up reclining fully dressed next to Ezra on a lawn chair. It was getting harder to be Zeke. I had to double up on my bindings lately and my boy pants were bunching up weird around my hips. I wasn't going to test my fate in trunks and a swim shirt.

"So what are you and Adam going to get up to for the rest of the week?" Ezra asked.

I shrugged. "This, most likely. I'll chill here and catch up on some reading while he practices."

He turned to look at me and once again I was struck by his eyes. They were hauntingly dark. Not even the blazing sun lent light to those inky, black pools.

"You don't have to spend the whole week in," he said. "You can come with me to the station on Monday. I'll give you a tour."

I perked up. "Really? That would be awesome."

"No problem."

"Daddy!" A sharp cry cut through our conversation. "Come play with me!"

Ezra winked at me. "If you'll excuse me, Princess Esme requires my attention."

I watched him go. Esme leaped out of the water and threw herself in her dad's arms. He promptly flung her back in the pool to Val's cry. Esme popped out of the water laughing her head off while Val splashed Ezra. He retaliated by jumping on her and bringing them both down.

A vision formed in my head as I watched them.

Landon grabbed me around the waist and pulled us under. I fought to get away as Cole shook his head at our antics. Riding his shoulder safely above the water was a blonde-haired beauty that looked just like her dad. Behind them, Michael taught our oldest how to swim. The little boy kicked his feet, his face scrunched up with determination as Michael held him.

Face warming, I shook the thought away. I had no idea where that came from. The world Val created for herself with her loves was unlikely to be my reality. Landon said he was okay with me dating other people but how long would that last now that things were getting more serious between us. There was also the fact that Michael and I were still dancing around this thing, and Cole kept every feeling other than pissed close to the vest.

I didn't know if they would be as cool with the two of us being the *four of us* long term. I also didn't know how to have that conversation. Did they want a future with me badly enough to accept it on my terms?

I sighed, letting my eyes flutter shut. "Future," I whispered.

Unbidden, the vision returned, but this time there was an addition.

"Watch it, Zee." Derek wiped off the splash of pool water. "I'm trying to read."

I escaped Landon's clutches and swam to the rim of the pool. "Well, stop trying and get in here. Your fifty nieces and nephews want to play with you."

Derek flashed me a grin. "Make me."

He was off and racing across the lawn before I heaved myself over the side.

The smile remained on my face as I pulled myself out of the scene. I wanted that. Ever since I found out my brother existed; I imagined every future with him in it. Trying to let go of that now made as much sense to me as letting go of my limbs. I needed them. I needed him.

The next thing I knew, my phone was in my hand. I held back from texting him for weeks. The dozens I sent him during the last week of school went unanswered and Jordan finally told me to give him some space. But I had given him as much as I could stand.

Me: You have every right to be mad at me. I know all of this is confusing, but believe me, what we have is real.

I never meant to lie to you. Please give me a chance to explain.

I wanted to say more, but I ended it there. I sent him enough texts to fill a book after he ran from me. All I wanted now was for him to let me say the rest to his face.

I dropped my phone in my lap and willed it to buzz. Screams, splashing, and laughter faded to a dull roar. Nothing else existed.

Please, please, please.

I reflected in the black screen. Anxiety etched lines around my mouth and eyes. I worried my lip between my teeth—a habit I broke myself of years ago.

Please, Derek.

My screen lit up.

I almost knocked the phone to the ground snatching it up. His name shone bold and clear on the screen and relief swelled my chest. Jordan was right. All he needed was time.

I opened his message.

Derek: Stop.

My face, my hopes, my everything sank.

That was it. One word. But I knew Derek Grayson by now. That one word said it all.

The screen blurred. Tears filled my eyes and I wiped them away quickly before anyone noticed.

My phone buzzed again.

555-9672: Is this Zela?

Wetness smeared across the surface as I typed a reply.

Me: Yes. Cole?

The day before, Landon came over to say goodbye and told me that Cole asked for my number.

Cole: Yeah. Where are you?

Heaviness settled in the pit of my stomach like a lodestone. More tears threatened to fall. All I could think about was him. *Should I say something to Derek? Should I call him? I can't leave it like this.*

After a minute, I texted Cole a reply.

Me: Adam's place.

Cole: What are you doing?

My exhales shuddered around the lump in my throat. I fought for every ragged breath. My body internalized the pain I wouldn't let it express and thousands of needles pricked my skin. The weight on my chest grew heavier.

I typed out a hasty reply as the attack came on.

Me: I'm trying not to let everyone see me cry as everything I've worked for over the last two years crashes down around me.

I couldn't say why I chose to go with honesty at that moment. All I knew was every ounce of strength went toward keeping me together. I had nothing left to lie.

My phone didn't vibrate for a full five minutes, then, his message came.

Cole: I'll be there in twenty minutes.

I sat up straighter. Surprise held back the tide of crushing sorrow for the barest moment.

Me: No, you don't have to do that.

I waited four, five, ten minutes, but Cole did not respond. At minute eleven, I called him. He didn't pick up the phone.

Getting to my feet, I gestured for Val.

She stopped pushing little Sammy in his tube. "Yes?"

"I think... my friend is coming over," I said. "Is that okay?"

"Of course it is. Invite him to join us for lunch."

I nodded and went out to wait on the front porch. On the way out, I realized the attack had passed.

Nine minutes on the dot, the gates of the manor rumbled open. A swanky, red convertible kicked up gravel over the driveway. Bass poured out of souped-up speakers, rattling the car and my teeth.

That can't be Cole. Who the hell did I just invite to Adam's house?

Peering through the window, a complete stranger looked back at me. I had a second of surprise before I slid off her face and noticed the guy sitting next to her. Even this far, I could see his scowl.

The woman killed the engine and thankfully the noise went with it.

I so rarely saw him out of uniform, I felt justified in being taken aback when he hopped out of the car. It wasn't his outfit. Everyone looked underdressed next to Landon, but something about Cole's style of simple jeans and plain name brands suited him in a way suits and ties never would. His true home was the water where he didn't need clothes, so why worry about them when he was on land?

No. What truly surprised me was the metal ring through his pink, bottom lip. Through magic only Cole Reed possessed, it elevated him from casually handsome to sinfully gorgeous. That ticked-off-with-the-world twist to his lips only added to the effect.

He climbed the stairs, only stopping when he was in front of me. "Zee," he said by way of greeting.

I couldn't take my eyes off his mouth. "When did you get that?"

He scowled and peered over his shoulder. "A week ago. I lost a bet."

I followed his gaze to the woman in the car. "Is she... your mom?"

"Fuck no. That's my older sister, Chris."

I started. "You have an older sister? Why didn't I know that?"

He swung back around. "We can talk about all the things you still don't know about me later. You ready to go?"

"Go? Go where?"

Cole gave me a funny look. "My place. Obviously."

"Oh, but— Val said you can stay for lunch."

He shook his head. "Too many people in that house and one of them is Moon." He made his way back to the car. "Tell her I said thanks, but you'll eat at my place."

"But—"

"Hurry up before Chris leaves us both."

Not knowing what else to do, I went back inside and asked Val to let me go with Cole. She said yes easily and that's how I found myself in the back of a red convertible, zipping off Adam's estate.

"This is a nice car!" I shouted over the music.

Chris beamed at me in the rearview mirror. She looked exactly like her brother. Or, her brother looked exactly like her. Seriously, if I slapped a wig on Cole, Christina would look back at me. "Thanks! Twenty-first birthday present!"

"It was nice of you to—!"

Cole flicked the music off.

"Nice of you to pick me up," I finished in a normal tone.

A snort caught my attention. "She had no choice," said Cole. "Not after running my car into a fucking *tree*."

Chris heaved a sigh. "When are you going to let that go, Chubs? It rolled down a hill. It happens."

"Not when you put the emergency brake on," he hissed. "Like everyone else can remember to do."

She shrugged. "Accidents happen. You should just be thankful I wasn't hurt."

"I said you couldn't drive my car at all!"

"What was I supposed to do? Trish threw an insane party back at school and I didn't have a ride. You're my little brother. What's yours is mine."

I jumped when Cole twisted around to face me. He jerked a thumb at his sister. "She loses her last car over unpaid parking tickets, comes home, swipes mine while I'm sleeping, wrecks it, and then Dad buys her a new one for her birthday. That's fucking typical."

Chris's laughter filled the car. "Yours will be fixed up in a couple days. Stop bitching and introduce me to your friend."

Cole spun around in his seat and directed his glare out of the window. It became clear I'd have to do the introductions myself.

"I'm Zeke," I said. "Nice to meet you, Chris."

"It's Christina." She swept her hand over her shoulder in a smooth move that sent a sweet waft of berry shampoo into my nose. "I'm Chubs's more talented, more attractive, and certainly more charming older sister."

I stifled a giggle at Cole's growl. It seemed I wasn't the only one who liked him riled up, but then, my reasons were different. "Why do you call him Chubs?"

"Don't answer that," Cole cut in.

Christina plowed on like he hadn't spoken. "Because he was the cutest little chunk monster when he was a baby. Rolls upon rolls of fat like that Star Trek guy."

"Star Wars," Cole corrected automatically, "and no, I wasn't!"

Chris turned around, unheeding of the fact that she was driving, and winked at me. "I've got pictures. Lots of them. I'll show you."

I didn't hold back my giggle this time. Christina teased and Cole sniped the whole ride back to his place.

It was a strange feeling watching them. The strangling sadness loosened its hold, but seeing them still made me think of Derek. I wondered if we'd ever go back to messing with each other like this.

Christina parked the car half on the driveway and half on the grass. She hopped out and skipped into the mansion without a backward glance.

"I'm sorry about her," he mumbled. "There's a 666 tattooed on her skull somewhere but I haven't been able to prove it."

Laughing, I shoved his shoulder. "Stop it. I like her."

"You would." He opened his door and got out. "Let's go. I'll give you the tour."

Cole pushed up his seat and reached in for me to take his hand. It seemed like he lingered a few seconds longer than necessary before letting me go, but I might have imagined it.

Clearing his throat, he shoved his hands in his pockets and strode off. "We'll start inside."

The outside of Cole's home was simple compared to Landon's and even Adam's. Beautiful of course, but understated in the simple white paint and gray roof and shutters.

"What do your parents do?" I asked.

"Mom and Dad both work for my grandad's fertilizer company." He pulled open the door and swept out a hand for me to go inside. "This is his place. Mom inherited it after he passed away."

"I'm sorry."

He shook his head. "I was two. I don't remember him."

I walked in and the first thing I saw was Cole. A miniature version of Cole with Christina's arms around him and a handsome older couple smiling with them. The portrait took over the wall of the entryway.

"Aw," I cried. "You were cute... and fat. Christina wasn't lying."

"Shut up." An arm hooked around my waist and dragged a chuckling me down the hall. I didn't imagine it this time, Cole's hand lingered on my hip as he showed me the first and second living room.

"This is the kitchen."

We walked into a bright, open, country-style space. Cole dropped his hand, but I grabbed it before he stepped away.

His head snapped around, eyes widening slightly as I slowly, but deliberately, put his hand back where it was. Something Adam said ran through my mind.

"I'm not going to deny what I want anymore."

"Thanks for picking me up." I molded my body to his side and heard his breath catch. "I was seconds away from losing it."

Cole didn't say anything for a minute. "Why?"

For the second time that day, I went for honesty. "Because of Derek. I ruined everything between us and I don't know how to get him back."

"You shouldn't have to get him back. If he's not a complete idiot, he'll come crawling back to you."

I smiled without mirth. "No, this time I screwed up. He has every reason to not want anything to do with me."

Cole fell quiet. I had the feeling he wasn't in the role of comforting someone often, but just having his warmth spread through me was helping.

"Are your parents home?" I asked.

"No."

"Good." I leaned my head back and met his eyes. "Then we can take this tour to your room."

Cole's skin was so fair there was no mistaking his reddening cheeks. "Yeah. Uh. It's— It's upstairs."

His hand disappeared from my waist and took mine. He led me up a staircase lined with more family photos. Scowling Cole was to be seen in plenty of them, but there were even more of him smiling with his sister, mom, dad, and a scruffy behemoth.

I paused. "What is that?"

"My dog. Toby." He tugged my hand. "My room is this way."

"You have a dog?"

Cole grinned down at me. "I told you there was a lot you didn't know."

"I want to change that."

There was a definite quickening of pace as he brought me to a door just off the staircase. Music poured out of the one across from his and I didn't need to ask who lived there.

Cole's room was how I pictured it and also not at the same time. Medals, trophies, and ribbons were showed off proudly in a case next to the window. There were more photos of his family and posters of Olympic swimmers on every wall. The room was light and airy like the rest of the house, but where it differed was the unholy mess.

His desk was covered in strewn papers and textbooks. There were shoes all over the place like he just came in, kicked them off, and let them stay wherever they landed, and the only explanation for the clothes covering his floor, furniture, and bed was that he threw dynamite in his closet.

I covered my mouth to keep in a laugh as Cole swore and sprang into action. He raced around the room trying to clean up while I strode across to the bed. The biggest dog I ever laid eyes on rested comfortably on his sheets. He lifted his head as I approached.

"Cole Reed." I slid a pair of boxers out from under Toby's paw. "I never in a million years would have pegged you for a slob."

I'd been in Cole's room at the academy and it never looked like this. He was right. Maybe I never really knew him at all.

"Fuck off." Cole snatched the boxers away and shoved them in the hamper.

I eyed Toby and the dog cocked his head at me curiously. "Will he bite?"

"Toby is a gentle giant. He wouldn't bite you if you attacked me. The lazy bugger would probably go back to sleep."

"That's good to know." I climbed up and laid my head on Toby. His fur was soft and comforting against my cheek. Toby twisted around to sniff me. He must have been satisfied because he put his head on the bed and continued his nap.

Cole watched the exchange from his desk.

"What are you doing over there?" I patted the spot next to me. "Come."

He took a step and hesitated. "Are you sure?"

I nodded.

Cole didn't ask again. He sat on the edge of the bed, but made no move to lie down. I grabbed his arm and pulled him down myself.

We gazed at each other across Toby's fur. The gentle rise and fall of the dog's stomach made us bob in time. I was close enough to count the imperfections on Cole's face... and close enough to see he had none.

"So..." he began.

I laughed softly. "So. You mentioned things I need to know about you. I'm listening."

"That's why you wanted to come up here?"

"Did you think there was another reason?" I asked, lifting a brow.

"Yes." Cole went with blunt honesty, recovering his hard, unflappable exterior.

I nudged his leg with mine. "Good," I said softly, "because there is."

Four words and tough Cole disappeared again. He flicked down to my lips and his mouth parted slightly.

If I was honest, I didn't know what I was planning to do, but I felt awful after Derek and Cole changed that without even trying. I wanted to make this contentment last as long as possible.

I snuggled deeper into Toby's side. "Tell me about the bet."

Forcing his eyes off my lips, he blinked at me. "What?"

"You said you lost a bet." I gently touched the cool metal. "Was it with Chris?"

"Yeah." His lips barely moved, as though he was keeping still so I could easily stroke his lip ring. "She bet I hadn't gotten good enough to beat her in a race. High stakes. If I won, I got her new car." He gestured at his mouth. "Unfortunately, my sister is still the fastest thing in the water."

"She swims too?"

He nodded. "She taught me how. Chris doesn't care about it like I do though. It got her a scholarship to Somerset, but she's more interested in her marketing degree."

"I'm impressed you went through with it," I said. "Didn't it hurt?"

"Like a bitch."

I laughed and, after a second, he did too.

"But," he continued, "when I say I'm going to do something, I do it." Cole cracked a grin. "The only thing that's ever stopped me is you."

"Me? What did I do?" I asked softly. I scooted closer until our noses hovered a hair's length from each other. My knee bumped into his, and Cole took the invitation to slide his leg through mine.

"You took the captaincy, presidency, and top grade point average away from me. Without mercy, I might add."

"I have a feeling you don't respect people who show mercy."

"Damn. Maybe you do know me."

I nuzzled his nose, breathing him in as he exhaled.

I did and I didn't. I knew what was important to him. I knew how to push his buttons, but what made him smile and laugh and cry was a mystery to me. Maybe Cole would lose control like Landon and take everything he wanted from me. Maybe I'd lose my virginity right here or maybe we'd just talk. Cole was still enough of an enigma that I didn't know what was coming next and it made the moment even more delicious.

"You'll have to take the ring out for school," I said as I skated my finger over his lips. They were surprisingly soft. "Now is my chance to find out what it's like to kiss a guy with a lip ring."

Cole caught my finger between his teeth. His tongue darted out and licked me and my nipples pebbled on the spot.

"What about you and Foster?" he asked as he took my hand and pressed my palm to his lips.

"He's my boyfriend, but we're not exclusive."

"That's all I need to know."

Heart pounding in my chest, I leaned in just as he pulled back. I blinked at him.

"What's wrong?"

"One second." He clicked his tongue at Toby. "I can't hook up with my dog in the bed. Toby, down."

The dog was up and off at the command. Cole got up to let him out. I heard the lock click behind him.

I shoved more clothes off and settled onto the pillows. Cole crossed the room and hopped on the bed in seconds flat, but instead of lying next to me, he swung his leg over and put his hands on either side of my head.

My pulse raced as I looked into his eyes. Common sense whispered in my ear.

What are you doing, Zela? Things are going way too fast.

Too fast, another voice spoke up. *How long did it take for Landon to put his hands down my pants?*

That's different. Landon never tried to keep you out while Cole has been guarded since the day you met. You were friends for a while in freshman year, but all you did was study. You don't know him. You're upset about Derek but this isn't the way to deal with it. We should get to know each other before—

Cole popped the top button of my pants open.

I immediately reached for his. We can get to know each other later.

"Anything else you want to know?" He grinned. "You should ask now while I'm in a sharing mood."

"Hmm." I yanked his belt out of their loops and tossed it to the floor. "What's your favorite movie?"

He laughed—a light, breathy laugh that tickled my lips. "That's what you want to know?"

"Yep and I expect an honest answer."

"Well, if lying is off the table"—Cole inched my underwear down my thighs—"then my favorite movie is *Limitless.*"

"Why that one?" I slipped my hand through the waistband of his jeans and enjoyed the tiny grunt as I wrapped around him.

"I love movies like that. The ones that make you think about what you would do if you could do anything? If it's not testing the way we think, why bother?"

"Does everything in your life have to be a challenge, Cole?"

"No. This isn't." Cole pressed his thumb to the most sensitive part of me. My lips parted on a moan and he bent and licked them like he wanted to taste it.

"Your... turn," I got out as he slipped a finger inside.

"Will you tell me what is going on with you and Derek?"

It took me a second to answer. We weren't going fast. This was nothing like my feverish romps with Landon, but his slow and sweet approach was scrambling my brain just as effectively.

"Yes." I was surprised to hear myself say that. I was even more surprised that I meant it. "I'll tell you about me and Derek, but I can't talk to you... before I talk to him."

"Fair enough." His voice was thick and husky. It dripped from his lips and made a shiver ripple beneath my skin. "Your turn."

"Why swimming? You're the kind who can do anything he wants, so why that?"

"I don't know. Why—"

I rose up and caught his ring between my teeth. I giggled as I brought him down to me.

Cole retaliated by picking up the pace. I released him with a gasp and sensed his smirk as he replied.

"Why math?" he asked. "You can do anything you want to."

"Because it doesn't come easy," I breathed. "I have to work hard for it, but when I get it, it's all worth it."

"That's why I love swimming."

"Why—"

"Shh." Cole bent and whispered against my lips. "No more talking."

I wasn't in the frame of mind to argue. I'm not sure how long we played with each other, but at one point I was on top of him, then he was back on top of me, and then we ended up on our sides, facing each other again. We stuck to below the waist but that was more than enough for our moans to fill the room.

"Shit, Zela."

I might have answered, but his finger hit that spot and everything went black. My nails dug into his arm and he hissed. Through a haze, his figure came closer and then his lips were on mine. Cole took advantage of my open mouth and gave me a kiss that was far from tentative. I never thought our first one would be in the middle of an orgasm, but whether the nerve-tingly sensations flooding my body were from the kiss or his misbehaving fingers, I couldn't tell nor did I care.

His free hand cupped the back of my neck, gentle even while our mouths tore hungrily at each other.

We both came down, breathing hard, rumpled, eyes cloudy. My wig came off at some point and strands of hair clung to my cheek and forehead.

"Wow..." I whispered.

"Wow is right." Cole wiped my hand on his sheets. "I wasn't expecting that when I brought you here."

I wriggled into my pants. "Neither was I." I buttoned up and then put my head on his chest.

Cole draped his arm over me. "We have to do that again."

"We can do it again right now."

His chuckle vibrated on my temple. "You don't know how badly I want to say yes, but my parents will be home soon."

My ardor cooled quickly. I was not in the mood for another interruption by parents.

"Should we go back to questions?" I asked. I lifted my head and propped my chin on his chest. "What would you do if you could do anything?"

He laughed. "Good one." Cole cupped my chin and guided me up to his lips. This kiss was softer, gentler. "Can I tell you in the shower?" he whispered.

"Um, yes."

Giggling like we were up to no good, we hurried to his bathroom, shedding our clothes on the way.

He turned on the water and we fell inside before it got warm. We couldn't keep our hands off of each other.

"What I would do"—he wrapped my legs around him and pressed me into the tile—"is take over Breakbattle Academy."

"What?" I was not expecting that. "Take over the academy?"

He nodded from the crook of my neck. "The battle system is a great concept taken in the wrong direction. It's too easy to abuse and it doesn't award potential the way Whittaker would like to think it does.

"There's something to be said for a little genius from Chesterfield going to a school that recognizes she's exceptional and gives her the teachers and tools she wouldn't be able to get anywhere else. The problem is the class system is too rigid and Cs, Ds, and Fs should have the same access to those teachers and tools. If I could, I would take over as principal and change things."

"Wow, Cole." I tilted his head back to look him in the eyes. "We should talk more about this. I'd like to hear more about what you'd do."

"I'll tell you, but for now... are you ticklish?"

"No," I said, much too quickly.

His grin widened.

"Cole, don't you dare!"

He attacked my sides. Searing water beat on my face and neck as I tried to escape Cole. He tickled me relentlessly, finding every sensitive part of my body and making me squeal for a different reason.

"C-Cole," I cried. "Stop!"

"I would but I bet you don't respect people who show mercy either." Water followed the lines of Cole's smile. A real smile—not a half one, or a smirk, or a twitch of the lips. What made Cole Reed laugh... was torturing me.

"I do! I totally do!"

We were enjoying ourselves too much, laughing, messing around, and making out in the shower. It was only his parents' impending arrival that forced us out.

Cole and I were dressed and sitting ten feet apart when his mom knocked on the door. He opened the door for her and Toby raced inside. He leaped on the bed and made himself comfortable.

"Hello." She shook my hand. "Are you staying for dinner?"

Our activities made us both miss lunch and my stomach was one angry growl away from announcing it to the world. Water dripped through the lining of my wig and traveled down my neck.

I really needed to go.

"No, I have to get back, but thank you, Mrs. Reed."

"Another time, then." She smiled and it struck me how similar it was to Cole's and Christina's. the family resemblance was strong in this bloodline. "Cole, you can take Chrissy's car to drop your friend home."

"Oh, she'll love that."

She didn't love it.

"Don't put one smudge on my car." She was hot on our heels as we headed toward the door. "Don't do anything to it. Don't even adjust the mirror."

He tossed her a grin. "Don't worry, I'll only roll it off a hill. It's not a big deal, right? You'll be over it in two weeks."

"That's not funny!" Chris snatched the keys off her brother. "I'm driving."

Cole's grin evaporated along with his dream of fooling around with me on the side of the road. He chased her out the door while I followed at a slower pace. Regardless of their arguing, I could tell they were close. I loved this midday distraction with Cole not just for what we got up to in his room. I needed to see him like this. The bullshit stripped away and what was left is a guy who likes to swim, has a dog, and an annoying big sister.

I held on to that feeling as Cole snuck me a kiss on the steps while Chris applied her makeup in the rearview mirror.

It didn't start to go until I returned to my room. What did I just do? I liked Cole but we were still feeling each other out since everything went down last year. He could take asshole to extreme levels, but the boy broke records until it finally hit him over the head that he needed to apologize.

I was still sorting through my feelings for him, and yet I hopped into bed with him for no other reason than it felt good at that moment.

And what about Landon? He agreed not to be exclusive but we never talked about what that means. By now he knew I was crushing on Michael, but I never mentioned Cole. How would he feel that I wanted not one, but both of his friends?

Not just wanted, I was prepared to let his friend claim my virginity before he did.

Oh yeah. He wouldn't like that.

A thought stopped me cold. What if Landon didn't have a problem with it? He gave me a sexual health test. Virgins don't have things like that at the ready. He's been with other people.

What if he's been with them while we were together? What if he is rubbing himself on some oiled-up French girl right now?

Jealousy like I never felt before roared up inside of me. I lit a match and burned that thought to ashes, then I collapsed on my bed. I was a hypocritical, panty-dropping disaster and I needed my cousin.

Jordan answered on the third ring. "Miss me already, Zee."

"Yes," I stated. "Can I tell you something without you saying I told you so?"

"No promises."

I groaned. "So... you were right about the willing young virgin lusting after manflesh. I have no clue what is wrong with me."

"I need you to go back to the beginning and explain this in detail."

I told her the whole affair with Cole.

"Dude, I leave you for *one hour* and you're getting naked with swim douche."

"Swim douche?"

"You can forgive them all you want but that's what I call them in my head," she replied. "Swim douche, track douche, and better-clothes-than-me douche. Although, track douche gets points for being there for you in Orlando."

"Can we get back to swim douche?" I asked. "Jordan, I did not wake up today planning to hook up with Cole. Tell me how this happens."

"You've been low-key crushing on him for months, Zee. The opportunity presented itself and you acted like any girl with a pulse would do when they're alone with someone they like, but..."

I buried my face in my pillow. She said but. Jordan's wisdom was incoming.

"But," she continued, "you don't want to get into the habit of hooking up because you feel bad. All those feelings will still be waiting for you after you get your clothes on, which you're experiencing right now."

As if heeding her, my eyes stung with unshed tears. "Stop. Jordan, I've been waiting weeks for him to talk to me and I get one word. Stop."

"You two have to talk."

"How?" I pushed myself up, rubbing my eyes. "I can't go to his house. I'd never make it past security."

"You're in the same class and dorm now. He can't avoid you. Corner him at school."

"I can attach myself to his ass, but Derek won't speak to me if he doesn't want to. Trust me, no one does the silent treatment as well as this boy."

"You'll figure something out, Zee. You will also get a handle on this three-muska-douches situation. Have you spoken to Landon about hooking up with other people? And what will Michael think about you getting hot and soapy with his best friend?"

I sank back into the pillow. This was going to be a long night.

Chapter Three

I promised Jordan I would go cold turkey on manflesh while I sorted out what I wanted. I broke my promise less than twenty-four hours later when Cole rolled up the next day in his sister's car and invited me over to his house to go swimming. We were in the pool for about twenty minutes and in his room for over an hour.

I had enough wits about me to not take it all the way, but everything else was fair game. By then I knew I wasn't doing it for any other reason than I liked fooling around with Cole almost as much as I liked talking to him.

He told me his favorite books, athlete, television show, and childhood memory. We ventured into the weird and played silly would-you-rather games and shared our strangest dreams. He even told me he slept with a nightlight until he was eleven. We talked about everything, except us or where this was going.

"Where do you want it to go?" Adam asked.

The sun peeked through the shades, rudely reminding us Saturday had come. Aunt Bev would be here in a few hours to take me away.

"I like Cole," I admitted. "I like him even more after this week, but it's complicated with Michael and Landon." I turned my head to look at him over the pillow. "Your mom makes this look way easier than it is."

He nudged my arm. "Do you want to talk to her about this?"

"No." I caught his arm and held it tight as I snuggled into his side. "I want to talk to my best friend. Tell me what to do."

"Okay, here goes. Stop hooking up with Cole until you talk with Landon about your relationship. That happens first. Figure everything else out later."

"That's reasonable," I murmured. "He won't be back until the day before school starts, but I'm leaving today. Distance between me and Cole would be a good thing."

"Speaking of school, are you ready to go back and face Cameron, Zach, and the Elites?"

My grip on him tightened. Hearing that name jolted me back to my porcelain prison—bound and screaming for uncaring captors. The grabbing and tearing at me. Ripping off my clothes on the sodden earth.

"Zela? Zee, are you okay?"

I pulled myself out of the memories, gritting my teeth. "I'm fine," I hissed, "and yes, I'm ready to face them."

I've done everything I could to push Cameron and the Elites from my mind so I could enjoy my summer, but I had not forgotten them and what the new school year would bring.

"Are you ready to be Elite?" I asked, shifting the focus to him.

"More than ready. Junior year is important for colleges. I have to step it up if I'm going to prove I'm ready to take over Shea Industries."

"You are—"

A knock cut me off. The door opened and Val stuck her head inside. "There you are, Adam. Here, baby. I forgot to give this to you yesterday." She came in carrying Jessie in one hand and a letter in the other. She deposited both on Adam's stomach, dropped a kiss on his forehead, and walked out.

Jessie leaned forward and stuck her finger in my eye without preamble.

"Ah," I cried. "Esme is rubbing off on her already!"

He chuckled over the sound of tearing paper. I picked Jessie up and moved her onto my lap. I cooed at the baby, battling her older sister's influence with sweet nothings.

"No way. This can't be for real."

"What's up?"

"Look." Jessie disappeared behind cream and gold-embossed paper. I pushed Adam's hand back for a better read. "Mr. Adam Moon, as a member of the Elite Class, you are cordially invited to a homecoming reception at the home of..." I trailed off, eyes widening as I read the name.

Jonathan Grayson.

I snatched the invitation from his hand and read it once, twice, five times. The sentences remained the same. Adam was invited to a party at Jonathan Grayson's house on Saturday night before school started. Adam was invited because he was in the Elite Class. I'm in the Elite Class. Does this mean there is an invitation waiting for me at home?

I sat up and gave Jessie back to her brother.

"Adam, I have to get ready. My aunt will be here soon." My phone was in my hand and I was dialing her number before I finished the sentence.

"Okay." He got up and headed toward the door. "If we don't see each other before then, I'll catch you up at the party."

"Yes," I said softly. I was glued to the stolen invitation. "Yes, you will."

AUNT BEV WAS CONFUSED about my eagerness to get home, but she kept the look on her face and the comments in her mouth. She turned onto my driveway and I was out the door before she killed the engine.

"Love you. Bye."

"Love you too," she called after me.

I bounded over the steps and dove for the mailbox. My panic was warranted. The letter Adam received was addressed from the academy. If Mom saw a letter from the school, she would naturally think it was for her just like Val did. Unlike Val, when she saw whose house I was invited to... Well, that's the thing. I don't know what Mom would do. All I knew was she hated Jonathan Grayson enough to make up an imaginary person so I'd never track him down. She could not get her hands on that letter before me.

I flipped open the mailbox and my heart leaped into my throat.

Empty.

I stood there for a long time, staring into the empty box.

"Zee?"

I jumped.

"What are you doing? Go inside."

Turning away, I waved to Aunt Bev and unlocked the door. I stepped in and paused on the threshold, listening for Mom.

Nothing. No hum from the blender. No music coming out of her office. No chatter from the television.

I gave up the thought that she wasn't home. Her car was in the driveway. Mom was here.

My footfalls were soundless on the hardwood floors. I passed by the kitchen entrance and there it was. Lying on top of the stack of mail, the letter lay safe and unopened on the island. I took a step toward it.

"Zela? Is that you?"

Mom. And she was close.

I didn't think. I raced inside and snatched the letter off the stack milliseconds before she appeared in the entrance off the living room. I hid it behind my back as I willed my heart to slow.

"Hello, Zela. How was your time with Adam?" Mom looked classy in a pair of slim, black pants and a white, linen top. Her hair was growing in. Still short, but more pixie cut than peach fuzz nowadays. But no matter what my mother did with her hair, she was a beautiful woman.

All traces of her youthful beauty remained and it might have been that beauty which drew in a married man ten years her senior. But that beauty wasn't enough to make him choose her or the child she carried.

Maybe I should hate him too, but all I wanted my whole life was to know him, meet him... talk to him. The letter crumpled in my grip. I couldn't let her stop me.

"It was fun, Mom," I said as I sidled around the island. "It's nice to be in my own clothes again, though." I tucked the letter in my pants and flipped my shirt over it. "How were you?"

She strode over to the cabinet and took down a mug. "Good. I finished up some edits on the book and approved the final cover. I was very productive." She poured herself a cup of coffee and then moved over to my side just as I inched out of the entrance. "But I missed you. Let's make dinner together tonight."

"Okay." I tilted my head up to accept her kiss. "I missed you too, Mom."

She continued on to her office. When I heard the door close and lock behind her, I bolted up the stairs. I flung my backpack off. It missed my bed by a mile but I paid it no mind as I yanked out the letter and ripped it open.

"Mr. Zeke Manning, as a member of the Elite Class, you are cordially invited to a homecoming reception..."

"ARE YOU NERVOUS?"

"Shh."

"Excited?"

"Shh."

"What are you going to do when you see him?"

"Jordan," I hissed. I cut eyes to my mother and aunt walking ahead of us. "Wait until we're alone."

She sighed like I was being difficult. "It's creepy here with no one around," she observed.

"No arguments here."

The Elite move-in day dawned dark and gloomy. It rained on and off all morning and we all managed to get wet. The squeaks of our shoes were the only sounds to pierce the hall as we walked to the dorm building.

"Did we get the wrong time or something?" Jordan asked. "Shouldn't other people be moving in? Where's Adam?"

"He texted me and said he's not coming until before—until tonight," I amended.

"I can stay with you until everyone comes," Jordan replied. "So you're not by yourself. Mom, can I spend the night with Zee?"

I knew why she wanted to stay and it wasn't to cure my loneliness.

"You can't have sleepovers on a school campus, JoJo. You'll see Zee next weekend."

Shoulders slumping, she grabbed my arm. "Promise you'll call me the second you get there."

"Again," I whispered. "Shush."

I don't know who was more nervous about tonight—me or Jordan. She thought I was walking into a world of rejection from the man who abandoned me and the brother who wanted nothing to do with me.

I felt so many tangled emotions I couldn't keep track. Tonight, I would meet my father. Not a picture, a replay of an interview, a glossy face next to a magazine article, or an ice cream shop employee. My father would be real and whole in front of me.

Does he know I'm coming? Derek must have confronted him by now. I would if a girl dressed as a boy spent the last couple of years worming into my life just to announce she was my sister. I'd demand an explanation from my father, so why wouldn't Derek?

How will Jonathan respond to me? Will he keep on pretending I don't exist? Denying my paternity has worked for him so far. Why not keep it up?

Questions I couldn't answer swirled in my head as we brought my things to my new dorm. The Elite floor was as quiet as the rest of the school. Students had all day to move in and it looked as though most of them decided to sleep in instead of rolling in at eight in the morning.

I set a picture of Mom, Jordan, and Aunt Bev on my desk and stepped back. These rooms truly were magnificent. My own computer, television, and bathroom. The furniture appeared brand new. No scuffs and chips reflecting years of use by teenage boys. They must replace it regularly. The same can't be said for the F dorms.

"This is Zach's room," I said to no one in particular. "He'll be moving into mine tomorrow."

"Unfortunate," my mom said, "but do not feel sorry for what you had to do. Women are made to feel like they should apologize for their success, but our counterparts do not. Anyone with the skills and talent would have done what you did, Zela."

"I don't feel sorry. I wish things didn't turn out this way, but I won the tournament fair and square." I took another photo out of my bag. "The same can't be said for Zachary Fields."

There was a time I would have felt sympathy for Zach. Those times were long gone. Bad blood existed between us now. Strikes against the other that could never be forgiven. I had more enemies than I could count this year, and whether I wanted him to be or not, Zach was included.

My family helped me unpack the rest of my things and readied to leave soon after. Black storm clouds hung over Breakbattle and they wanted to get home before the skies opened again.

"Just pick me up tomorrow morning," Jordan pleaded. "Who is going to know I'm here but us?"

"Have you forgotten you have school in two days too?" Aunt Bev returned. "The answer is no. Get your stuff and say bye to Zee."

Huffing, Jordan hugged me tight. "Just... promise you'll call," she whispered.

"I will."

The hours before the reception, I sat beneath the windowsill and watched the storm rage. Water trickled down the pane like tears. Jordan called me five times since she left despite my promise to call her.

I appreciated her worry. She was doing it for me, experiencing all the emotions I should be feeling while I sat still and blank, listening to the rain.

"YOU LOOK GREAT."

Adam did a twirl on my carpet. He skipped the traditional black and donned a slim-fitting gray suit that accentuated a body honed by years of swimming.

"Thanks," he said. "You look nice too."

I kept it simple. Black suit, white shirt, black shoes. What I wore on the outside didn't matter as much as what was going on inside. I still passed for a boy, but the price of double bindings was becoming costly. I could hardly breathe in this thing.

"Ready?" he asked. "We're supposed to meet in the cafeteria."

"Yep." I followed him out into a hallway that was livelier than it was a few hours ago. Boys streamed in and out of their friends' rooms—some of them dressed up like us, but most not. The reception was for juniors only. Cole, Landon, Michael, and Derek would be there.

Derek.

"Why do you think they're having it at their house?" I asked, voicing the question on my mind since I saw Adam's letter.

"No clue. The Graysons are notorious for never throwing parties, having meetings, or letting anyone on their property. Especially after..."

"It's okay," I said when he trailed off. "Derek told me what happened to his mom."

"He did?" Adam was genuinely surprised. "Wow. You two did get close."

A fist closed around my heart and squeezed. I didn't speak as we headed for the cafeteria, but my mind could not be silenced.

We walked in to see guys in handsome tuxes and girls wearing glittering dresses and strappy heels. I didn't know until that moment the junior girls were invited too. Two people peeled themselves out of the pack and came for us.

"Adam." Melody captured his lips in a bold kiss uncaring of the students, teacher, vice principal, and principal watching. Melody was radiant in a pale pink strapless dress and pink pumps. Declan and Henrietta could try, but I doubt they could improve her in any way.

"Hey, baby." Landon hooked an arm around my waist and pressed his forehead to my temple. "I missed you."

I relaxed for the first time that day—for the first time in weeks. "I missed you too."

"After the party, we'll come back to my room and... catch up."

A shiver went up my spine. "Can't wait."

We pulled away to join the group and my eyes landed on Cole and Michael propped up on a table to the side. A sharp reminder of the texts I shared with Michael and my bedroom activities with Cole made my cheeks warm. There was something else I needed to do with Landon tonight.

"Attention, juniors."

Landon's hand fell off my hip as I turned to face Principal Whittaker. My principal was a handsome guy, that was never in doubt, but he'd outdone himself in a suit that rivaled Landon's in expense.

"The Graysons honor us by inviting the juniors to their home to celebrate the coming year."

Not all the juniors.

"I will not hear of anyone disrespecting themselves, our hosts, or this school by acting out in any way. Am I understood?"

"Yes, sir."

I scanned the room while he went on about what was expected of us. I was disappointed, but not surprised, that Derek was nowhere to be found. It didn't make much sense for him to leave his house only to drive right back.

Whittaker clapped. "Excellent. Let's go. The cars are waiting outside."

The "cars" turned out to be four stretch limos.

I shook my head. Elites truly lived a completely different life.

Adam slid inside first and I came in after him. My butt hit the seat for all of two seconds. Landon came in, picked me up, and put me in his lap.

"Landon, I can't ride there like this."

"Says who?"

Sighing, I surrendered without a fight. I was a tight bundle of nerves on the way to meet my biological father for the first time. The little kisses he was dropping on my neck and jaw were a welcome distraction.

Cole and Michael ducked into our limo and then locked the door.

Michael met my eyes and smiled. Just for me as though he didn't see Landon at all. "Hey, Zee. How was your summer? Did you get to New York?"

"No," I replied, picking up our last text conversation. "Mom decided to stay in and get some writing done, so Aunt

Bev took us out for a beach weekend instead. How was Scotland?"

"Great. Mom's meeting with potential investors went well, and we freaked people out racing down the sidewalk. Her wheel caught a loose cobblestone and she almost took me out. People screamed."

I tumbled off Landon's lap laughing. I may not have seen him, but I got plenty of insight into Michael's life through our texts.

His parents divorced when he was little and his dad relocated to Germany for work. Despite that, the three of them were on great terms and every school break Michael and his mother went to Europe to stay with him. This summer, they took a detour to Scotland for his mom's work and Michael sent me daily updates of their antics.

I wiped my eyes. "What about you, Cole? Is Chrissy back at college? Is your car fixed up?"

Cole leaned back in his seat, eyes fixed on the roof. "Yeah."

Was that yeah for one of my questions or both? I didn't get a chance to ask.

Cole took out his music and headphones and shut us out.

The rest of the hour drive to Evergreen was fun. Michael, Landon, Adam, and I talked and messed around. The pall over our trip was a stiff and silent Cole brooding in the corner of the limo, and of course, the tight knot twisting my stomach as we got closer. I grew quieter and quieter until I stopped speaking at all.

"We're here," Adam spoke up. "We—"

I cut him off climbing over his lap to peer out of the window. A tall, metal fence came into view. Through the bars, a lonely mansion sat on the hill. Lonely was the only description I could give. There were no dancing topiaries, no colorful gardens of jewel-tone flowers, no line of sports cars that I had come to know as accessories to the Evergreen life and home. The setting sun cast orange and gold over a bare manicured lawn.

It fell out of view as the driver turned onto the driveway. The murmur of voices floated back to us as the driver spoke to the security guard. Eons passed waiting for the gates to finally open.

Soon, we were let through and the limo parked at the top of the circular drive. I shot back and clambered over Landon and Michael to get out.

Three stories of columns, arches, balconies, and white brick shone in the glory of balcony and floor lights. Palm trees were everywhere, placed in the path of windows and to the height of balconies. Their palms whispered in the breeze, adding a touch of beauty to their function of obscuring a crafty paparazzo's shot.

I took a step toward the door and a hard wall of muscle and polyester blocked my path. The guard swept out his hand.

"Phones, cameras, listening or recording devices of any kind are to be handed to this gentleman over there. They will be returned to you at the end of the night."

I blinked into mirrored sunglasses. Put three of me together and this guy could bounce us down the drive without breaking a sweat. I backed up and put my phone in the waiting hands of the guard without protest.

Again, I made for the house and found myself bouncing off his chest.

"Arms out, please."

I endured my pat-down in silence. Cole not so much.

"The hell with this shit," he snapped. "This isn't the damn Pentagon. They invited us here, not the other way around."

"Mr. Reed," Argyle said sharply. "That is enough."

I bounced on my heels as the unnamed man stuck his hands in my pocket, came away with a piece of gum, and confiscated that too. Over his shoulder, I stared at the door picturing my father and brother inside.

After all this time... I'm only ten feet away.

"You may go in."

I was off and running before he finished the sentence.

"Mr. Manning, slow down."

Argyle's cry barely registered. The doors flew open when I reached the top step, the butlers moving in tandem to welcome us inside.

"Zeke," Argyle hissed. "Stop running."

I did. My shoes made an audible squeak as I skidded to a stop on the polished floors. I stopped... because he was here.

At the top of the grand staircase, stood two people. Naomi Grayson was dazzling figuratively and literally. Her gold sequined dress sparkled under the light of the chandelier and drew every eye to a body that was fitter and a face that was lovelier than the cameras could ever capture.

I spared her the barest glance and honed in on the man holding her.

Jonathan Grayson.

"Welcome, everyone." His smile was wide and charming. "It's a pleasure to have you here with us tonight."

My feet moved of their own power, bringing me closer to him. I knew what he looked like. I must have found every single article and photo of him there was on the internet, but yet, I drank him in. If I didn't capture him now, he might fade away.

"The party is confined to downstairs," he said. "We have food, drinks, music…"

Thin lips formed his words. Jonathan looked plain next to Naomi, but I'm certain every living being in the world could say the same. A touch of gray graced his brown hair and when he smiled, the lines around his aquiline nose wrinkled. I pictured him eighteen years ago, young and handsome, and holding the woman my mother used to be—instead of his wife.

"Please, join us in the living room." Jonathan and Naomi descended the stairs. "Refreshments are waiting to tide us over until dinner. I'm looking forward to speaking to all of you and hearing your plans for the future."

My chest strained in my bindings, my breath speeding up as he stepped off the stairs directly in front of me. Jonathan was so close all I had to do was reach out and touch him. So I did.

"H-hi."

His eyes snapped to me and the hand reaching for him. He clasped it and shook warmly.

"Hello," he said kindly. His eyes sparkled with good nature, but not recognition. "Nice to meet you."

My father dropped my hand all too soon and continued walking. I lurched to go after him when movement flickered out of the corner of my eye.

Derek stepped out of a shadowed hallway. All thoughts of following Jonathan fled as he paused at the top of the stairs and locked eyes with me.

Angel.

No, it couldn't be. Not him. But yet that word floated through my mind as I took him in. Derek stood illuminated beneath the crystal chandelier. Rainbow prisms of light danced on his pristine white tux and golden-brown hair.

I put my foot on the step and found my new friend's arm in my way once again.

"The party is confined to the bottom— Hey!"

I ducked beneath him and raced up. "Derek."

Heavy footfalls charged after me, but one raised hand from Derek halted the guard in his tracks.

Derek watched me approach completely expressionless. I didn't stop coming until I was two steps away. A million things went through my mind as we looked at each other, but all that came out was,

"Hi."

He said nothing. Did nothing. A still, perfect statue.

My heart sank to my stomach as the silence stretched. I lifted my hand, desperate to touch him, prove he was real, but I fell short inches from his sleeve. Somehow, touching him was even more impossible than Jonathan.

"Derek, please..."

He came alive. He shifted, crooking a brow. "Please what, Zee?"

"I called you," I said softly. "I called and texted and tried to talk to you so many times."

"I know."

I stepped closer and he let me. Over his shoulder, two guards stood before both entrances to the hallways. I felt their eyes on us and my anxiety heightened. This wasn't right. The way Derek was acting and the audience watching us. We needed to go somewhere and talk properly.

"I want to explain everything," I said. "Can we talk in private?"

"No need." He smiled. "You don't have to explain, Zee. I get it now."

"You do?"

"Yes, I do. That's why I convinced my parents to throw this party. For you."

Hope swelled in my chest for a moment, until he uttered those final words. "For me? What do you mean?"

"Everything you did was to get here, right? Becoming Zeke, getting into the academy, befriending me—all of it was so you could use me to get close to my father."

I reeled back and tipped off the step. My hand flew out to grip the banister before I could fall. "That's not true!"

My shout made one of the guards step forward.

"It is true," Derek replied. He didn't sound angry, harsh, annoyed, or anything like the Derek I've known for the last two years. "You wouldn't have taken it as far as you did—lying to me all of this time—if you didn't have another endgame.

"Well, you've gotten what you wanted. He's right in there." Derek pointed at the door our father disappeared through. "I hope he's everything you've dreamed of in a daddy."

Tears spilled over. My knuckles went white under my hold of the banister. It was the only thing holding me up. This was so much worse than him yelling or cursing me out.

Derek walked past me. "Goodbye, Zee."

This was worse because I knew deep in my soul, Derek was done with me.

I WAS LATE JOINING the party. The guard prepared to tackle me was the one who led me to the bathroom so I could cry in peace.

My shoes scuffed the blue tiled floors as I kicked around the pile of tissues I made on the floor.

What am I going to do now? Jonathan didn't bare his teeth at me, the girl in the costume who came in and blew up his life. Did Derek not confront him? Did he not tell him about me?

The idea that he went against his parents' stringent rules for privacy and threw this party so I could meet him was hard for me to take in. It's exactly what the secretly kind-hearted Derek would do, but the boy who spoke to me tonight was not him.

"He can't be done with me," I whispered into the chilly room. "He's my brother. My family. He can't leave me too."

A knock sounded on the door, jerking me upright.

"Zee? Are you in there?"

"Yes," I croaked.

"Are you okay?"

"I'm fine, Landon." I got up and hurriedly tossed the tissues in the wastebasket. "I'll be out in a minute. You can go back to the party."

I washed my hands and splashed cold water on my face. I came out and wasn't surprised to find Landon on the other side.

"They're about to serve dinner." He took my hand and kissed it, pushing back against my dark mood. "Sure you're okay?"

I nodded. "I am." I looked across the hall to the sitting room where everyone gathered. The lone white suit was stark in the sea of blacks, reds, pinks, and grays. "I just need to talk to Derek."

Landon heaved a sigh. "Derek again. Alright, I know how this goes." He brushed his thumb along my cheek. "Settle things with him and, if you need me, find me."

"Thank you."

I took off across the hall, fire lighting my nerves. Derek was not going to write me off before letting me explain. The irritating dummy thought he had me all figured out but I was the one who knew him. He was protecting himself from getting hurt again, but I wasn't those disgusting bastards who betrayed his trust and violated his mother. I'd make him see that.

The party was wonderful. Soft music played in the background to polite conversation and hushed laughter. Servers flitted through the space carrying trays of food that smelled heavenly. I veered around one as I zeroed in on Derek.

I was in arm's reach when another server appeared out of nowhere. "Would you like one, Master Derek?"

"Thanks." He turned away from the junior girl he was talking to, saw me, and promptly walked off—cucumber canape forgotten.

Huffing, I went after him and so began our game of cat-and-mouse. I stalked Derek all over the room until Naomi announced dinner was ready.

The group streamed out and I was two steps behind Derek. The tight lines in his neck and shoulders told me he sensed my presence.

Derek claimed a seat next to Michael and I pulled out the empty chair on his right.

Someone blew past me. The junior girl Derek was chatting up earlier boldly sat in my seat and pulled it out of my hand as she scooted up.

I gaped at her as she twisted around and smirked. "Fs sit at the bottom of the table."

I was not a violent person, but I seriously considered wringing her neck. Someone grabbed me as I opened my mouth.

"Zee, sit with me."

Adam dragged me off to the opposite end away from Jonathan—away from Derek.

"What's up with you?" Adam asked softly as he pushed me down on the chair.

"I need to talk to Derek."

"Talk to him or kill him? You've been chasing him around the party with crazy eyes."

"I have not," I snapped.

Adam gave me a look. "Play it cooler, or you'll have security on you."

"I have to get him alone."

"Again... to talk or commit homicide?"

I shoved a laughing Adam away. Although, he did have a point. I didn't want to draw the wrong kind of attention. I was going to talk to him and I didn't need anyone interrupting.

Jonathan, Naomi, Argyle, and Whittaker kept up a steady stream of conversation throughout dinner. They went around the table encouraging us to talk more about what we wanted out of the coming year, and our plans for the future.

My classmates' answers were irritating noise until he spoke.

"And you, Mr. Manning," said Jonathan. "What do you want to do?"

It was the first time since they put the bowl of cucumber soup in front of me that I took my eyes off Derek.

Jonathan smiled—open and curious for my reply—and I sensed he wasn't the only one. Derek was watching me too.

"I... want to be a mathematician," I began. My hands began to shake, so I moved them to my lap. "And then one day, a professor. I'm looking forward to this year and taking Calc II."

His eyes warmed with his chuckle. "Not something you hear many students say."

I found myself laughing too. "I get that a lot, but I've always loved math."

"People made fun of me as well and said I had as much chance of directing a blockbuster as I did of marrying a movie star." He held out his hands. "Look at me now."

The room erupted into laughter. Naomi used the same hand to swat him as she did to pull him in for a kiss. They broke apart and Jonathan moved on to Adam.

Dinner was delicious. Our dessert of baked apple rose tarts was even better, but that wasn't why I inhaled it. I wanted to finish first and then get to Derek before he got up from the table.

I swallowed the last bite and stood. Derek was on his feet before I pushed in my seat.

"May I be excused?"

"Of course, sweetie," said Naomi.

He ducked out of the room, slipping past security.

I followed at a slower pace. The guards watched me openly as I stepped into the opulent grand foyer and walked over to French doors just off the sitting area. I caught the white of his pant leg as Derek went into the bathroom I had been crying in earlier.

Pushing aside the white gossamer curtains, I ducked into the corner between the wall and the door and gazed outside. Nothing moved out there. This tiny corner of space was still and frozen in time. I felt for the handle and cracked open the door, letting a wisp of cool air wash over my face. Behind me, I heard a creak, and then footsteps.

The guards were no longer in the doorway. They must have trailed the rest of the party out of the dining room.

I pressed tighter into the corner. Derek walked past me unaware until I whispered his name.

He spun on me. "What the fuck?! What are you— Why are you following me?!"

My response was to grab his sleeve and shove him out the door. I slammed it shut behind me, encasing us in the privacy of the empty estate.

"What the fuck are you doing?!" he raged. "You're—"

"No!" I screamed. "For once, you're going to listen to me!" I advanced on him so fast Derek backed up and stumbled over the patio chair. "I did *not* use you to get close to your father! I would never do something like that and, to be honest, it pisses me off that you don't know that!"

Derek's surprise morphed into anger in a blink. His lips peeled back. "You're pissed at me? Me?! You want to pretend I'm the one who did wrong!"

"You did!" I shoved the chair aside. It crashed to the ground in an ear-piercing clang that should have brought security down on us, but no one came. "You should have listened to me! Let me explain instead of inventing your own version of the truth so you could push me away!"

Derek wasn't blank now. Fury burned in his eyes with the heat that made his cheeks flush red and beads of sweat collect on his forehead.

"Let you explain?" he repeated. "Explain that my dad cheated on my mom and knocked up another woman? Explain that he's a deadbeat who abandoned them instead of owning up to what he did? Explain that the man I thought I knew is a complete fucking stranger! Do you have any idea what your little revelation did to me?! What it will do to my family?! Do you care?!"

"I—"

"Of course, you don't, because this is all about you!" Derek's hand flashed out and I jerked back, but he wasn't coming for me. He yanked his phone out of his pocket and waved it in my face. "'Derek, I had no choice.' 'Derek, this was the only way.' 'Derek, this is hard for me too.' Me, me, me!"

He flung the phone. I let out a scream as it shattered against the wall, one of the pieces striking the back of my neck. "You only care about your fucking self, and that's why you didn't give a shit about lying to me for two years!"

"That's not true! I hated keeping the truth from you, but I thought you'd act *exactly like this* if I told you."

A harsh bark of a sound mimicking a laugh came out of his mouth. "So this is my fault?"

"No!" I fisted my hands in my hair and almost pulled off my wig. Derek was maddening! Why wouldn't he listen to me? Why was he twisting everything? "That's not what I meant."

"It is what you meant, Zela. You didn't tell me because you knew it would wreck me and how I'd feel didn't matter as much as what you wanted." He stuck his face in mine. "I fell in love with you," he whispered, "but you were never real."

I trembled. I was right before. Derek came as an angel tonight, filled with avenging fury that poured inside of me and burned away my defenses.

"I had to do it," I said once more, voice thickening with unshed tears.

"No, you didn't."

"Yes."

"No," he snarled. "There is no good reason for you fucking up my life because of what my dad did! You shouldn't have brought me into this."

"Getting close to you wasn't about him." I blinked and wetness stained my cheeks. "I didn't use you."

"Liar." His voice was soft, and it was worse than his shouts. "You're done with me, Zela. Stop following me—"

"No."

"Stop texting me."

"No!" I surged forward, arms out, but I crashed into a wall that wasn't there. He was right in front of me but I couldn't touch him. I felt him ruthlessly cutting me out of his life and the chasm opened between us. If I didn't do something, he'd get too far away, and I'd lose him for good.

"After tonight, you and I are—"

"I did it because you're mine!" I screamed, and I leaped across the gulf and grabbed him. His white suit crumpled in my fist. "I've been alone my whole life wishing for you. For someone I could talk to. Someone who knew what I was going through. Someone who had been denied what I had... family."

I shook him. I wasn't strong enough to hurt him, but the pain of the last few months burst out of me in a torrent that I couldn't control.

"I wanted you, and then, one day, I found my birth certificate and you were real. You've been there all along and all I had to do was get into one stupid fucking school, wear these stupid fucking clothes, and lie to my mother and aunt and everyone I know, but I didn't think twice about doing it because of you! Because going another minute without knowing my brother made me want to scream! So don't tell me I don't care about you!"

I threw him away from me as hard as I could. We stumbled away from each other, eyes huge, chest heaving.

Derek said nothing for a long time. His cheeks were still stained, his hands were still balled, but the fire behind his eyes was changing into something else.

"What does that mean?" he rasped. "You lied to your mom and aunt. About what?"

I swiped across my eyes, collecting tears on my sleeve. "About why I wanted to be at Breakbattle. She doesn't know it's about you. She still thinks it's a grand experiment."

His brows shot up his forehead. "Hold on. You were serious about that?"

Derek's surprise confused me. "Yes," I croaked. "She hates the gender separation and lost her mind when I said the name Breakbattle. She only agreed to let me go when I told her Zeke would be fodder for her book. I told you all of this last year."

"Yeah, but after the tournament I figured that must have been a load of bullshit like everything else you've told me since we met."

I bristled. "Everything I've told you was true."

"Right." Derek was putting himself back together before my eyes. He straightened his suit, fixed his hair, and cleared his face. He leaned against the banister, all trace of his explosion gone. "If you're so honest, tell me what your mother said when you asked her about the birth certificate."

Frowning, I fixed myself up too. I replied as I set my wig to rights. "I never told her I saw it. She still doesn't know that I found you or Jonathan Grayson."

"Why?"

Derek's gaze bore a hole in my skull, as if daring me to lie, but there was no reason for me to.

"I was afraid of what she'd do. She might've pulled me out of Breakbattle and put me in Chesterfield. Or taken me to another country. I'd never see you again."

"And you couldn't have that."

"No," I snapped. "We shouldn't have been kept apart in the first place. I wasn't going to risk her doing it again."

He bobbed his head like he agreed. "So what you're saying is... your mother never confirmed that my father is yours."

I blinked. Of all the things I thought he'd say, that was not on the list. "What do you mean?"

"I mean, you saw that name, looked it up, and decided he was your father. It doesn't mean he is. The name Jonathan Grayson isn't very unique."

A cool breeze blew through the summer night. It passed over my damp, heated cheeks and played with my fringe as we gazed at each other. It was too nice a night for this. The thunder and storms that passed through the day would have better suited the fight coming.

"I'm not stupid, Derek," I said tightly. "I did my homework. Somerset University. Eighteen years ago. Your father taught a guest lecture on screenwriting. My mother was an English major with a minor in film studies. It wasn't hard to put those pieces together."

He shook his head. "It still doesn't prove we're related. Did you find a DNA test with those important papers?"

I stalked closer. "Stop it, Derek. I'm your sister and you know it. We look alike."

He barked a laugh. "No, we don't."

"We have the same hair."

Amusement shone in his eyes and it annoyed the hell out of me. What was so funny?

"Millions of people have dirty blond hair, Zee."

"This isn't about those people!" My voice rose, spurred by his smirk. "We have the same ears too."

"What the hell does that mean?" Derek grasped my shoulders. "Zela Rae Manning, you and I look nothing alike."

I knocked his hands away. "Okay, so you look like your mother, but—"

"—and you must look like yours because you sure as fuck don't look like my dad."

Lifting my chin, I met his smile with a hard set to my jaw. "Don't do this. You're not going to push me away, and definitely not going to logic me away. They met while she was in college and his name is on my birth certificate. You're my brother."

"I am, am I?" Derek was still smiling and it made me angrier by the second. "You sound ridiculously possessive."

"Because you're mine," I repeated as though it was the single thing in this world that was true. Why should I feel weird about saying it? I didn't have any other siblings and I most likely never would. There was only him. "My brother. My Derek. Get used to it."

He chuckled. "What if I don't want to?"

"That's not an option."

"Hmm." Derek lifted his hand. His fingers were gentle on my cheeks, wiping the traces of my tears away. "Okay."

I froze. "What?"

"Okay," he repeated. "I'll get used to it."

I didn't move. *Was this a trick? He couldn't be saying...*

"What do you mean?" I pressed.

"I'm not pushing you away anymore, Zee, and I'm sorry I did. I'm mad you kept this from me, but I should have let you explain a long time ago." He held open his hands. "I'm sorry."

My breath lodged in my throat. Was this real? Could it be?

I took a step, then another, then I flew into his arms.

Tears sprang to my eyes again and stained his shirt as I burrowed my face in his chest. I wrapped my arms around him and squeezed, making him grunt.

"You forgive me?"

Derek rested his cheek on top of my head. "I do."

"We can go back to how it was?"

"Yes."

I bounced up and down—so happy I might have floated away if he wasn't keeping me anchored. "I love you."

"I love you too."

Derek pressed a soft kiss to my forehead, and I knew everything was going to be okay.

"I should have told you sooner," I admitted. "I did not want the truth to come out how it did, but years in the future, this could be a funny story we tell our kids."

His chest rumbled with a laugh. "We'll for sure tell our kids about this. Luckily, I can afford the therapy they'll need afterward."

Giggling, I leaned my head back to smile at him. "We survived our first real fight as brother and sister. I hope the next ones aren't this bad."

Derek rested his forehead on mine. "I'll bet my inheritance we'll have plenty of crazy fights ahead... but not as brother and sister."

"No?"

His head moved on mine as he shook. "No. You're not my sister, Zela."

The smile froze on my face. "What?"

"You're not and I would have known sooner if I had talked to you."

I dropped my arms. "Derek—"

"Your mother never told you my dad was your father, and even if she backs it up, a name on a birth certificate isn't proof. I know my dad and he loves my mom so much it's nauseating sometimes. He'd never cheat on her, and if he did, he wouldn't abandon his kid."

I tried to pull away but his arms were secure. "Listen, I know this is hard but—"

"I'm not in denial," he said firmly. "I know it's not true, and deep down, you know it too."

"What are you talking about?"

"You're obsessed with me."

He released me but I didn't go far, too stunned to move.

"Obsessed. Possessive." He waved a hand at my clothes. "And willing to do all of this to be close to me."

I took a step back. This was not good. We had taken a crazy turn and I didn't remember getting in the car.

"You don't act this way over a sibling. You do it for someone you're in love with—"

"Stop."

"—and I know, because I'm in love with you too."

"Derek!" My happiness burst and burned away in the acid of my writhing stomach. "You can't say those things to me! You're my brother whether you want to admit it or not."

"No, I'm not." Certainty laced his voice. "You came to Breakbattle looking for a brother but you found me instead. You want to believe the connection we have proves your beliefs true, because if they don't, you're back where you started without a brother and a father."

"Derek, stop!"

"But it's not true," he plowed on relentlessly. "You know it's not, because your obsession with me isn't sisterly, baby. It's love."

I wanted to hit him. I wanted to rage and scream and pound every awful thought out of his head. My blood sibling could not be in love with me. I'd destroy myself before I let that be true.

Calm down, Zela. Talk to him. Get him to see sense.

"Derek," I tried in a softer voice. "You're going to hate yourself when you have to accept that we share a father. I don't want that. Please, *stop*."

He shook his head. "We don't share a father, Zela, but this is important to you, so I'll help you figure out who your father truly is." He leaned in and kissed my forehead too quickly for me to get away. I staggered back like his kiss was a slap.

"I'll start now." Derek moved toward the door. "I'll see you at school on Monday, Zela. I love you."

He slipped inside before I could find the words to tell him off.

I backed up until I hit the wall. My legs gave out and I slid to the floor.

I stayed there until a guard found me forty minutes later.

Chapter Four

"Zee? Zee?"

The edge of the textbook dug sharply into my palm, but the pain was a buzzing gnat in a storm. Undefined figures and shapes moved around me as I trudged down the hall.

"Zee, are you okay?"

Adam grasped my arm, pulling me up short. The world came into focus on his handsome, worried face.

"Jordan said I needed to look out for you today and she was right. Did you sleep at all last night?"

I scoffed. "Sleep? Yeah, I think I did that for an hour. Maybe two."

"Why?"

Because my brother announced he was in love with me. Again.

Clutching my stomach, I leaned on Adam's chest. "I need to sit down."

"Come on."

Adam pulled me close and walked us both to the cafeteria. The first day of junior year arrived and brought all the people, sounds, and smells with it. The scent of sizzling bacon and melted cheese hit the back of my throat, but instead of tickling my appetite, my stomach heaved.

Derek sat at our usual table, casually eating his breakfast like it was no big deal. Around him, Cole, Michael, Landon, Tanner, Nico, Justin, Owen, and Hunter were engaged in conversation and laughing it up.

I wanted to run back to my oversized dorm and hide under the bed.

Nothing was right. I was too messed up after the party to fool around—let alone talk—with Landon. I was past due for a conversation with Cole and Michael. Not to mention finally being in the same room as my father, but I spent all night chasing Derek around. And Derek...

Adam tugged me toward the food line.

"No, I can't eat," I said.

"Jordan also told me to make sure you get some food in you."

I pulled a face. "Can you guys stop talking about me? Please."

"We love you the most. We're going to make sure you're okay when the other can't be here." He kissed my temple. "Don't worry. Jordan will take over cheering you up this weekend."

His words were sweet, and yet the urge to cry overwhelmed me. Adam's kiss was that of a brother's without question. I wish I could say the same of the ones Derek gave me Saturday night.

Adam picked up two trays and piled them with food despite my protests. Landon relieved me of the apple when I set mine down. I barely noticed. I was fixed on Derek.

His seat was next to me. Everyone knew this. No one fought it. If I sat somewhere else, they would think something was wrong and I could *not* explain what was going on with us.

"Dude," I heard Justin say as I slowly lowered myself in the chair. "I've always wondered what's up with you and the apples."

"Henrietta says…"

I tuned everything out as I stared at him. My aggravation grew with every passing second. Derek was just sitting there, eating his bacon, like the world wasn't fucking ending, because that's what it felt like to me.

"You have to stop."

I blinked. "What? Stop what?"

"Stop staring at me like you want to telepathically explode my head," he said calmly. He didn't even look up from his bacon. "You're freaking me out."

I gaped at him open-mouthed. "*I'm* freaking *you* out?! Are you kidding me?" I grabbed his shoulder and turned him around. "What you said to me the other night—"

"Are you okay?" Derek dropped his smirk. "You don't look like you slept."

"That's because I didn't," I clipped, "because of you."

"Well, that's payback because I didn't sleep because of you either."

Derek's new phone rested on the table between us. He tapped the screen. "Eighteen years ago. Somerset University. English major. I've started looking up the guys your mother went to school with at that time."

"Why would you— You can't—" Exploding his head was sounding tempting. I took a deep breath and tried to get something out that made sense. "I don't want you doing that."

"Why not? I said I'd help you."

I looked him in the eyes, more serious than I'd ever been. "Because you're in denial and this useless project of yours is delaying the inevitable." I glanced around and chose my words carefully. "You need to accept what our relationship is now. Please."

I moved under the table and took his hand. "I love you like a brother," I whispered, "and that's all you'll be to me."

Derek leaned in, pressing his forehead to mine. I went rigid like his touch electrocuted me, but I didn't try to pull away.

"That's not all I am to you," he whispered. "Only one of us is in denial and I won't stop until I prove it."

"I'm telling you to stop," I forced through clenched teeth.

He shrugged. "But you don't tell me what to do."

"Ugh!" I shoved him off. "You're so—! So—!"

"Yours?" he finished. His smirk made me flush.

"Go," I ordered. "Now. You and I need some space until you get your head straight."

"Alright." Derek got to his feet. He didn't look as bothered by this as I expected. "If that's what you want."

"Really?" His agreeableness cooled my ire. "Thank you."

"No problem. I can give you space, but we both know you can't stay away from me."

Embarrassment lit my face on fire at how loudly he said that.

"I'll be with my breakfast buddies until you change your mind."

With that, he walked off and sure enough plopped down at a table of sophomore girls who were all over him in seconds.

"What was that about?" Adam asked.

"I don't want to talk about it."

I stabbed at my food for the rest of breakfast. A few people tried to make conversation with me but gave up when they got clipped, one-word answers in reply. Landon was most persistent.

He caught up to me as I stomped out of the cafeteria. Hooking his arm around my neck, Landon made me stop.

"Things are clearly still weird with you and Derek."

"I don't want to talk about it," I repeated.

"Then we won't talk," he said easily. Landon brushed his lips along my skin—a kiss so featherlight as to hardly be there. "You're mad. Let me take your mind off of it."

"Yes."

My reply was so quick he chuckled. Jordan warned me against getting naked as a means of avoiding my problems, but she also told me Derek just needed time and that my life wasn't a festering shithole. She was wrong about a lot of things.

"We have class now, but we can take our lunch upstairs and eat it off each other."

I curled into his side, breathing him in and letting his sweet appley scent calm my jangled nerves. "You don't have a problem with me shamelessly using your body as stress relief?"

"That's literally my dream. Use me all day and six times on the weekends."

Giggling, I snagged his collar and pulled him down for a kiss.

"I love you," I whispered.

"I love you too."

"Told you that's how he became Elite."

A snide voice popped our bubble. A group of Elite girls posted up against the wall, watching us. Shannon's lips peeled back in a snarl that didn't look good on her pretty face.

"He fucked around until he got a few of the Elite guys to train him and feed him answers. Disgusting," she spat. "Argyle and Whittaker should never have approved the tournament."

I wasn't surprised Zach's girlfriend was being awful. What shocked me was her little posse nodding their heads.

"Shannon, why don't you go and get some business, so you can stay out of mine."

"Why don't you go and get some dick?" She laughed. "But I'm sure you're on your way."

My tone was as sweet as my smile. "You're right. I am."

I grabbed Landon's hand and dragged him away, leaving Shannon to shout nonsense at my back.

"Damn, that was hot," he said. "Were you serious because I can be late to class?"

I bumped his shoulder. "We're not missing our first day, but we have a date for lunch."

Landon and I climbed the six flights of stairs, our flirting getting filthier the whole way up. We stepped through the E-marked double doors and Landon slipped.

I shot forward to catch him and my foot went flying. We fell hard, landing face-first on a sticky substance coating the floor. I peeled open my eyes and before me lay a used, bloody tissue.

"Uck!"

I batted the nasty thing away and scrambled up for a proper look at the magnificent Elite Wing. The floor was covered in garbage and whatever Landon and I were coated in. Bulletin boards had been ripped up, their butcher paper in shreds on the floor. Only one was still intact. On the sign-up sheets for the school clubs and activities, was a huge up-side-down A.

The door opened behind us.

"Wow," said Cole. "I think class is canceled."

THE TEACHERS ORDERED us back to our dorms while the custodians cleaned up the mess. Everyone went back to theirs while I went to Landon's and took up his offer of stress relief.

"Why did they do that? How did they do that?" I pulled the covers up to my chin. "For All's pranks were harmless last year, but this was just... nasty. What did junking up the hall-way and soaping the floors prove?"

Cool air wafted over my chest. Landon was craftily tug-ging the sheets off my breasts.

I flicked his nose. "Stop it. I'm cold."

He grinned wolfishly. "I know."

I rolled my eyes. "Can you behave yourself for one second?"

"You weren't saying that ten minutes ago."

"I'll take that as a no," I replied, smile playing at my lips.

With first period canceled, we got a cool hour and a half to explore each other's bodies to our hearts' content. I took losing my virginity off the table though. When we finally did it, it wouldn't be while my head was wrecked over a dozen different things. I wanted our first time making love to be the sweet, perfect experience it almost was that night at his house.

"Maybe he has something else to prove," Landon offered. He pushed the covers down some more. My breath hitched as he trailed his finger along my lower belly. "Whittaker and Argyle didn't hear him when he played nice. Now, he's stepping it up."

"I don't like the sound of that."

I wanted things stirred up at Breakbattle. I wanted Whittaker—and the board of education—to accept this system hurts more students than it helps.

I wanted to rip the expansion out of Cameron's hands and tear his plans up like confetti. I wanted him to know it was me who took it away from him.

What I didn't want was anyone getting hurt.

Turning over, I took hold of Landon's chin and kissed him.

I wasn't concerned about new For All until now. It's clear his crusade was against the system while the true For All,

Cameron, was against me. I knew what Cameron wanted. I didn't know what this new guy's actual end game was.

"I love you," I said softly. "Will you warm me up?"

"Yes, please."

We fooled around in his room until the chime for second period forced us out. I left Landon's room and practically ran into Michael and Cole heading out to class. It was plain on their face that they guessed what we were up to.

Cole picked up his feet and kept going without a word. Michael stopped me when I tried to do the same.

"Hey. Can we talk?"

I glanced over my shoulder. Landon tossed textbooks into his backpack.

"I'll see you in class," I called to him.

Michael and I set off. "What's up?"

"I'm sure you can guess."

Michael switched his backpack to the other shoulder. His free arm hung between us and brushed against mine as we walked closer than needed down the stairs.

"I had fun talking to you this summer," he said. "I usually love seeing my dad, but the whole time I wished I was with you."

Warmth grew like embers inside of me, stoked by every deliberate touch. Landon was fierce. Cole was Cole. But Michael was sweet. He left me presents in front of my door. Sent me silly text messages. And spent hours comforting me when he could have been enjoying Orlando with his friends.

"I missed you too." Any other day, I might have been strong enough to hold that confession in, but that day

Michael's pinky was hooked through mine, and it rendered me helpless.

"What are you doing this weekend?"

"This weekend?"

Smiling, Michael held my gaze as he brought my hand to his lips. "We have a date."

"Date?" I squeaked.

"Is Friday or Saturday night better for you?"

"Date?"

I was repeating things like a moronic parrot and the kisses he was dropping on my fingers were entirely to blame. I pulled away to allow my brain to function normally again. Michael looked at me curiously.

"I think we should talk before we make plans for a date," I said.

Leading him off to the side, we pressed against the wall while the other Elites headed to class.

"Is this about Landon?" he asked. "I thought you guys weren't exclusive."

"We're not, but we are serious. I love him."

Michael didn't blink. "I respect that. But if you still want to be with me, then I want to be with you."

I dropped my head. "It's not as simple as that anymore."

"Why?" He gently took hold of my chin, refusing to let me look away. "It's that simple for me."

"It's not just you, me, or Landon," I whispered. "This summer, I... I was with..."

"Cole."

My eyes flared. Michael stroked my chin, his sweet smile still in place.

"I know you hooked up."

"How?" was all I managed.

"He told me. He felt guilty for being with you when he knew how I felt, but he shouldn't feel guilty and neither should you. You can hook up with whoever you want. I never had a claim on you." He found my fingers once more and brought them to his lips. "But I would like to. So tell me... Friday or Saturday?"

"Friday." The moronic parrot took a holiday. Things were incredibly messy, but I wanted him, and Michael saw me at my worst and wanted me too. Like I said, I wasn't strong enough to say no that day.

"Seven or eight?"

"Seven."

"Italian or Greek?"

"Greek."

Michael was smiling so brightly it was infectious. We stood there giggling at each other like loons—until Landon walked past us.

He took one look at us huddled together holding hands and a muscle in his jaw ticked. He said nothing—just rounded the corner for the stairs and disappeared.

My smile slipped. I was overdue for a talk with him. I had a feeling we wouldn't be spending lunch eating off each other.

Michael and I headed upstairs hand in hand. The Elite Wing was spotless once again. The only trace of For All was the bare bulletin boards.

I pulled away as we stepped in front of Mrs. Peterson's door. I didn't want to rub our budding relationship in Cole's and Landon's faces.

Mrs. Peterson squealed when I walked inside. She hopped out of her desk chair and gave me a hug that wasn't teacherly, but entirely welcome. She was the only one in the Elite camp who rooted for me from day one.

"It is truly an honor to be your teacher, Zeke," she said. "I'm looking forward to this year and seeing all that you achieve."

She spun me around to face the class. "Everyone, this is the newest addition to the Elite scholars, Zeke Manning."

Adam scrunched up his face in the back and I smothered a laugh.

"We have to jump right in due to this morning's... delay, but I expect you all to make sure Mr. Manning knows the ropes." She patted my shoulder. "Zeke, your desk is between Mr. Porter and Mr. Grayson."

Two rows, ten desks. I headed for the one second from the last and passed Sullivan Porter.

"I'll show you the fucking rope."

I halted. Sullivan shot me the filthiest look behind his textbook. "You don't belong here, F. You and your bitch boy stole Zach's and Rhys's places, but trust me, we'll send you back where you belong."

I opened my mouth.

"Is something wrong, Zeke?" Mrs. Peterson asked.

I replied without looking at her. "No, ma'am."

Calmly, I raised my hand, using my body to conceal me flipping him off. "Everything is fine."

I continued to my desk and met Derek's look as I set down my things. He put two fingers to his temple and saluted.

"Is this enough space for you?"

THE ROCKY START ASIDE, the rest of the morning went smoothly. Mrs. Peterson went over the syllabus, discussed what she expected of us, then passed out a study guide of lessons we needed to know for the review test—the next day.

"At least I remember most of this from studying for the tournament," I muttered to myself. I headed out of the wing, seeking lunch. "I wish I had the textbooks."

"I have them."

I snapped my head up. When did Cole get here?

"You can borrow mine," he added.

I tucked the guide to my chest. "Or we could study together."

Cole looked away. "That's not a good idea."

"Why not?"

"Summer is over, Zee."

"It doesn't mean we have to be."

His jaw clenched. Saying this was hard for him. He avoided this—avoided me—so he wouldn't have to.

"Michael likes you."

"So do you."

"I never said that."

"You didn't have to."

He gripped my arm and made me stop. We stood in the middle of the hallway, the only two people who existed in a sea of noise.

"Don't make this difficult." Cole's struggle reflected in his eyes. The part of him that always gave him away no matter how tough or cruel he acted.

"I am going to make this difficult," I said with a smile. "You want me to end this. Michael has always chosen you, and you want to do the same, but I won't make that choice for you. If you want to end this with me, Cole, then do it now. Tell me you don't want to be with me again. Don't want to touch me, kiss me, or tickle me in the shower."

His breathing picked up with every word I said. "Why are you doing this?" he growled.

I raised my hand and he grabbed my wrist just short of his lips. "Because everything in your life is a challenge to defeat. Why should we be any different?"

A dozen emotions flashed across his face. Cole voiced none of them. Dropping my hand, he stalked off.

"We'll study after dinner," I called.

"Fuck you!"

Chuckling, I continued on to the cafeteria. My laughter dried up when I turned the corner and discovered Landon waiting for me. He pushed himself off the wall.

"Hey. About that lunch date..."

I held out my hand. "Let's go."

We didn't speak on the walk back to his dorm. Everything that came to mind was wholly inadequate. Landon was first. My first crush. First kiss. First to claim my heart. Now I wanted him to make room for someone else.

I pulled him over to the couch and took a seat. He didn't sit next to me. Landon moved over to the window.

His back was to me as he said, "So you and Michael are a thing now."

"No, but we are going on our first date this week."

Landon made no move. "I hope you guys have fun."

"Landon..."

"Really, Zee. We're not exclusive. You can date who you want."

I rose and encircled him from behind. My heart hammered in my chest and I pulled him closer, wanting him to feel it. "Will you sit with me, please?"

"If that's what you want. I'll do whatever you want, Zela." He slumped over, body giving in, and me the only thing holding him up. "I love you."

"I love you too." I turned him around and cupped his face, feeling the tempting prickle of his stubble against my palm. "I could be with a hundred other guys and I'll still love you so much it makes my heart burst."

"Yeah?"

I rose on tiptoe and kissed him until our lungs cried out for air.

"Yes."

Landon gripped my thighs and lifted me up. He carried me to the couch and sat us down, me in his lap.

"You're not planning on being with a hundred guys, right?"

"Definitely not," I said with a laugh.

"Tell me what you do want."

"I can't." I buried my face in his neck. "It's awful and self-ish and I hate myself for even thinking I have a right to ask."

Landon was gentle as he took off my wig and cap. His fingers were soothing running through my hair. "Tell me anyway."

"I want you to be with me... only me." I squeezed my eyes shut. "I kept picturing you in Europe with another guy or girl and it drove me crazy, and I know that's not fair because I was here with someone else."

His hand stilled. "Someone else? But Michael was in Europe too."

"I was with Cole," I whispered.

"Oh."

That was it. Oh. I waited for Landon to say something, but as the silence grew, I pulled back. He didn't appear angry or disgusted with me. Honestly, I hadn't seen this expression on his face before.

"Are you mad?" I asked. "I should have told you sooner—"

"Zela, there was another girl."

I stiffened. "What are you talking about?"

"In Europe," he explained. "She was one of Dad's models. We were both trapped in the hotel, bored with nothing to do, so— Baby, are you okay?"

It was a fair question. My hold on his collar was getting pretty tight. "Did you sleep with her?" I rasped.

"No," Landon said clearly. "We kissed and she wanted to take it further, but I couldn't do it. All I could think about was you and the way you stroke my jaw while we kiss and make those soft breathy moans that I swallow like candy."

Heat flooded my cheeks. My stranglehold eased as he wrapped his arms around me. "You don't have to ask, Zee. I'm yours, and only yours, for as long as you'll have me."

"I plan on having you for a long time, Landon Foster." I kissed his cheek, then his nose, and jaw, and every inch of him I could reach. "And there won't be one hundred guys. Just one. Maybe two."

"Can I ask you something?" Landon tipped his head back. "Just once and I'll never ask again."

"What is it?"

"Why Michael and Cole?" he asked softly. "Why can't it just be me?"

"Look at me," I whispered.

He did.

"It's not because you're not enough," I began. "It's me, Landon. A time ago, I was broken and there're parts of me that are gone or will never fit quite right."

"That isn't true." He pushed the hair from my face, tangling a strand around his finger. "You're perfect."

I smiled. "I love that you think that. You don't see the girl who goes to a therapist every two weeks and is so taken over by her past, she doesn't know what's real most days. I never thought I could be the person I am when I'm with you. Being loved by you has given me a piece of myself back.

"And even though it's new and complicated..." I thought of Michael and me safe on the Hogwarts Express, shielded from the world. "I believe Michael has another piece."

"And Cole?"

I nodded.

Landon took a deep breath and held it. I was quiet as he came to terms with our future.

"Okay," he said, "but I have a condition."

Sitting up straighter, I steeled myself. "I understand. Do you not want me to talk to you about them or see us in public?"

He frowned. "What? No. I don't want you to hide anything from me. Ever. But there is one thing I do want and I'm not moving on this."

"Tell me."

Landon looked me in the eyes. "I'm going to be your first."

I couldn't help it, I laughed. "Landon, are you for real? That's your condition."

"Henrietta and Declan ruined it for us. I'm not letting Michael or Cole get there first."

Shaking my head, I straddled him and pushed him back into the cushions. "I accept your condition."

His grin made me shiver. "We can take care of it right now. Just to be safe."

"There are ten minutes left for lunch."

"Hmm."

I yelped as he shot off the couch and raced us toward the bed.

"We'll just have to think of another way to spend our time," he said.

FRIDAY MORNING, I'M a bundle of nerves. I snuck glances at Michael all through breakfast which weren't very sneaky because Cole got up halfway through and made up some nonsense about needing to study.

Things had been weird between me and Cole to say the least. We studied for the review test together, but didn't do more even though we both looked at the bed multiple times. We hadn't been alone together since.

"What's up with you and Derek?"

I tore my eyes off Michael. Tanner jerked his head at Derek's new table.

"You got into it on Monday and now he doesn't sit here. You not friends anymore?"

"We are. There's nothing going on with us, but you know how Derek can be."

He blew out a breath. "For real."

I was thankful Tanner accepted that easily. I didn't want to touch the situation with Derek at all, not even to make up a convincing lie.

He seems to be his old self though.

Derek lapped up the attention from the junior girl who snubbed me at the party.

It irritated the hell out of me.

He has me in stomach-twisting knots over getting him to let go of his feelings and be my brother, and this guy was licking cream off some mean chick's fingers and laughing at her no doubt terrible jokes. He didn't look like he was in love with anyone but himself.

A weight settled on my shoulder.

"We staring at Derek again?" Adam asked.

"No." I pointedly looked away, knocking off Adam's chin. "We're not. There is something else I need to do. You ready?"

"Yep. You take that side and I'll take this side."

I glanced at Cameron's table as I got up. I promised him a fight and that's what he was going to get.

I started with my old friend Noah first.

"Hey, Noah."

He looked up from the girl he was nuzzling and that heart-melting smile lit up his face. It was good to see they were still together. Noah did literally go to battle for her. "Zeke! Hey, man. What's going on?"

"Nothing much. I just wanted to let you know that if you ever need help preparing for a battle again, I'd be happy to do it."

"Seriously?"

I returned his smile with a big one of my own. "Yep. I may be Elite now but I'm not going to forget my friends."

"Damn, thank you. I'm going to take you up on that real soon."

Laughing, I said goodbye and moved on to a table of Ds. I gave them the same message. The Battle Doctor was back in business.

Adam made the rounds to the Fs while I spoke to the Ds and Cs. At one point, I caught Cameron watching me but I slid off him and kept talking like nothing happened.

Adam and I met up outside of the cafeteria and went up to class together.

"Are you sure you want to do this?" His question was so soft his lips barely moved. "Cameron got in your face after the tournament. He'll hit back if he finds out what you're do-ing."

My eyes bugged. *Jordan? She told him even though she promised— No, wait.*

It hit me that Adam must have been talking about our public showdown on the basketball court.

"The beauty of this plan," I replied, "is Cameron won't know what I'm doing until it's too late."

Adam dropped it. By now, he trusted me.

He changed the topic. "Do you know what clubs you're going to join?"

"Archimedean Club is a given. Future Leaders was also a lot more fun than I thought it would be. Those, plus whatev-er else Cole signs up for because it'll piss him off and make it impossible to avoid me."

"You guys are brewing up one weird-ass love story," he muttered.

"Says the guy in love with two women at once."

"Touché."

We topped the sixth-floor landing and Adam stepped forward to hold the door for me. Stepping inside brought on the unfamiliar feel I thought would never pass.

Life as an Elite was the same as being in the F Class in exactly one way. Mrs. Peterson taught us all subjects and as-signed what she knew was a ridiculous amount of home-work. That is where the similarities ended. The way they treated students on the sixth floor was night and day.

Peterson handed out the MT tablets half the school walked out over and basically told us they were ours to do with as we pleased. Also, if we lost or broke our tablet, the school would have it replaced free of charge.

It didn't end with the perks. With our small class size, the coaches were able to give us individual attention. Instead of endless practice games where Coach Singh bellowed from the sidelines, he'd have us come up one by one and talk through form, technique, and lead us through drills to put his critique into action.

There was nowhere I couldn't go. No passes. No battles. No asking for permission. I strolled in and out of the library as I pleased. I had my pick of clubs and volunteer opportunities. Next weekend there was a movie night for weekenders and Peterson put me down before I asked.

It's an entirely different life for those on the sixth floor, I thought as I looked around.

A hard shove from behind sent me flying. I tripped over my heel and Adam caught me before I hit the floor. We whipped around on Lars Johansson, Wyatt Wharton, Jose Dimas, and Sullivan.

"Oops," said Jose.

Sullivan's smile was nasty. "How did you become Elite when you can't even manage walking?"

Adam lunged at him and I hopped in his path.

"You realize you're insulting Zach more than me," I shot back as I struggled to hold my best friend back. "He's the one who lost to someone who can't manage walking."

"Fuck you."

I laughed. "I hear that daily from someone a lot tougher, and cuter, than you. You're not going to get to me, Sully, so give it a rest."

I turned my back on my new classmates and dragged a steaming Adam away.

"Don't give those guys the satisfaction of landing you in detention," I told him.

Adam shot them a filthy look as he protectively put his arm around me. "I'm not letting them hurt you again either. I'm serious, Zee. If Sully touches you, I'm getting detention for the rest of the year."

I should have argued him down but part of me was grateful to have him watching my back. One awful day in the locker room showed me Sully wasn't above violence.

Adam walked me to my seat, kissed my cheek, and then went to his desk. Derek watched the whole exchange.

"What's going on with you and him?" he asked as I unpacked my bag.

"Why does everyone ask that?" I muttered. "We're friends."

"Good."

I lifted my head, narrowing my eyes on him. "Why is that good?"

"No reason."

My anxiety heightened, but Derek was the picture of innocence looking back at me.

"Do you miss me yet?"

"How can I miss you?" I snapped. "You're behind me every day."

Derek grinned. He didn't look so innocent now. "Kinda seems like you miss me from the way you stare at me across the cafeteria."

I ignored that. "I have a question. Have you accepted the truth?"

"Yes," he replied without hesitation.

"I'm not talking about your version of the truth." I sat and scooted closer to his desk. "I want things to go back to the way it was, Derek. *You* have to let it."

He just smiled. "I'm not the one in our way."

"I—"

"Attention, class," Mrs. Peterson cut in. "Eyes front."

I reluctantly turned away from him. I should have known he wouldn't make this easy. Derek never made anything easy, but this was a situation most members of the human race did not have to deal with.

I spent most of the day with my eyes on the clock. I'd never wanted it to be the weekend more than I did that day. I had to get out of this place.

Eight hours later, the final bell rang and I beat it out of class with a hasty bye to Adam. My things were already in my backpack, so I skipped the stop at my dorm and went straight outside. The cool September breeze washed over me as I trekked across the lawn. I was the first one out here, but soon the grounds would be filled with people tossing the ball around, spread out on blankets, bunking in for a weekend of whatever treats their class would allow.

I preferred Breakbattle like this. Quiet, empty, peaceful. It was easy to pretend we were a normal school when students weren't out here in groups separated by the letters on their chests. As and Elites on one side. Fs on the other. Everyone else in between.

Mom honked the car to signal me. I climbed inside and leaned over to kiss her cheek.

"Hello, my only one," she said. She must have been in a good mood. "How was your first week in your proper classes?"

"Great, Mom. Mrs. Peterson gives me extra assignments from some of her advanced math classes." My excitement bubbled out of me. I couldn't help it. I loved math that much. "She also mentioned that she has colleagues from Somerset U who'd be happy to let me shadow them. Could I do it, Mom? I'd miss a day of school, but they would count it as special credit. Mom, please."

She laughed. "Of course, Zela. I don't see why not."

Smiling, I leaned back in my seat and shifted to watch the academy grounds fall away and be replaced by the thick, dense trees that blanketed our town.

"Mom, can I ask you something?"

"Yes?"

"What was it like at Somerset U? Do you miss it?"

"Oh, dear. Do I miss it?" She fell silent, considering her answer. "I guess I miss staying up late roaming the campus with my friends. I miss the debates over my favorite literature, eating my lunch in the quad, and feeling like I had my whole future in front of me. I miss being young." She stroked my hair. "Why do you ask?"

"No reason. We just... have to think about which colleges we'll apply to soon."

She tugged my ear. "Somerset would be a fine school for you, Zela, but don't limit yourself. You could easily get into the Ivy League." Suddenly, we veered off conversational and returned to the business of molding my life on the right course. "This weekend we'll sit down, research universities, and go over your options."

"Okay." There was no point fighting Mom. She'd do that research with or without me and I wouldn't be surprised if she filled out the applications herself. "Not tonight though," I spoke up. "I have a date."

"Ah yes. With this Landon fellow? Why haven't I met him?"

"You will meet him."

Very, very far in the future. Preferably after we're married with five kids and I know he won't run away.

"But I'm not going out with him tonight," I continued. "I have a date with another guy, Michael."

"Excuse me? You're not cheating on him, are you?"

"No!" I cried. "Of course not. Landon knows about the date. He's cool with it."

There was a pregnant pause during which I kept my gaze fixed firmly out of the window. I knew there was no avoiding this conversation, but I didn't need to see the look on her face while we did this.

"I'm dating them both," I announced. "At the same time."

"I see."

I held my breath, waiting for her to say more. Mom always had more to say.

"It seems you've picked up quite a bit from your sessions with Miss Valentina."

The side mirror gave me a perfect view of my pink cheeks. "This isn't because of Miss Val. I like them both and it's my choice—"

"Do not justify yourself, Zela."

I flinched. *Oh no. She is going to forbid me from seeing them, but I'm not lying down on this one. It's my life and my choice and—*

"I'm proud of you."

Eyes flaring, I whipped around to goggle at her. "I'm sorry. What now?"

"Every day, I see you growing into the woman I hoped you'd be." She blew a raspberry. My mother—Andronika Manning—blew a raspberry. "This nonsense that women should be chaste and have one partner is based on an outdated belief rooted in men's need to control our desires so they could keep track of which child was fathered by who. A non-issue nowadays due to birth control and DNA testing, so there's no reason women should be constricted to one partner."

My mouth hung open. *What the hell was happening?*

"You might not know that Val and I have had many conversations about her and her partners and how they've made it work. Truly fascinating," she said brightly. "I've included some of it in the book."

"You— You have?!"

"Oh yes. Along with my own experiences with multiple sexual partners."

I blinked. "Wait. Hold on—"

She plowed on. "You're old enough now that I can discuss this with you."

"No, I'm not."

"I let go of societal beliefs on single partners a long time ago." She waved her hand. "My twenties were filled with exploration and not just with the opposite gender."

Holy hell! Where is the off switch?!

"I had a brief affair with this lovely lesbian couple—"

I clapped my hand over my ears. "La, la! La, la, la, la, la!"

Mom clicked her tongue. "Honestly, Zela. I'm still a woman. You didn't think I lived in celibacy, did you?"

"I absolutely thought that! In my mind, you're a genital-less nun and I was conceived through immaculate conception!"

She gave me a look, lips quirked in a teasing smile. "Actually, you were conceived on a school desk after a few too many strawberry pom mojitos."

My head fell hard on the dash. "Mom, can you just let me out here... and then run me over?"

Mom's laughter filled the car harder and louder than I had heard in a while. She teased me the whole way home, sharing more about her adventurous life than I ever wanted to know.

We pulled into our drive and I scrambled for the door handle. "Seriously, Mom! I don't need any more therapy!"

Her guffaws chased me as I ran in the house.

Hours later, I was recovering on my bed while Jordan ran through my options.

"Did he say what kind of restaurant?" she asked. "Is it formal? Will they kick you out if you show up in jeans? What are you doing after? Is hooking up on the table? Why didn't you get details, Zee?!"

"I didn't know first dates came with a questionnaire," I cried. "Henrietta and Declan took over dressing me for the first one and they hit it out of the park. Let's go with that."

"That dress was incredible and nothing in your closet is fit to be on the same rack."

Laughing, I grabbed a pillow and flung it at her head. "Real nice."

She giggled as she danced out of the way. "We'll just have to make do with what we got. I'm thinking the blue dress you bought in Florence with a brown belt and brown flats. Classy, comfortable, not too formal, but still nice enough for any restaurant."

"This is why I need you."

She winked. "And don't you forget it."

I moved over to the vanity and picked through my make-up options. "JoJo, be honest. Can I call what happened in the car child abuse?"

"Oh my goodness. Cringe." She came up from behind and hugged me. "I'm not even going to tell you about when Mom gave me the sex talk. She started going on about the things she and Dad got up to and I promised I'd never have sex if it'd get her to stop."

I lifted a brow. "How long did that resolution last? Two weeks?"

"One."

We fell over, clutching our sides. I was fizzling with a heady mix of nervous and excited energy. Michael would be here in an hour and I'd been thinking about little else but tonight all week.

Jordan slinked her arms around my neck and propped her chin on my head. "Can I tell you something without you freaking out?"

I riffled through my lipstick box, searching for the right shade of pink. "You're the one who does the freaking out, remember?"

"True. Very true." I felt her chest expand as she took a breath. "I'm going out tonight too... with Adam."

The box slipped through my fingers. "Oh my gosh, really?! Why didn't you tell me?!"

She chewed her lip. "I don't know. You have so much going on right now. Is it weird for you to have your cousin dating your best friend? Tell me if it's weird."

"It's awesome," I said firmly. "Adam is a great guy and he'd treat you like a queen. Also, you've seen Moon babies. They're adorable."

"Don't start calling yourself Auntie yet," she said with a laugh. "It's just a first date. We'll see how it goes."

Jordan leaned forward and plucked a tube out of my scattered mess. "This one with the gold earrings and wear your hair up."

"I love you." I immediately started doing up my hair. "What are you wearing?"

"If I'm lucky, nothing by the end of the night."

This time we did fall over laughing. We hugged tight, busting up on the carpet. I needed this. This week had been a confusing mess that I couldn't yet see myself out of. I wanted one night with a cute, sweet guy where I could pretend everything was okay.

Jordan helped do my makeup and then left to get ready for her own date. Six fifty-five on the dot, I was downstairs pacing in the kitchen. Mom eyed me as she stirred the quinoa.

"Are you nervous?"

I paused. "To be honest, no. I've always felt safe and comfortable with Michael."

She hummed. "Bring him inside before you leave."

"What? Why?"

"I want to meet him."

"Mom, no—"

Her eyes narrowed. "No? Are you ashamed of your mother?"

"Of course not," I said, groaning. "I don't want him to be nervous. Mother, I love you, but you're kind of intense."

I braced myself for a frown and a lecture. What I got instead was a smile and a chuckle. "That's a part of my charm, only one."

I gaped at her. "Who are you today?"

She came over, flicked my nose the way I picked up from her, and followed with a kiss. "Bring him inside. I meet him or he doesn't leave the house with my daughter."

That sounded more like her. I considered testing her but the bell rang before I plucked up the courage.

I opened the door on Michael's beaming smile glinting in the porch light. I bit my lip to stop myself grinning too wide. It was insane how handsome he was. Michael kept it simple with gray slacks, a V-neck sweater, and a white tee underneath. One of those effortlessly casual outfits that probably cost more than most people saw in a month. Michael's mom was a CFO for a fitness company and she supplied him with the money to buy the clothes and the genes to work them.

"Hey, Zee." Michael slipped his hand into mine as he brushed his lips over my cheek. A light, chaste kiss, but I blushed down to my toes. "Ready to go?"

"Not yet," I whispered. "My mom wants to meet you."

"No problem," he said easily. He kissed me again. "Don't worry. Moms love me."

I had a feeling his streak was about to be tested.

I led him into the kitchen as she finished plating her dinner. She dusted off her hands and then reached for his to shake.

"Hello, Michael. It's nice to meet a progressive young man such as yourself."

For the love of all that's good, if Mom brings up her sexual adventures right now...

"It's nice to meet you too, Ms. Manning. I read your book, *Sunrise Nation,* and loved your descriptions of Africa."

She straightened, looking at him in a new light. "You read it? Most people don't get the true point of the story isn't the romance but—"

"—finding the strength to leave her home and accept that she had to become someone very different," he finished. "I passed it on to my mom and she now owns everything you've ever written. She'd die if I brought her a signed copy. Would you mind?"

Mom was smiling ear to ear now. She agreed on the spot and her chest puffed up as Michael heaped more praise on her. She let us go with a "have fun" and "stay out as late as you want."

I stared at him open-mouthed as he held the passenger door for me to go in.

He winked. "I told you I give good mom."

"How did you do that? I've never seen her take to any-one that fast. I'm serious," I deadpanned. "I'm still growing on her."

Michael propped himself against the door. He let it swing in a little, bringing himself closer to me until the smell of his cologne tickled my nose. "I looked her up a while ago. I wanted to know more about you, your family, and your life. I brought it up in the letter you threw away."

I laughed softly. "When are you going to forgive me for losing your presents?"

The door swung even closer and my lungs emptied as his lips hovered over mine. His breath was warm on my mouth as he said, "I just did." Michael twisted and kissed the tiny corner of my lips. "You look beautiful. Have I told you that yet? This is the first time I've seen you as you."

"Thank you." I held still, waiting for him to kiss me for real.

He pulled back. "Ready to go? I haven't eaten since lunch and this place has the best Greek food in a hundred-mile radius."

I tamped down on my disappointment. "I'm starved. But I've been to Greece. My expectations are high."

"I'll meet those expectations. I promise."

You already have.

But I didn't say it out loud. Michael was there for me at my lowest. He charmed my mom, and he was being so amazing about my relationship with Landon. The night was perfect and it had just begun.

The drive to Evergreen was an hour long but there was never a lull. We talked the whole time about whatever came to our minds.

"So after you claim gold in the Olympics, Michael Young, what's next?"

Michael released the wheel and threaded his fingers through mine. He dropped a kiss on my knuckle, then another, then another. I clenched my jaw lest something embarrassing like a moan escape my lips. How could such an innocent act be so sexy?

"You know what?" He tucked our hands on his lap. "It's you who helped me decide that I want to go into sports medicine. I thought at first I'd be a trainer because of how much I love helping with you, but I don't just want to teach people how to run. I want to make sure they can do it for as long as they want." His thumb swirled on the back of my hand. "You go after exactly what you want and you don't stop fighting until you get it. You helped me see that I could do more."

I rested my head on the seat, enjoying the sensations his thumb was enticing. "You were amazing before I came along, Michael."

"I'm even better with you."

Michael asked me the kind of math I wanted to study and we launched into a conversation about advanced mathematics that he didn't know a lot about, but listened with real interest as I explained.

In no time at all, we pulled through the gates of the Promenade and parked in front of a cozy little blue-and-white stucco restaurant with brown slats on the sloped roof. A small fence covered in flowers and ivy set them apart from the other places in the plaza.

Michael came around the car and opened the door for me. The perfect gentleman.

I was the one to lace our fingers together and lean into him.

"Can I know what else you have planned for tonight?"

He smiled down at me. "The usual. Dinner and a show."

A bell chimed overhead as we walked in, signaling the host to step out from his podium.

"Good evening. Table for two?"

"Ye—"

"No," Michael said. "I'm here for pick-up. Young."

The host inclined his head. "Certainly, Mr. Young. If you'd like to take a seat, I'll have your order out in a moment."

Michael and I shuffled off to the bench on the side.

"Why are we picking up?" I asked.

"There's somewhere I want to take you that's even better than this. Trust me."

"I do."

It didn't take long for a server to come out bearing our food. My mouth watered at the heavenly smells wafting out of the bag but Michael took it and walked it out the door.

"I hope you like souvlaki, spanakopita, and stuffed grape leaves."

"I do." We held hands, swinging them over the cobblestones. "What's for dessert?"

"You'll find out."

Tingles lit my nerves. I was suddenly thankful I let Jordan talk me into sexy underwear.

We got back in the car and headed out of the Promenade. Evergreen was a town made up of mansions and the thick, deep woods that surrounded them. My curiosity piqued as we turned off the main street and onto a dirt road. The trees narrowed on us as we got deeper in, and eventually, I couldn't spot the town except for the faint glow of traffic lights rising over the horizon.

Michael suddenly pulled the car off the road and parked on the edge of the tree line.

"We're here."

Making a face, I peered through the dash looking for a clue. "Is here the spot where you murder me and bury me in the woods?"

Michael's laugh was smooth and rich. "Here is the place where I seduce you and make you mine."

"Oh. I'll get out of the car for that."

He chuckled as he met me in front of the car and drew me to his chest.

"Why are you so damn cute?"

Our eyes caught and, for a moment, we stopped laughing.

His hands glided down my arms and stopped on my waist. My heart beat against my chest—loud in my ears and probably in his. Tilting my head back, I rose up to meet him.

But he wasn't there.

Michael stepped back and gestured to a small gap in the trees.

"It's not too far. Right through here." He held out his hand for me to take. "Just stick close to me."

My mind was a swirl of confusion as I let him lead me through. I wasn't a naïve little girl anymore. I wanted to kiss him and I sensed that he wanted to kiss me too.

So why did he pull away?

I couldn't come up with an answer.

I held his arm to my chest, resting my forehead on him as we drifted deeper and deeper into the woods. Thick shadows pressed on us, plunging the forest in serene darkness only penetrated by the buzzing hum of hundreds of critters settling in for the night.

After a few minutes of walking, I made out light shining ahead.

"What's that?"

Together we broke through the trees and came out on to a well-trodden path. Overhead, a string of lights weaved through the branches and lit our way.

"Wow," I breathed. "Is this part of a park?"

"No."

"But someone hung this up. It must be someone's property. Won't we get in trouble if we're caught?"

He shook his head, smile tugging at his lips. "I promise you won't get in trouble. This is my backyard."

"It is?" I looked around. "Where is your house?"

Michael pointed off in the distance. "Through there. We actually bought this place for the running path. Mom had the lights put up so I could run at night."

"Is that safe? This path is accessible from the road and we've established this is a great place to murder and bury your dates."

"Don't be scared. I'll protect you."

Michael kissed the shell of my ear and I promptly forgot about serial killers.

If only I could get him to drop those lips down a bit and to the left.

He set off, tugging me along. "We're just up here."

The path seemed to go on forever through the darkness. We walked for what felt like a long time, holding each other and stealing glances and dancing on the edge of flirting, but it couldn't have been more than a few minutes before I noticed a break in the lights.

The string lights on my side veered off, leading down another path, and we curved to follow. A few more steps and I sucked in a breath.

Lights went around the trees, encircling a tucked-away space of soft grass and the blanket that had been laid upon it.

Michael guided me inside and I lay down, looking up at breaks in the swaying branches to see the stars.

"I found this spot while running," he said as he tucked himself next to me. "I like to come here and read, listen to music, just be alone." His finger traced a pattern on my palm. "I thought you might like it."

"I love it." Our noses brushed together as I turned to face him. I liked us like this. Breathing the same air, stealing the heat from each other's bodies, narrowing my world until I could see nothing but his eyes.

"I've never brought anyone else here."

"Really?" I said.

"No one. Not even Cole."

I ran my finger along his chest and heard the slight hitch of his breath that made my pulse quicken. "Why did you bring me here?"

"Because you let me in. I wanted to do the same with you."

I didn't need to ask what he meant.

And even though it's new and complicated... I believe Michael has another piece.

"Hungry?"

"Yes," I whispered. But neither one of us moved.

"We should eat before it gets cold," he offered.

"Yeah, we should."

His eyes traced my face like he wanted to commit every part of me to memory. The thought made me smile and Michael flicked down to my mouth.

Michael slipped his hand out of mine. I mourned the loss for all the time it took for him to take hold of my chin. Slowly, unhurried, Michael kissed me.

His lips were soft on mine. He didn't push or demand, but the gentle, deliberate pressure made sweet, raging heat burn beneath my skin.

I moaned—just a soft exhalation of breath—and Michael took his chance to deepen the kiss. Our tongues teased and played with each other as the kiss headed into different territory. I cupped the back of his head and drew him on top of me.

His hands traveled the length of my body and he wrapped my legs around his waist. Our moans got louder as we rutted against each other. Michael nipped my bottom lip and I squeaked, laughing through the kiss.

This is what I'm talking about.

I slipped between our bodies and grabbed his belt.

Michael broke the kiss. "Whoa, Zee. Wait." He caught my hand and pulled it away. "We can't."

I blinked up at him. "We can't? Why? Do you not want to?"

"Fuck no." He squeezed his eyes shut like he was in pain. "I *want* to."

"Then what's wrong? You've been holding back all night, but you don't have to. I want this. I want *you*. We won't have sex but"—I rose and dropped kisses along his jaw—"we can do everything else."

Michael's groan rumbled low in his chest. "Fuck, that sounds— But we can't," he said. "I want us to take things slow."

He drew up out of my reach. His chest heaved as he caught his breath and I couldn't resist splaying my fingers over his heart. It pounded wildly out of control. His lips said slow, but his body told another story.

"I taste sweeter than any dessert you've got in that bag."

Michael's breathing picked up as his eyes darkened. His control hung on by a thread. The old Zela couldn't say these things, but Landon and Cole were good teachers. I knew how to make him snap.

"I don't doubt it," he rasped, voice husky. "But this is important to me, Zee. We need to take things slow."

Moving up to his face, I traced the lines around his mouth. "Why?"

"Because I need to know what we have is real." He caught my hand and kissed the palm. "You're in love with another guy, and you're involved with my best friend. But I'm not going to be another hookup or second-best. I want a real relationship with you, Zela. A real connection that isn't confused by sex."

I swallowed, my desire cooling as I took in what he said.

"Michael, you're already more than a hookup or second-best to me."

He smiled—that perfect, breath-stealing smile that weakened my limbs. "Good."

I smiled back, but it quickly turned teasing. "Are you sure I can't convince you to put me on my knees on this blanket?"

"I'm sure you could."

I laughed until he came in for another kiss. Honestly, I wouldn't push him if this is what he wanted. Every fiber of my being screamed for him, but it wouldn't be right if we both weren't ready. I wanted perfect with Michael. When the time came, Michael would not doubt that I cared for him just because he was him.

We eventually stopped making out and sat up to a dinner that was cold, but delicious. Michael fed me French fries and more than my share of the souvlaki. Then he surprised me with sweet, sticky baklava for dessert.

"I heard you mention once that you liked it," he said as he took it out of the bag. "This will be the best you ever had. I promise."

"Want to put a bet on it, Young?"

"Yes, I do. What do you want if you win?"

I waggled my eyebrows.

"Fucking hell, woman."

Laughing, I tipped over and fell onto his chest. "I'm just kidding. If this isn't the best baklava I've ever tasted, then you have to move our running time from five a.m. to six. That's plenty early to be awake."

He grunted. "Fine. And if I win… you let me take you out again next weekend."

"That's cheating." I slid my arms around his shoulder as I straddled him. "Now I want to lose."

I held his gaze as I slowly opened my mouth. Michael placed a sticky treat on my tongue. I uttered a soft sigh of pleasure as I chewed.

"Wow. Not joking. This truly is amazing." I pecked him on the lips. "You win."

"Thank you," he said with a grin. "For the final part of the night, I promised you a show."

"Are we leaving?" I breathed in the earthy, mossy scent and let it fill me with a calm I rarely felt. "I like it here. It's so peaceful."

"It's about to get even better. Look up, Zee."

Puzzled, I leaned back and gasped. Flying overhead, dozens of fireflies flitted through the trees, lighting among the branches like Christmas lights. It was the most incredible sight, and their beauty filled me up.

"This is amazing," I breathed. "I can't believe I didn't notice them up there."

Michael held me to him as he lay back on the blanket.

For a while, we just lay there, watching the fireflies flit through the trees and relaxing with each other. We didn't talk, but we didn't need to.

Michael's finger trailed a slow path up and down my body, a touch incredibly intimate without straying anywhere more interesting. As I lay there with my head resting on his heart, I knew everything I needed to about how he felt about me.

And I felt the same.

Chapter Five

"**T**hings are going really well with you and Michael," Adam said.

"Yeah." It wasn't a question, but I answered anyway. I peeked through my lashes at Michael lacing up his shoes across the court. "We've been on four dates so far and each one was better than the last."

I finished tying my shoes and glanced around for listeners. "But between you and me, this kissing-only thing we're doing is driving me crazy. You have no idea what it's like to run behind that boy and *not* be able to grab his ass."

"You're right," Adam deadpanned. "I don't."

I made a face at him. "You don't know my suffering. You're getting some."

His grin turned wicked. "You're right. I am."

"Adam, yuck! That's my cousin you're talking about."

I rained swats down on him.

"You brought it up," he cried, trying to shield himself. "I am getting some. I'm getting *a lot*."

"Ah!" I jumped him, climbing his back like a spider monkey. I wrapped my fingers around his neck and shook. "Take it back!"

"Every chance we get!"

"Zeke," a dry voice interrupted. "Kindly stop strangling Adam and join your team."

"Sorry, Coach," I said between giggling.

The truth was I couldn't be happier that Jordan and Adam were together. Their first date went extremely well. Adam took Jordan to a skating rink and then they walked around the Promenade talking and eating cotton candy. After that, the night ended how she hoped it would. They've been out every weekend since, but on the weekdays, Adam sat cuddled up with Melody and disappeared with her after dinner. I was happy it was working with them. I only wished things were as smooth with my boys.

Cole, Michael, and Landon were on the other side of the court warming up for the scrimmage game. They laughed about something that must have been hilarious because Cole rolled off his seat howling. Their friendship was intact despite me, but their relationships with me were a different story.

We were five weeks into the new year and Landon and I still hadn't had sex. They were piling on so much work to prep us for standardized tests that we hardly had time to eat or sleep, let alone study. On the weekends, he was either out of town modeling for Declan or volunteering at a teen center outside of Evergreen.

While I had my plate full with my regular homework, extra assignments from Mrs. Peterson, shadowing her university colleagues, and fulfilling my promise to help students win their battles. I signed up to be a tutor to tackle the academic side, and spent the rest of the evening on a field, court, or mat working on the physical battles.

We both agreed we didn't want our first time together to be rushed, so we kept waiting for the right time. And waiting... and waiting... and waiting.

Between that, Michael's insistence that we take things slow, and Cole fighting his attraction for me like hooking up would kill him, it had been a stressful few weeks with no relief.

I let my best friend up but he grabbed me as I jogged off.

He curled me in his arm and kissed my temple. "You won't have to wait long," he whispered. "Michael is crazy about you. Anyone can see that."

I leaned back and pecked his cheek. "Thanks."

We split up and went to our teams. Cole, Michael, Landon, and Derek gave me a funny look as I ran up.

"What?" I asked, slowing down. "What is it?"

Cole's face crumpled in a scowl. "What were you and Moon kissing about?"

"I thought you said you were just friends," Michael added.

Landon nodded along. "The guy is always all over Zee."

I ping-ponged between them, not knowing what to make of this.

"Tell me about it," Derek said under his breath.

"Don't you start," I snapped at him.

Chuckling, he jogged onto the court and left me to the rest of the jealous crew.

Planting my hands on my hips, I shook my head at them. "If you want to know, we were kissing about my sexual frustration. So, if you want us to stop... you know what to do."

I turned my back on triple looks of shock and ran off to get in position behind Derek.

Playing sports at the Elite level was intense, especially when you played against Lars, Jose, Sullivan, and Wyatt.

I raced down the court, weaving through bodies friendly and foe. The hoop loomed in front of me. I skidded to a stop and raised the ball—

Someone streaked across my vision and pain exploded in my hand. I cried out, losing my hold, and Sullivan followed his vicious smack by snatching the ball on the first bounce and beating to the other side of the court.

"Zee."

Derek stopped everything and ran over to me.

"Are you okay?"

I quickly stopped nursing my hand. "I'm fine. Don't do anything," I added, catching the look he shot at Sully's back.

"I'm not going to do anything. I know by now that you can take care of yourself." He jerked his chin down the court. "That fucker thinks you don't belong with us. Prove him wrong."

I couldn't help it. I smiled. "I will."

We rejoined the game as Landon ran. He faked like he was going to shoot and Jose sailed through the air trying to catch nothing. Landon passed me the ball and I made the shot with the most satisfying swish.

Derek grinned as he ran backward across the court. "Good to see those practices weren't a waste."

"You're not taking the credit," I called. "That was all me."

His laughter bounced off the walls and filled my ears. It had been a while since we laughed. It had been a while period.

My smile dimmed as I fixed on the back of his head.

Day after day, sitting two feet from each other but never talking or reading or putting up with his moods. This isn't what I want.

The game played on until we were fourteen and fourteen. Derek was without question the best basketballer in the group which is why the other team had three guys on him at all times. He struggled to find a way out amid the waving hands in his face.

"Derek!" I shouted. I ran around the fringes of the group. "I'm open!"

Sullivan broke off like that was his cue. He barreled toward me, hands out, instead of up, and I braced myself to be fouled. The next thing I knew, Adam was in front of me and Sully was on the floor.

"Ow! What the fuck?!" Sullivan bellowed. "You're on my team!"

"Sorry, man," Adam said mildly. "I was trying to cover Derek and you came out of nowhere."

"Coach!"

Singh wasn't having it. "Stop whining, Porter, and get in the game!"

I was off before the boy got his bearings. The hole he left allowed Derek a chance and I caught the basketball as it sailed over Adam's head.

Jose came running at me. I twisted out of the way and kept going. The rapid *thump, thump, thump* of the basketball didn't mask the streaks and pounding of the team chasing me down.

I reared up, my feet hovering inches off the floor, and threw the ball in a perfect arch that I knew would make it before my feet hit the ground.

A sharp screech cut through the gym. "Nice job, Manning! Red team wins!"

Shrieking, I jumped up and down giving into the high. "Nice, Z—"

I spun on Derek and threw my arms around him. "Did you see?" I squealed. "I did the move you taught me. That was the first time I got it!"

His breath was warm on my ear as he chuckled. "Well, you were going up against an inferior player. My moves work on everyone but me, Zee."

I laughed. "Very true. Going up against you always reminds me of how much I suck."

"You don't suck. You're amazing." Arms encircled my waist. "I knew you'd embarrass the shit out of Sullivan."

Alarm bells clanged in my mind as Derek pulled me closer. I scrambled out of his hold.

Clearing my throat, I put a respectable distance between us. "Sorry. I shouldn't have—"

"How long are you going to hold out?" Amusement shone clearly in his eyes. "You miss me. It's obvious."

"Like I said before," I replied. "This stops when you let it."

"Okay. If it's up to me, come by my room tonight and we'll watch a movie." He backed away. "If you don't, I'm going to start thinking you don't like me at all. It'll really hurt my feelings. It may even take me another four years to trust again."

I clenched my fists. I was stuck between the urge to tell him I would always care about him and the urge to knock him upside the head for emotionally blackmailing me. I loved my brother, but the 666 was tattooed on his scalp, not Christina's.

Derek winked like he could read my thoughts. "See you after dinner."

Shaking my head, I walked over to get my stuff and head back to the dorm. I had to shower and then go to tutoring. I caught Cole on the way to the locker room. He was the last one to go because I suspect he was watching my exchange with Derek.

He narrowed his eyes on me as I stepped into his path.

"I'm going to take a shower," I announced.

"Okaayyyyy..."

"Want to do something about my sexual frustration?"

Cole dropped the scowl immediately. He licked his lips as he looked me up and down, no doubt recalling our previous sudsy escapades.

He shook himself. "I can't."

"Why not?"

"We have tutoring."

I closed the distance between us and felt no small amount of pleasure at seeing him stiffen. "We can be late," I whispered. "I have this new cherry shampoo. You can wash my hair with it while my hands are busy with... something else."

Cole's knuckles turned white as his grip on his gym bag tightened. "This isn't going to work, Zee."

"It's already working, Cole." Smirking, I lowered my eyes to the obvious bulge in his pants. "You have five seconds to make up your mind before I take blow jobs off the table."

"Resorting to ultimatums?" he hissed.

"They seem to work around here."

"Zee—"

"Five, four, three—"

"Fuck!"

I yelped as he snatched my hand and raced us out of the gym. We tripped on the stairs twice running up and collected strange looks from guys loitering in the hallway when we burst through and hurried to my room. We started tearing off our clothes before the door swung shut.

Cole and I were both very late for tutoring. We ambled into the library, mumbling apologies to the class advisor, and found our tutorees waiting for us in the back.

"Hi, Zee." Maddox Dane, one of my former F classmates, pushed his textbook across the table as I sat down. "Help."

"That's why I'm here, my friend." I took out my notebook and got to work. "Rational expressions aren't so bad. You first need to..."

Maddox listened intently as I explained how to solve the math problems. When he was working quietly on the first one, I glanced at Cole.

He's so cute with that serious look on his face. He's even cuter laughing as I shampoo his hair into crazy styles.

Cole glanced up and our eyes met. I waved, a grin on my lips as I thought of what we got up to, and was treated to his cheeks pinking and his glare returning full force as he dropped his head.

Either way, he's cute.

"After this, will you help me with wrestling?" asked Maddox. "I want to challenge Bertram from the D Class for his SAT prep slot and he chooses wrestling every time."

"Sure, I'll help," I replied without having to think about it. All students had access to after-school SAT prep, but because this was Breakbattle, Fs were limited to one hour, once a week. "I can give you an hour after tutoring. Does that work?"

He beamed. "You're the best, Zeke. The only decent Elite in this whole place."

"Can't get the F out of me that quickly."

We finished going over his homework and moved the tutoring to the wrestling gym. Afterward, he shouted thanks at me as we went our separate ways.

I was feeling good about life until I entered the cafeteria and saw the empty seat next to mine. An ever-constant reminder that Derek and I were on the outs.

Maybe it's time to do something about it. You're overdue to have it out and settle this. Whatever he feels, nothing will happen between us and he'll be forced to get over it. I don't want things to be this way until that happens.

I thought that, but I must have changed my mind a dozen times over dinner, and six more times as I climbed the stairs.

What if he never lets this go? What if he's still searching for the father you found years ago?

I couldn't go further than Derek's door. I paced in front of it, mind whirling.

How was I supposed to know what to do? There was no advice column for this, and no one I could talk to but Jordan—who kept telling me to forget about him and focus on Jonathan.

I just want my brother back. Why is that so hard? If only we could—

"Dude! Are you coming in or not?"

I jumped.

"I know you're out there, Zee."

A flush crept up my neck, but I beat back my embarrassment and pushed open the door. Hunter waved at me from his spot at Derek's desk.

"Hey, Zee."

"Hi, Hunter." I cut eyes to Derek. He was in his usual position—reclined on the bed with a book in his lap. "Are you having mentor time? I can go."

"It's over," Derek said. "See you tomorrow."

Hunter rose with his backpack.

"Why don't you stay?" I asked quickly. "We're going to watch a movie. You should join us."

"Ooh. That would be—"

"He can't," Derek said firmly. "He's got a project to finish up."

Hunter's shoulders slumped. "Derek's right. I have to finish my section or my partner will kill me." His cherub face suddenly lit up. "Can I watch a movie with you guys tomorrow night?"

"Sure thing, man," Derek said before I could open my mouth. "Zee will be back tomorrow night."

"Great."

Hunter let himself out, saying a goodbye that wasn't returned. Derek and I were too busy locked in a stare down.

"I'll be back tomorrow, will I?"

Derek dropped the book on the side table. He didn't break eye contact as he drew one leg up and draped his arm over his knee. "You're here, aren't you? You missed me." He gestured with his foot at the laptop on his bed. "You want us to go back to how we were. Let's do that."

I moved around the bed, eyes on him like he would strike any minute. "Fine. Then get up and we'll watch the movie on the couch."

He didn't make a move. "The couch is harder than the bleachers."

"I'd feel more comfortable on the couch."

Derek raised a brow. "Why? You chilled in bed with me when you thought I was your brother."

"You *are* my brother."

"If you believe that, there's no reason for you to be uncomfortable." He grinned. "Your big bro wouldn't pull anything."

Why did this feel like some kind of test? It seemed to him refusing to get in the bed was admitting I thought something could happen between us, instead of the actual gut-wrenching truth.

"Let me make this clear," I began, "you having romantic feelings for me is taboo in every country I've lived in, including this one. If you still have those feelings, you need to let them go. Now."

He put up his hands. "I got it. Say no more."

I inched toward the bed. "You have to accept Jonathan is my father," I continued. "I know what that means for your family and it sucks. I don't want to blow up anyone's life which is why I never went shouting about it or tried to hop your fence."

I put one leg on the bed, and when Derek didn't do anything, I drew up the other and crawled up to the pillows. I took a deep breath, holding his gaze steadily.

"I just want to know him, Derek. That's what I've always wanted. You more than anyone else know what I've gone through... trying to find my dad."

Derek curled his fingers over mine. "I know. I hate what you've gone through. It should never have happened."

My first thought was that I should pull away. I didn't. It could have been wishful thinking, but right then Derek's touch felt nothing more than comforting.

"Can I ask you something?" he said after a pause.

I nodded.

"What's the plan, Zee? My father isn't an easy man to get to—not even for me. How do you plan on getting close to him and what will you do if you get the chance?"

I blew out a breath as I leaned against the headboard. "You want the truth? I didn't think that far ahead. I had my hands full getting through your porcupine shell to the gooey center."

"I don't have a gooey center. Stop spreading that around or these people will start thinking they don't have to be afraid of me."

I let out a giggle. "I'll keep your secret."

Derek mimicked me, resting against the headboard. "So you just want to get to know my father?"

"Our father," I corrected. "He didn't want me before. There's no reason he'd want me now even if I showed up at his door with a birth certificate. But if he got to know me and saw that I don't want money from him or—"

Derek made a noise in his throat. "Pretty much the plan you had with me," he finished. "And how did that go for you?"

"We're here, aren't we?"

He sighed. "Fair enough." Derek was quiet for a moment. "Alright. I'll help you. I'll come up with ways that you can get close to Dad. Talk to him. Get to know him."

I shot up, eyes flaring. "You will? Derek, that would be great. Thank..."

I trailed off as he raised a hand. He looked at me seriously. "Conditions," he said. "You never *ever* say a word about this to my mom."

"Of course not," I cried. "I don't want to cause problems for anyone."

"And," he continued, "if you get it in your head to tell my dad he's your long-lost father, you warn me first."

"Why?"

"Because I want to be there with you."

"To stop me," I said, voice hard.

"To support you when you get the news you don't want to hear."

The silence spread between us. My expression couldn't have been kind, but Derek didn't flinch.

"You still don't believe me," I croaked.

He shook his head. "My dad wouldn't do this, Zee. You want to get to know him, but I already do. He's not that kind of guy."

"My mother wouldn't have written down some random guy's name," I clipped.

"Two words. Jeremy Holt."

Wincing, I snapped, "That's different."

"How?"

"She had to lie to me so I wouldn't have been able to find him as easily as I did, but making up a name after what happened at the mall is very different than putting one down on a government document. He is my father."

Derek was unmoving. "You may think that, and your mom may even believe he is, but that doesn't mean it's true."

Heat surged to my face. "What is that supposed to mean?"

Derek was still holding my hand. He squeezed it as his face softened. "I'm not trying to say anything bad about your mom, but I've spent the last five weeks looking up her old classmates and professors. All of her professors except one were male. Also, a few local businessmen came in that semester and taught special lectures, not just my dad."

"Who told you that?"

He jerked his head at the laptop. "I found an old friend of your mom's on Facebook. She was very clear that your mom didn't have a boyfriend around the time she got pregnant with you and didn't want one. She was dating around."

I tugged my hand free. Anger licked at my self-control. "So my mother slept with so many guys that she doesn't know who knocked her up. She just put your dad's name down because she saw him in the lecture hall once. Is that what you're trying to say, Derek?"

"No."

"Then what are you saying?!" I exploded. "You don't know my mom! You don't know anything!"

"I know that I don't have any more proof than you do," he said calmly, "and I won't believe you're my sister until I do."

Derek picked up the laptop and turned it on. "I don't want to fight anymore. Let's watch the movie."

"Fuck the movie! You can't just—"

"Zela, please." His voice was soft and weary. "I missed you too."

The rant lodged in my throat, stuck between my anger and my missing him. In the end, I yanked the blanket up to my chin and settled in with a huff.

"Fine. But you promise me you'll stop digging into my mother's past."

"Zee—"

"Promise me, Derek, or I'm leaving."

"Okay. I promise." Derek shuffled down and laid himself on my pillow. "What do you want to watch?"

"Something funny," I replied after a beat.

"Feeling old school?"

I gently tapped his skull with my forehead. "You mean *Ace Ventura*? I'm not sitting through another Jim Carrey marathon."

"Those are the classics right there. They'll be studying him in future film classes. Mark my words."

I chuckled and the tight knot I'd been holding on to inside began to loosen. "If you want old school, we can watch *Clueless*."

"Are you still pissed at me? Because you're taking the revenge too far."

I couldn't hold back my giggling now. "Let's say I am and put it on."

He groaned like a dying animal. "Fine. I've got root beer in the fridge. Want some?"

"Ooh. Yes, please."

Derek stood to get our drinks while I queued up the movie. I snuggled into the sheets, falling into an uneasy truce, but one I'd hold on to for as long as I could.

"REMEMBER THE TOP OF your laces," I shouted. "You've almost got it, Brandon."

My D charge waved as he hurried to the other side of the field. Brandon asked me to help with his game, but once we got out to the field, the group of Cs that were playing dropped everything and asked if we'd hook up with them.

My pen skittered across the page as I watched them from my place in front of the bleachers. It was difficult to watch, calculate, and give tips at the same time. I loved it all the same. Sitting at a desk with a graphing calculator wasn't nearly as thrilling as seeing math happen before my eyes.

"Austin, don't play scared," I called. "Steal the ball!"

"Exactly what I would've said." Coach Fineman stepped to my side. "I heard about a student taking it upon himself to coach, but I didn't believe it."

I froze. I wasn't sure what to make of this and his blank expression didn't give me a clue.

"I'm not coaching, sir."

"No?" He gestured at my notebook. "Then what do you call this?"

"It's just that my friends helped me when I came here after being homeschooled and couldn't kick my way out of a sack. I thought I'd use what I learned and help others."

He gazed out across the field. "This is quite different from sharing tips with your friends. You're not in the same class as any of these boys."

"That doesn't mean we can't be friends."

To my surprise, he inclined his head. "You're correct, but listen, Zeke, I'm sure your intentions are good, but Breakbattle pays me more than the average high school coach's salary to be out here shouting at the students. You're making a habit of this, but it isn't your job. Leave coaching soccer to me."

"It's not just about helping," I said, thinking quickly. "I'm also learning more about sports math and testing it out in action. We train and help each other all the time, sir. What's the harm?"

He lifted his chin, peering at me over his nose. "There is no harm that I've seen and it's not technically against the rules, but it is unnecessary. As I said, I'm the coach. If students need help, I'm here." Fineman jerked a thumb over his shoulder. "Head out, Zeke. I'll watch the rest of their game."

I wanted to argue but insisting would seem strange and most likely result in laps around the field. Reluctantly, I grabbed my backpack off the bleachers and walked off.

"Too bad."

I jerked to a stop. My lips curled before I saw him—hearing his voice was enough. He and his friends stepped out from their hiding spot behind the bleachers. Zach smirked at me as Jose, Sully, Wyatt, and Lars fanned out behind him.

"You ratted me out to Fineman," I said. It wasn't a question. Not when his snitching was written all over his self-satisfied face.

"I'm not standing by while you help your buddies cheat. Not after you fucked me over."

"It's not cheating. It's called training and practicing."

Sully scoffed. "That's like saying it's not cheating for one team to be coached by a major leaguer and the other to get lessons from the guy who doesn't know which end to hold the bat. You got Moon and the Elites to help you and it's the only reason you won the tournament. Admit it."

I glared at him. "Their spirits didn't inhabit my damn body. It was me out there running, throwing, swimming, and playing. And I did it while *sick*."

Zach's smirk widened.

"It was also me who kicked butt on the academic tests."

"They tutored you," Lars put in. "They told you what would be on the test."

Folding my arms, I stared them down. "You know that isn't how it works. You can't be this stupid. You're Elite." I returned Zach's smirk. "Or most of you are."

Zach launched at me and had to be restrained by his friends.

"Cool it," Wyatt snapped. "Fineman is right here."

He shoved out of their hold. "Here's how it's going to work," he growled. "Everyone will stay in their lane, you'll quit this Battle Doctor shit, and *I* won't let the rest of the coaches as well as Whittaker know what you're doing."

Shrugging, I replied, "You do what you have to do, Zach."

I strode off. None of them tried to stop me, but I wasn't foolish enough to think it was over.

An hour later, I was sitting in Derek's room while he read and Hunter worked on his homework at the desk.

I closed my history book and tossed it in my bag. My work was spread out on Derek's comforter. It was crazy how quickly I made myself at home.

"Hunter," I spoke up. "What exactly do you get from this mentor/mentee relationship?"

"Basking in my presence," Derek replied without looking up.

Hunter laughed. "Derek is a great mentor. He passes on his basketball skills and helped me plan how to ask out Sloane. Plus, his room always smells like vanilla."

"But you just sit here in silence." I gave Derek a look. "You could at least help him with his homework."

"The kid didn't become Elite by needing homework help."

Hunter nodded. "It's true. I don't need help. I actually finished my homework a while ago." He reached behind him. "I've been working on this."

"Hunter, oh my goodness."

He placed the notebook in my hand. Looking back at me... was me.

Hunter's sketch was amazing. I sat hunched over my textbook, cross-legged and forehead scrunched as I read a passage. Next to me was Derek doing what he did best, reading. A few black lines and crafty shading and the two of us were made real on the page. Hunter even added in little details like the name of Derek's book and the part in my bangs.

"This is great," I said. "Can I keep it?"

"No way." The notebook was out of my hand before I could blink. "It's really rough. I haven't had a chance to color it and your nose is all wrong."

"Can I have it when you're done?"

"You really like it?"

"I love it."

He smiled. "You two do look nice together."

"That's what I keep saying," Derek muttered.

"Hush."

I threw a pillow at him. Derek tucked and rolled just in time.

"Too slow, Zee."

Knock. Knock.

Derek went to open it while I got back to my work.

"What's this?"

Cameron's honeyed voice slid inside the room before he did. I slowly raised my head, jaw clenching as he walked in.

"A study date?" he remarked. "Good to see you, Hunter. And you, Zeeeee-*ke*," he drew out. "That's right. It's Zeke. Almost called you something else."

"Why don't you go practice saying it in your room? Get out."

He smiled. "I'm not here to see you." Cameron made his point by giving me his back and facing Derek. "Let's go."

Derek glanced at me over his shoulder. A quick one that I would have missed if I wasn't watching them hard. "I told you I'm not going. I know you've got something to prove, but we've been over it fifty fucking times. Ease up."

"You have something to prove too," Cameron shot back. His charming tone was fading fast. "Your dad told you the same thing mine did. We have to make this happen."

"We will," Derek said through gritted teeth. "Go, Cameron. I'm not talking about this anymore. We both know what we have to do."

"We better"—Cameron turned his head a fraction, peering at me over his shoulder—"understand each other."

My pencil shook in my hands. Flashes of kneeling in the dirt with his camera in my face made my stomach twist. Hunter just watched the exchange in wide-eyed confusion.

Cameron backed out of the room. He didn't resist tossing me a wink in the second before Derek slammed the door in his face.

"Hunter, pack it up and leave," Derek announced. "We'll meet for practice at six."

"Okay. Bye, Derek. Bye, Zeke," he said brightly.

Derek pushed aside my stuff and sat in front of me. "Is something up with you and Cameron?"

"I was just going to ask you the same thing."

"You know what's up with us," he said easily. "Network business. Members of the board are coming back to give Breakbattle another shot and Cameron is obsessed with making sure nothing goes wrong." He gave me a hard look. "He's also obsessed with you. He's been hounding Michael, Cole, and Landon about what you're doing, eating, reading, and saying every minute of the day."

"What do they say?"

"They tell him to fuck off. Cameron's been hinting that you're the new For All and you'll ruin everything, but we know that's bullshit."

I nodded slowly. "I'm surprised they haven't been kicked out because of me by now. Cameron's painting me as enemy number one."

"Trust me. He's tried to get them out, but I stuck up for them with Dad. It helps that he's hanging on to his position by the skin of his teeth."

I was quiet for a spell, studying him. "Derek, why are you going along with this?"

"Why are *we* going along with this," he corrected. "Cameron's shitting himself over the fundraiser my dad is throwing next week for the Worldwide Literacy Coalition. Half the school board is going to be there and so will you."

"What? Who told you that?"

He leaned in. "You want to spend time with my dad, don't you? This is your chance. He's between movies and using this time to push forward the expansion. There are more fundraisers, galas, and events coming up throughout the year. You can come with me."

I swallowed around the hard pit lodged in my throat. This is what I wanted. I'd get to see Jonathan. Talk to him. Get to know him. Let him get to know me. But...

"I'd have to pretend I support the expansion," I stated. "Or my invitation will be revoked."

Derek's expression remained neutral. "You have to decide what's more important to you."

I dropped my head, breaking the hold his gaze had on me.

He's right. This is what it comes down to. What are you going to do?

"Okay," I whispered. "I'll be there."

Cold fingers brushed my forehead. Derek gently removed my wig and cap. My blonde strands tangled as he weaved them through his fingers.

"I wish you could come as yourself," he said softly. "He should know the real you, not the costume."

"I hope he does one day."

Derek dropped his hand. "I'll get you an invitation without my dad's name on it, so you can give it to your mom."

"Thank you."

"Sure." He reached for his book but my hand on his arm stopped him.

"I'm serious, Derek. Thank you."

"I'll do anything for you, Zee." He tugged out of my hold and reclaimed his spot.

I didn't know what to say to that, so I picked up my homework. We didn't speak for the rest of the night.

THREE DAYS LATER, DEREK dropped an invitation on my tray. I broke off kissing Landon.

"What's that?" he asked.

I glided my fingers over the cream paper as I read.

You're invited to the Worldwide Literacy Coalition's first annual fundraiser.

This black-tie event will be held at the Evergreen Country Club.

Prepare for a night of great food, great company, and giving.

"Hold on," Landon said as he read over my shoulder. "You're going to this?"

"Are you?"

"Yeah. We"—his eyes darted to Cole and Michael—"have to go."

I nodded. The four of us didn't speak much about the Network. It was a certainty that they didn't know what Cameron and the senior Elites did to me the night of the tournament. Derek couldn't have known either.

They'd lose their minds if they knew, but Cameron was my fight. I would handle this myself and screw up his plans for the expansion at all costs. Telling them what I planned would put them in the position of choosing between me and the future the Network could offer them. It was better we didn't have that talk. It was better I didn't find out what they would choose.

"Why are you going?" he asked.

"Derek invited me," I replied. "I thought it'd be nice to meet people and network." I cracked a smile. "Not a pun."

Landon didn't laugh with me.

"What are you guys talking about?" Melody plucked the invitation from my hand. "A fundraiser? Who is throwing it?"

"My parents," said Derek. "It's small. Just some people from school and their families."

"Adam, are you going?"

My friend shook his head. "Far as I know, none of my parents got the invite. Zee is partying without me on this one."

"All five of you are going?" Hunter piped up. "Derek, can I come too?"

Landon took hold of my chin and brought me in for a kiss. The table's chatter faded in the background. "Want me to pick you up?"

"You don't have to. Derek said he'd send a car."

"I want to." He gave me another soft kiss. "This party got ten times more bearable now that I know you'll be there. I want to sneak in every second I can with you."

I smiled through another kiss. "When you put it like that..."

Adam was happy to let his lack of invite drop, but I caught up to him outside the cafeteria and pulled him away from Melody.

"See you after class, Mel." Adam twisted around and draped his arm on my shoulder. "What's up?"

"The party is more than a fundraiser," I said, lowering my voice. "Members of the board will be there. The Network is planning to win them over off campus where For All and Stand Up can't get in the way."

"What are you going to do?"

I sighed. "There's nothing much I can do. If I make a fuss about the expansion, Derek won't be able to wrangle me any more invites."

"Does it matter if you go to these things?"

It matters more than anything.

"Yes," I said aloud. "We want to know what they're up to and Derek isn't always forthcoming. Plus, me and the guys are doing a great job keeping the peace by not talking about the Network at all. If I can be there while it's happening, I'll find out which way they're leaning and if we need to step it up."

Adam nodded along. "If they're whipping out their checkbooks and throwing events at the country club, then we do. You've been doing your part alone, but I can help."

"I'm already getting heat. Coach Fineman called me out for helping the guys at practice."

I don't know what it was, but something made me look over my shoulder. I landed on Cole, Michael, and Landon immediately. They trailed us with enough distance that they couldn't overhear, but all three were openly watching us.

Adam turned to see what I was looking at and waved. Their response was as different as their personalities.

Cole scowled. Landon didn't react. And Michael waved back.

"They're being so weird," I mumbled. "Seriously, seventeen years of living with my mother gives me the urge to lecture them on how men and women are capable of being friends."

He chuckled. "I guess I can't blame them. Cole has it in his head that me and him are competing for everything.

Landon hasn't forgiven me for going along with your plot to make him jealous."

"And Michael?"

"He just wants to be the one by your side all the time."

I tucked my head under his arm as a smile tugged at my lips. "Well, damn. That's adorable."

"Really? Even Cole?"

"I'm finding his need to win incredibly sexy. It translates pretty well when our clothes are off."

He hummed. "You know, when Jordan and I—"

"I will kill you."

Adam burst out laughing. He leaned on me as he guffawed, our faces cheek to cheek as I snickered in return.

"Babe." Hands grabbed me from behind. "Walk with us. We want to talk about the party."

"I saw that coming," Adam whispered in my ear. "We'll talk about what we're going to do later, but I'm serious about helping. I'm not worried about Coach."

"What was that about Coach?" Landon asked as he got me loose and plastered me to his side. "Something up?"

I went with the truth. There might be things I leave out so Landon doesn't land himself in prison for beating Cameron to death, but I wouldn't outright lie to him.

"Zach went to Coach Fineman about me helping the other classes improve their game and stuff. Coach said to leave it to him but it's important to me."

"Why?" Cole asked.

"Because I don't think being on the sixth floor means I should forget everyone else exists. Also, it's fun. I get to tutor math on and off the field."

Cole accepted the explanation.

"You really coming to the fundraiser?" Michael asked.

"If my mom says yes."

"Did Derek... tell you what it's for?"

"Yes," I said simply.

"And you still want to go?" asked Landon.

I slipped out from under his arm. "Can I ask why you want to go?"

The boys shared a look.

"Mr. Dupre promised a few leaders from local nonprofits will be there," Landon confessed.

"Also, some of the faculty from Somerset University," Michael added. "Coaches included."

"Okay," I said.

Landon stroked my cheek. "Babe, if it—"

I held up a hand. "No, stop, please. You don't have to feel weird about it. I understood your reasons for joining then and I understand now. I don't want to get in the way of your dreams because I believe in you guys way too much."

It was Michael who grabbed me first and squeezed me to his chest. He kissed me hard, pouring every ounce of what he felt into it.

Landon got his hands on me when we broke apart and he was next. I clung to him as heat spread through to my toes.

Cole didn't kiss me, but the look in his eyes screamed how much he wanted to. He glanced at Michael and the look vanished.

"We should get to class," he muttered.

Cole picked up his feet and strode off ahead of us. I let him go. We were in the same class and all the same clubs. He couldn't shake me that easily.

After classes, Adam hung back to finish our conversation.

"I'll sign up for tutoring too and tell Tanner and Nico to spread it around that I'm open to help people up their battle game." He waggled his fingers at me. "I can't use your math magic on them but I should still be able to help."

"It's not magic if it's math," I said, "and you're the best. Thanks."

"Of course." His eyes drifted over my head. "I'll see you at dinner. I'm meeting up with Melody."

"See you."

After he left, I turned to find what he was looking at. Cole lingered by the bookcase, skimming his fingers along the spine but making no move to take one down.

"Hey," I said softly.

Cole didn't give a sign that he heard me.

"Almost time for Future Leaders. Want to go together?"

"Sure."

We walked out of the class, heading for the classroom at the opposite end of the hall. Cole was content not to speak, but that was the natural flow of our relationship. I made the first move like a person holding out their hand for a wounded animal to know their scent. Cole wouldn't stop snarling until he knew he was safe.

"We should talk," I stated. "After the meeting. Come up to my room, okay?"

Cole's gaze fixed straight ahead. "Talk about what?"

"Us."

"Us?"

It stung me to hear his derisive snort.

"So I get the talk now?" he continued. "Weeks later, after you've confessed your feelings to Landon and Michael and told them you want a real relationship with them both. Now you want to chat about us? And here I thought all I was good for was a hookup."

"Hey." I snagged his collar none-too-gently and spun him around. "Don't even try it, Reed," I said, getting in his face. "Yes, I like hooking up with you. We happen to be very, very, *very* good at it, but don't pretend that's all we're about. I love talking and laughing and spending time with you just as much."

I shook him and imagined his fool brain rattling around in his head. "You don't get to keep me at arm's length and then blame me that our relationship isn't further along. If you want to figure out what we're about, talk with me after club."

Cole ripped my hand off. "Fine!" he growled.

"Good!"

We squared off—nostrils flaring, eyes blazing.

In the next breath, Cole yanked on my wrist and I crashed into his lips. His kiss poured molten heat into my soul. He pushed me back, slamming me into the wall, but I barely registered the faint pain as I ran my hands over his body.

If I get him back to that room, we're going to do more than talk.

"What on earth—?! Mr. Manning! Mr. Reed!"

Cole flew off me like I burst into flames.

Miss Lewis, Future Leaders' new advisor, gaped at us, clutching her chest. "What do you think you're doing?! This is a school hallway, not a back-alley bordello! Inside! Now!"

"Yes, ma'am."

"Sorry, ma'am."

We shuffled inside, enduring her frequent glares of disapproval all through the meeting. The minute it let out we hurried to the dorm building, burst into my room, and picked up where we left off.

"WE DID TALK AT SOME point," I relayed to Jordan as we huddled on my bed that Saturday night.

We were an odd pair. Jordan was cute in skinny jeans and a chiffon crop top. While I was the sight to see in a jet-black tuxedo and matching bow tie.

"Are you two together?"

Sighing, I tipped over and fell face-first on the sheets. "He admitted he wants us to be more than casual, but he can't think about it until he knows for sure his friendship with Michael can handle it. He said he doesn't want to lose either one of us because we're the only two people in his life he's gotten close to. It was so sweet I couldn't help but understand even though I'm disappointed. It looks like we're taking it slow too."

She patted my head. "At least you talked. Wherever you go from here, it'll be forward."

I let out a slow breath. "You're right. I just need to give him time."

"Exactly." Jordan's touch was soothing on my hair. "That's my method with Adam. Eventually, he'll accept Melody's decided their relationship has an expiration date and choose me, right?"

I sat up and hugged her. "I'm not the one to ask about choosing, but I do know if it ever comes down to one, he'd be crazy not to pick you."

"It's true," she said. "He would be."

I laughed, thankful to hear her sounding like herself. "What are you guys doing tonight?"

"Nothing crazy. His mom invited me over for dinner. We'll end up watching a movie/making out in their theater until we're inevitably interrupted."

"It won't be traumatically mortifying as long as you're caught with your clothes on."

"Good tip," she teased, tweaking my nose. "But how are you? Are you sure you want to go to this thing?"

My smile melted away as the conversation shifted. "I have to go. Jonathan will be there."

"This can't be how you pictured getting to know him. He'll spend the night schmoozing his rich friends and playing the host. He probably won't talk to you for longer than is polite."

"That's longer than I ever had."

She sighed. "Okay. I get it. Just... don't expect too much."

"I don't." I nudged her with my shoulder. "I know you and Adam have appointed yourselves guardians of my physical and emotional well-being, but you don't have to worry about me. I'm doing a lot better now.

"I think the stress of Breakbattle, being Zeke, and hiding who I was from Derek brought the voices and everything back. Telling him the truth caused new problems, but it also lifted a weight off me. Derek and I have things to sort through, but we will. He's helping me get close to my father.

"And Cameron and Zach don't know it, but they have nothing to hold over my head now. I will stop the expansion and piss Zach off doing it." I rubbed her forearm. "I'm good, JoJo. I promise."

She gave me a lopsided smile. "Does that mean you don't need me?"

"I will never mean that. Slap me if I even think it."

We fell against each other, hugging and laughing.

"Zela!" Mom's shout echoed up the stairs. "Your date has arrived."

"I should hurry and save Landon." I pecked her on the cheek. "Have fun on your movie/make-out date."

"I will," she called after me as I hurried out. "You have fun too."

I hit the top step of the stairs and smiled down at Landon. Sometimes I believed the day would come where I'd see him and my heart wouldn't do flips, but the next time our eyes met he'd prove me wrong. His blue, floral tuxedo was the right blend of formal and off-beat. Everywhere Landon went, he stood out.

"I love your tux," I said as I slipped into his arms. "Did you design this one too?"

"Declan gets the credit for this." He kissed me. "You look cute too. Not even my parents could improve upon your perfection."

Smiling, I rose for another kiss.

"It was nice to meet you, Landon."

I froze lips puckered.

"I'm certain we'll have more time at the end of the night to talk and get to know each other better."

Landon let me go and turned on my mom with a smile. "Looking forward to it, Ms. Manning. I'll have her back no later than eleven."

She nodded sharply. "See that you do."

He laced our fingers together and we escaped outside. Michael and I got a "stay out as late as we want." Can't say what prompted Mom to cool on Landon and most likely never would. She was nothing if not unpredictable.

I whistled as we stepped off the porch and saw the huge, black luxury truck parked in front of our house. The front wheel was longer than my torso. "Wow. Whose car is that?"

"Henrietta's." He opened the door and helped me up. "She has a few clients whose makeup she does personally and she likes to bring her own stuff right down to the vanity."

"It's nice." I rubbed the warm leather, unsurprised the seat was a black and dark red with the initials *H.F.* stitched in gold behind my head.

I leaned out of the car to wave bye to Mom as we pulled out of the drive. Her figure grew small in the mirror until we turned the corner and she disappeared from view.

The tiniest twinge panged my heart after she was gone. I didn't like lying to her about Jonathan. I wished more than anything I could sit down with Mom and talk about the man who left all those years ago.

But I can't. She closed that door a long time ago and sealed it with a false name. She wanted me nowhere near him but I'm done letting her decide.

Landon teased my knuckles with a gentle finger. "You okay?"

"Yeah." I turned my palm up and played with his in turn. "Thanks for picking me up."

"It's worth it to steal a few hours with you."

"We have been so busy. Why don't we stop off after the party? Get some dessert. Just sit and talk."

"Love to."

We spent the rest of the ride listening to music and singing along at the top of our lungs. Landon had the worst singing voice I'd ever heard. It was criminal that such an awful noise could come from those perfect lips.

He had me laughing so hard tears ran down my face. It was the best way to relax me and he wasn't even trying.

We pulled up to the country club and rolled out of the car giggling like we had a secret. Landon grabbed my waist and peppered my lips with tiny little kisses like treats through our mirth.

"I love you, Zela Manning."

"I love you too."

"Aren't you guys cute?"

Derek emerged from the double doors. One look at him and I was reminded why I was here. Derek held out his hand.

"Landon, I have to go with him," I said. "I'll see you inside."

"What's up?"

I curled my fingers around Derek's. "Derek is going to take me to meet his father."

"Okay. I'll catch up with you later."

I smiled at him over my shoulder. "Good luck."

The Evergreen Country Club was a lot like how I imagined. A mansion like all in this town, uniformed staff manning grand double doors welcomed us inside. We stepped into a circular lobby. Soft lighting shone down on us and the indoor wishing well in the middle of the foyer.

I peered over the rim. Coins glinted on the bottom of the basin, representing the wishes of those who seemed to have it all.

But no life is perfect.

Derek touched the small of my back. "He'll love you, Zee."

My lips trembled. I couldn't voice it, yet Derek knew what to say. He led me away.

Tinkling music poured out of the ballroom as we approached. Through the entrance, people flitted in and out of view, some carrying trays and others carrying wallets. Derek told Melody the party was small, but dozens of round, white-linen-covered tables took up every space that wasn't taken by the dance floor or stage.

"Where is he?"

Derek pointed through the crowd. "Over there. I can introduce you, but he won't have time for more than the required 'hello' and 'how are you.' He's working his way through greeting all the guests."

I bobbed my head, heart pounding its way up my throat, as Derek tugged me closer to the crowd of people shielding Jonathan.

"If you really want to talk to him, find him during the dancing. Dad hates to dance and pretends like he's tired as soon as the music kicks up."

"Okay, okay," I breathed. "M-maybe I should wait until then." I dug my heels in. "I d-don't know about this. I—"

"I'll be right next to you." He held up the hand I was squeezing. "Even if you break my fingers."

A soft laugh sneaked out of me. It took a bit of my tension with it and I picked up my feet. "Okay. Let's go."

Derek found a break in the crowd and pushed us through. In the center of it all, Jonathan Grayson stood with Naomi. Derek's mom was first to notice us.

"There you are, my love. Stay close. We're going to take a picture as a family." Naomi grasped his jaw and planted a smooch that left bright red lips on his cheek. "My handsome boy," she said fondly.

"Mom," Derek hissed, red-faced. He tugged me to his side. "You remember Zee."

Naomi turned stunning blue eyes on me. "How can I not? My son talks about you all the time. I'm glad we got another chance to meet you."

"Me too. Whenever you have time, I'm dying for those embarrassing childhood stories. Don't feel like you have to hold back."

Naomi's laugh was as beautiful and refined as her.

"That conversation will never happen," Derek said.

"No?" She rubbed the lipstick from his cheek, smiling mischievously. "You don't want me to tell him about the time my baby mistook a set toilet for a real one? He was so proud he used the potty on his own I couldn't be angry."

A snort ripped out of me at Derek's beet red face. I knew in that instant I liked Naomi Grayson.

"Looks like I'm missing the fun."

My mouth dried up in a snap. Jonathan moved away from the couple he was speaking to and joined our group. His eyes lit up when he recognized me.

"Zeke Manning. Good to see you again." Derek lifted my hand before I thought to raise it and Jonathan shook warmly. "I was looking forward to talking at the reception and now we have another chance. I'm dying to get to know my son's best friend."

"I can already tell you he's a delight," Naomi said.

Jonathan smiled at me. "High praise. You've won my wife over. I'll be a piece of cake."

I brimmed with so many emotions at once I couldn't tell one from the other. My father was speaking to me. He was smiling at me. He was happy to see me.

"Why don't you join us at our table?" Jonathan offered. "I must continue making the rounds, but we can pick this up over dinner."

Naomi and Jonathan strode off.

"O-okay," I said at their backs.

"That went well."

"I know," I squealed. Happiness bubbled in me like fizzy soda.

"I was making fun of you," he deadpanned. "You didn't say a word to him."

I shoved his shoulder. "One step at a time," I said, fighting a laugh. "I'm looking forward to more of those baby Derek stories."

"Hm. No. I'm about to threaten my mother with emancipation if she tells you another one." He backed away. "Our table is at the front. See you in a minute."

Derek went after his parents while I headed for the table.

"Zeke? Zeke Manning, is that you?"

I pulled up short. "Mrs. Jeong?"

The member of the board of education happily waved me over. Standing at her shoulder was Principal Whittaker.

"What luck," she said. "We were just speaking about you."

"You were?"

She beamed. "Your principal was telling me that you transferred into the Elite Class. Congratulations. Are you finding the math classes more your speed?"

"They're incredibly hard and it's great," I replied. "I'm learning so much from Mrs. Peterson and from my self-study."

"How are you adjusting to being in a new class? Was it hard leaving your teachers and friends?"

"A little," I admitted. "But we eat together every day and we practice and study after school. If they need help preparing for battles, I'm always there and not only for my friends." I shot Whittaker a smile. "I practice with the Ds and Cs too and they started calling me the Battle Doctor."

I made a face like I was embarrassed.

"The Battle Doctor," Jeong repeated, sounding impressed. "Quite a title."

"It's weird, but I love helping out and using math to do it. I've discovered a whole world of sports math since I've been at Breakbattle."

"Sports math? Fascinating." She looked over my shoulder and waved to someone. "I'd like to hear more about this later tonight, Zeke. I don't know if you heard, but we'll be dropping in again this year as we decide on integrating the battle system into our public schools."

"Oh, wow. I didn't know."

She nodded happily. "Yes, yes. I expect to see you very soon. I have to go but it was a pleasure as always."

Jeong left and Whittaker was right behind. He didn't leave before giving me an approving nod.

Sitting at the Grayson table, I watched the party go on around me. Landon was in a corner engrossed in conversation with two women I assumed ran nonprofits. Cole was near the refreshment table with Christina. They both spoke to a well-built man in a sharp, gray suit.

Across the room, Michael sat with a woman I recognized as his mom. He grinned when he saw me and beckoned me over. I talked with them for the rest of cocktail hour until someone came on the mic and announced dinner was ready to be served.

By the time I weaved through the crowd to get to the front table, Derek, Naomi, and Jonathan were seated and both seats on either side of them were taken. I grabbed a seat two heads away from Jonathan but it was no good.

As dinner went on, he spent most of his time talking to Naomi or the man next to him, Rolando Martin from the board of education.

This is what tonight is about. Jonathan isn't going to let me steal too much time away from Mr. Martin.

I picked at my food, one eye on him and one on my plate. If Jonathan planned to bow out of the dancing, I'd draw out every course so we'd be the only two left at the table.

I pushed my seafood-stuffed salmon filet around the plate while everyone ate their dessert. As if it was the cue, Jonathan set his fork on his clean plate and the music turned up. He rose and held out his hand to Naomi.

"May I?"

He swept her out onto the dance floor and soon other couples followed. I waited... and waited... and waited for Jonathan to make his exit, but he seemed content to twirl Naomi around the room all night.

Derek spoke to Mrs. Jeong just off the dance floor. I shot him a desperate look. He shrugged helplessly, mouthed something to me, and then pointed at the door leading to the terrace.

I got the hint and rose from the table. A fresh, cool breeze wrapped around me as I stepped outside. A stark difference from the heated, packed room in there.

The terrace was empty. All that met my sight was a stone bench set beneath the railing. I sat and rested my head against the metal. The cool and silence brought soothing relief.

Eventually, I will get a chance to talk to him. He has to take a—

"Needed a bit of fresh air too?"

I stopped breathing.

"Nice night, isn't it? It seems the storms have finally passed on." Jonathan moved to my side. "This is lucky. I've been hoping to get a chance to speak with you all night."

"With me?" My voice was barely above a whisper. "Why?"

"You've caused quite a stir, Zeke. Since the first week you started at Breakbattle Academy."

"You mean..."

Shadows cast over him, obscuring the side of his face, but as he peered at me out of the corner of his eye, I trailed off.

"You can't be my biggest fan, then," I forced out.

"Why would you say that?"

"I've caused a lot of trouble for your Network."

The sound shocked me so deeply it took my mind a minute to register Jonathan laughing.

"Trouble for us? No." He grasped my shoulder. "The casualty of your battle was the person it was with. And if I can be honest, I appreciate how you handled yourself in response to Dupre's test at orientation."

"You do?"

He nodded. "I wasn't aware of what he had planned, or I wouldn't have ordered Derek to go along with it. Refusing to cover up the death of my son may not have earned you a place with us, but it won you Derek's trust and my respect. Loyalty is an important trait in our members, but integrity is valued even more."

I couldn't believe Jonathan was openly speaking about the Network. This was my chance to ask him more. Get him to explain why Cameron was allowed to craft his own twisted punishment for me in freshman year. Why did he get his position back? Why did his position exist in the first place? And most importantly, what was Dominick Dupre's role, and how would he use it to make you richer?

My opportunity to ask these questions had come... and I didn't take it. I had no desire to speak about the Network, Dominick Dupre, or Cameron. I just wanted to speak to my father.

"Earning Derek's trust was worth everything," I said. "He's been a good friend to me."

"I'm happy to hear that. I admit, I've been worried about him. The world has given him reason to be closed off, but over time, it will punish you for the barriers it forced you to erect."

"I never thought of it that way," I admitted. "If you're too trusting, people line up to take advantage. If you close your heart, you keep out those who want to love you for you." I shook my head. "Screwed either way."

Jonathan laughed—a light, genuine sound that made me smile. "I couldn't have put it better myself. The reason I'm glad he let you in."

I made a face. "I don't think you should stop worrying about him just yet."

"What do you mean?"

Shifting to face him, I gave Jonathan a serious look. "He's your son, but he calls Ace Ventura movies classics. How did you let that happen?"

He laughed short and sharp like it startled him. "I did my best with the kid, but at some point, you just have to accept them for who they are... and pass the blame onto their mother."

I giggled. My heart fluttered in my chest, racing away on a happiness I never felt before.

"Tell me your favorite movies, Zeke." He winked. "I hope a few of mine are in there."

"Of course. I loved *Flamingo* and *A Good Neighbor*. I've got a weakness for action, so I've seen *Die Hard* twenty times, but I also love Studio Ghibli."

He hummed. "Hayao Miyazaki is an inspiration. He weaves heartfelt tales, and at the center of each are strong female characters."

My lips quirked up in a small smile. "My mom says the same thing."

"Does she? Well, it's obvious she's doing a better job imparting her film taste. Have you seen *Howl's Moving Castle*?"

"Only twelve times. It's one of my all-time favorites."

Jonathan and I talked movies back and forth as the music floated out of the cracked door. Slow to fast to dance to classical. The party went on unheeding of our absence.

"Adam's grandma introduced me to the world of film noir," I told him. "They don't make movies like that anymore."

"They sure don't. That was a great time for film." He tossed his head, passion lacing his voice. "I remember staying up late with my father and Humphrey Bogart. We used to—"

Light swept over us.

"Darling? Where did you— Oh. There you are." Naomi strode across the terrace, hands out. "You're very sneaky slipping out here while I was speaking to Katelin, but you're not getting out of dancing with me."

Jonathan gathered her in his arms and kissed her deeply. I looked away.

"There's nothing I want more than to dance with you, my love."

Naomi giggled like a teenager.

This is what Derek meant when he said his parents were so in love it was nauseating.

I felt a tap on my shoulder.

"He says that now," she replied. "Let's see how long it takes before he slips away."

Some giggling and the sound of more smooching followed that.

"It was great talking to you, Zeke," Jonathan said as his wife pulled him away. "We have to pick this conversation up again another time."

"I'd love to." Excitement lifted me off the railing and tugged me after him as though we were connected by an invisible string. "Anytime."

"I'll tell Derek to bring you around more often."

The door closed in my face and finally, I didn't have to hold back my smile. I talked to Jonathan Grayson and it went great. It went better than great. He liked me.

Squealing, I plopped down on the bench and kicked my feet in the air. He said he wanted to continue our talk and I prayed he meant it. There was so much more I wanted to know about him. I needed to hear the stories of watching movies with his dad. What was his favorite breakfast? His favorite music? Does he jiggle his foot when he's nervous like I do? I wanted to know it all.

My mother had every right to be angry with him for leaving us. *But I wanted to know my father on my terms, not through her eyes.*

"You're going to pay for this, fucker."

A sharp, cold hiss made my head snap up.

I dropped my feet.

Just off the steps of the terrace was a path that led around the building. I squinted through the gloom, listening hard.

"Get the fuck off me!"

The shout was followed by a grunt and then a loud thump.

I frowned. *I know that voice... Cameron?*

"I told you what would happen if you didn't stop," a second voice snarled.

A loud cry ripped through the night and I was off the bench. I raced for the steps of the terrace just as someone tore around the corner. We crashed into each other and I tripped, falling back and crying out as a heavy body landed on top of me.

Cameron scrambled off me. "What the fuck are you doing out here?"

I flinched in the face of his fury, and the blood weeping from the cut on his forehead.

"Are you okay?" I croaked, struggling to sit up. "Who was that? Who did that to you?"

I reached for him.

Cameron jerked back like my touch burned. "Fuck off! I don't need your help!"

He flung open the doors and ran inside. I went after him. I grabbed his arm again and Cameron roughly shook me off. The force made me stumble into a table, drawing the attention of the crowd.

"Sweetie, are you okay?" A woman with light-pink hair tips to match her pink dress pointed at me. I glanced down at the blood staining my shirt.

"I'm fine," I replied.

I took off after Cameron. He stormed out of the room and was gone when I stepped out. There was no one in the lobby. The only sounds were the gentle splashing of the wishing well.

I went into the bathroom and did the best I could to get the blood off, but all my scrubbing was leaving a huge, pink wet stain on my shirt.

The door banged open and I jerked. My hand slipped beneath the spray and wet the front of my pants.

"Zee? Zee! Are you okay?" Landon took my face in his hands. "I saw you get into it with Cameron."

I kissed the tip of his nose. "No. For once, Cameron didn't do anything to me. Except bleed on me. I'm a mess. Do you mind if I wait in the car? I can't go back in there like this."

"No way." Landon released me and yanked out some paper towels. He took up the task of drying me off. "I'm not leaving you in the car. Let's just get out of here."

"But what about the people you wanted to talk to?"

His cheekbones were sharp, sculpted perfection. Sometimes I wondered if they would cut me if I trailed my fingers along his dips and curves. But not when he smiled. Landon's smile softened him and made him the regular boy I fell in love with once again.

"I talked to them, got a lot of great advice, and now I want to spend the rest of the night with you. Let's go."

He didn't have to ask me twice.

I texted Derek on the way out that I was leaving. In the car, I stripped off the jacket, shirt, and finally my bindings. I breathed a sigh of relief when I was down to my tank top.

"Don't stop there." Landon tugged the hem of my tank. "Not when it's getting good."

I smacked his arm. "Will you behave yourself?"

"I'm so tired of behaving myself, baby." He caught my fingers and threaded them through his. "Do you still want dessert?"

I hesitated, unsure of how those two sentences connected. "Yes. I never got to mine."

"I know just the place."

The drive was short, but the route unfamiliar. Landon drove through a part of Evergreen I had never been. We pulled into a tiny plaza housing a grocery store, daycare, and an ice cream shop.

"You can stay in the car," Landon said as he unbuckled. "I'll be quick."

My phone buzzed in the depths of my pocket.

Jordan: How is it going? Everything okay?

Me: It's great. I got to talk to him. Just the two of us.

Jordan: You got the great Jonathan Grayson alone? Wow. Is he what you expected?

**Me: I don't know what I expected. Mom used to say he was arrogant, selfish, and full of himself. That's when she'd speak of him at all. He doesn't seem to be that guy anymore.

A few minutes passed before her reply came through.

Jordan: Are you hoping that is true because you want this guy to accept you? He can be all nice and smiles to his son's best friend. But what will he do when he finds out you're his daughter?

Her text settled like lead in the pit of my stomach. I felt my good mood leaking away.

Me: Where is this coming from?

Jordan: I've just been thinking of all you've done to find him and what it's cost you. But he's always known you've existed, Zee. If he's a different man now... why didn't he find you?

I stared at the screen for a long time.

Me: JoJo, what's going on? What happened?

A couple of minutes passed before she replied.

Jordan: Malcom called.

I hissed low under my breath. Malcom St. James. Jordan's ex-boyfriend. All-around bastard.

He cheated on Jordan and then made her feel like the crazy, distrustful one when she confronted him on the rumors. Their breakup was nasty and, unfortunately, public. She caught the piece of trash upstairs with some girl at a party.

Me: What the hell did he want?

Jordan: He heard I was seeing someone and "it finally hit him he could lose me for good." He tried to get me back but I told him I wouldn't trust his cheating ass even if he cut his dick off.

He turned the charm off real fast after that and said all this horrible stuff. Including how he spent a month while we were dating hooking up with Lucia.

My jaw dropped. *That can't be true.*

Lucia Reine was one of Jordan's best friends since Chesterfield Middle. She wouldn't do that to her.

Me: He has to be lying. You know Malcolm. He's a manipulative piece of shit and he wanted to hurt you for rejecting him.

Jordan: I don't know. I called Lucia but she hasn't called me back.

Me: Where are you?

Jordan: Home. I ended up canceling on Adam.

Me: I'll be there in an hour.

I peered over the hood, looking for Landon. He accepted his card from an employee in a bright yellow shirt.

My phone went off again.

Jordan: No, Zee. Seriously, no. I love you, but I'm a mess right now. I've already picked a fight with Adam and got on you about Jonathan. I'm not good company right now.

Me: I don't care. You need me. I'll be there soon.

Jordan: I swear you're the best cousin in the world. Come over tomorrow and cheer me up, but tonight, I need to talk to Lucia and I have to do it alone. You get it, right?

Me: I get it. I'll be there tomorrow first thing.

Landon let himself in and put our dessert behind his seat. He saw my face as he drew back. "Everything okay?"

"Come here." I gripped his lapel and pulled him in for a kiss that tasted like chocolate cherries. Someone sampled a few before they bought.

He hummed low in his throat. "Better than okay."

I smiled despite myself. "That was for being wonderful. You're so good to me, Landon. Never let me take advantage of you."

"You don't and you wouldn't." He kissed me again. "Tell me what happened."

I shook my head. "The human garbage my cousin broke up with couldn't resist another chance to bring her down."

"Oh, I'm sorry, babe. Do you need to go back?"

"She said she needs space, so I'll give it to her." I rubbed his forearm. "Let's have dessert."

I twisted around to reach for the ice cream and Landon stopped me.

"Not here. We're having dessert somewhere else. It's not far."

I relaxed as Landon started the truck. "Do I get a hint about where we're going?"

"Nope."

"Can I sneak my ice cream on the way?"

He laughed. "We're five minutes away."

"Five minutes is long in ice cream time," I said. "What did you get me anyway?"

Landon took his eyes off the road to grin at me. "You have a hard time being surprised, don't you?"

"Jordan and Aunt Bev tried to throw me a surprise party once. I screamed and ran out of the house."

"It's a good thing we're in a moving car."

Laughing, I attacked his side with tickles. He yelped, trying to squirm away from me, and almost crashed the truck.

"Stop trying to kill us," he said, chuckling. "We're here."

The car veered off the road and climbed a gently sloping hill. There was nothing around us but grass, trees, and the road we took to get here. My confusion rose the higher we did.

"You're taking me to the top of a hill?"

"That's right."

He sounded very proud of himself. I didn't understand until the truck crested the hill.

Beneath us, couples, families, and friends stretched out on blankets. The movie screen rose stories high, the fresh-faced actors clear even from our private spot overlooking the clearing.

"We can't hear anything," he admitted, "but we used to come up here and make up our own stories."

"We?"

"Me, Henrietta, and Declan."

"That's so cute."

"It was when I was little," he added. "I come up here alone now when I need some space. Do you like it? If you want to watch the movie for real—"

I stopped him when he reached for the ignition. "I want to be up here with you."

My heart pounded as he leaned in to kiss me.

"I was hoping you'd say that," he whispered against my lips. "I've got blankets. We can lay them out in the back."

I flicked his nose. "You knew you were going to get me here, didn't you, Foster?"

"It was all a part of the plan."

Landon drove around and faced the truck bed toward the screen. We got out and I riffled in the ice cream bag while he spread out the blankets.

"Is this...?" Beaming, I popped the lid off the container. "Cookie dough ice cream with chocolate syrup and gummy bears. How did you know this is my favorite?"

"I heard you tell Derek once. You guys get into your own world sometimes, but lucky for me, I sit right next to you." He winked. "I pick things up."

I strode around the car, meeting him before the truck bed. "What else have you picked up?"

"I'm not saying," he whispered. Landon gently pushed my wig and cap off. I shivered as his fingers tickled my scalp. "I'm going to save it for times like this so I can impress you."

"Crafty move."

Landon gripped my thighs and lifted me on to the bed. "I gotta be crafty. I'm competing with two other guys for your affections."

"You're not competing." I snuggled into his side. "You already have my affections."

An old black-and-white movie played down below. An actor fitting the tall, dark, and handsome type in every sense of the stereotype gazed intensely through an office window, monologuing.

I nibbled on a gummy bear. "Do you know this movie?"

"Oh yeah. The guy is an amnesiac. He wakes up one day in that office but he doesn't know how he got there. The door says private investigator and the man in the pictures are him.

But when he asks the people around him, no one knows who he is. Is he the fake, or is the life created for him?"

"Wow. That sounds interesting. I have to—" I leaned back and caught his grin. "And you're messing with me."

He laughed. "I don't know this movie, but half the fun is pretending we do."

"Okay, I'll play." I sat up, squinting at the screen. "His life isn't fake... he just isn't a part of it yet. He moved to a new place but ran into an old enemy."

Landon picked up the thread. "An enemy determined to finish what his bash on the head started. Our hero has to find a way to stay ahead of a killer he can't recognize."

"Plot twist," I cried. "Our hero is actually the killer and the target his identical twin brother. He attacked him in his office, got knocked out, and assumed the man in the photos was him."

"And she"—Landon pointed at the curly-haired beauty giving an impassioned speech to the hero—"is the woman who set them on their dark path. Only one can have her hand."

I snapped my fingers. "But she loves the first brother, so our forgetful killer goes after his twin so he can steal his life and the girl."

We took one look at each other and fell into a fit of giggles.

"We have to pitch this to Jonathan Grayson," I said. "I'm really into this idea."

Landon stretched out the width of the truck bed. He propped up against the hump over the tire and patted his chest. That was all the invitation I needed to lie on top of him.

We didn't see much of our silent movie. I fed him chocolatey gummy bears in between dropping kisses on his jaw. Every now and then he'd twist at the last second, capturing my lips.

Landon nipped the tip of my nose. "What do you think they're saying?"

"I think she's saying... she loves him," I whispered, "and she's happy that despite everything they've gone through, they made it here. Together." I wasn't looking at the screen. "What is he saying?"

"That she is the most beautiful thing he's ever seen." Landon caressed my bottom lip and my mouth parted for him. "He'd bash a million brothers over the head for her."

I wrapped my lips around his finger and moved down to his knuckle. He sucked in a sharp breath as my head bobbed.

"What else will he do for me?" I asked softly.

"He's... not so good with words. He'd rather show her."

Our lips met in the same breath. I clung to Landon as he tipped me over on my back, laying me on the blanket. I ran my hands up his chest and pushed the jacket off his shoulders. Our clothes came off in a feverish rush.

Landon broke our kiss only to trail soft pecks down my neck and through the valley of my breasts. He reached my lower belly and stopped. Glazed sapphire eyes locked with mine as he lowered his head. His tongue teased and tugged out moan after moan. Pressure built in my core at a fever pitch, faster than before. It was wickedly hot and I didn't try to quiet myself. My cries echoed over the hill as he brought me to the edge and then pushed me over.

My heel dug into the grooves of the truck bed as my body contorted. I came down with black spots dancing in my eyes like fireflies in the trees.

Landon grasped my thighs and spread them apart, pulling them off his ears. "One of these days, you're going to pop my head like a grape. But damn, what a beautiful way to go."

I laughed hoarsely and held out my arms. Landon came. He licked a stripe up my belly before claiming my mouth. He wrapped my legs around him and I gasped in the middle of our kiss.

This is happening. It's happening right now.

"Ready, baby? We don't have to if you don't want to."

"She says she wants to," I rasped. "She really, really wants to."

The final word barely passed my lips before he pushed inside. Crying out, my nails dug into his back as sharp pain broke through my high.

Landon kissed my cheek, nose, and pressed two soft kisses on my closed eyes. He whispered sweet nothings as he waited for me to adjust.

My body slowly relaxed and he moved. Landon whispered in my ear as I clung to him.

"I love you, Zela," he said hoarsely. "I loved you first, and I'll love you last."

"L-look at me," I forced out. "Please."

His lips brushed along my cheeks as he raised his head and pressed our noses together. Hot, molten pleasure hummed beneath my skin. I felt every sensation so keenly as though my nerves had just come alive. The cool breeze drying the sweat on my temple. The hard ridges of his back, slick and smooth beneath my palm. His warm breath on my lips as I swallowed his moans. I can't believe I waited this long to be with him.

Pressure built in my core and I got louder as my body was wracked with wave after wave of mind-bursting sensations.

Landon collapsed on top of me. Our chests heaved, pushing against each other. I lifted his head and grinned into his dazed eyes.

"Let's do that again."

"Okay," he croaked. "I might... need a minute though."

I tossed my head. "No minutes. No more waiting. Again. Right now." I grasped his shoulder and threw him on his back.

"Fucking hell, woman," he cried. Landon gaped at me as I straddled him.

I settled on top of him and smirked as I placed his hands over my breasts. "Think we can make this big truck bounce, baby?"

His eyes darkened. "We're gonna fucking try," he growled. "Minute over."

I shrieked happily as he reared up and put the challenge to the test.

LANDON PULLED UP TO the curb and parked the car. He leaned across and kissed me mid-giggle.

"Is that what it's like to be drunk?" I asked as I nuzzled his neck.

His laugh rumbled against my cheek. "Before the puking starts." Landon tangled in my hair and pulled my head back. "Are you okay? I know we said we wanted it to be perfect—"

"It was perfect."

"We did it on a hill in the back of my mom's truck. It was hard and dirty and we could have been caught." He pressed a lock of my hair to his lips. "You deserved music, candles, and a real bed for your first time."

"I didn't need all of that stuff, Landon. All I wanted was me and you together with no interruptions. It was special because it was you."

"I love you."

We kissed long and slow. The need for air eventually pulled us apart.

Landon glanced at the dash. "You should go in. It's almost eleven." He smirked at me. "Wipe that goofy grin off your face before your mom sees you."

"I can do that, but tomorrow night, I want you to put it back on."

"Yes, ma'am."

I said goodbye and practically floated inside. It was incredibly sweet that Landon wanted my first time to be flowers, candy, and candles, but I couldn't think of anything better than hard, dirty, and dangerous with him in the back of a truck. Tonight had gone better than I could have ever imagined.

Flickering light poured out of the living room. I peeked around the corner and found Mom engrossed in her show.

"I'm home," I called.

She replied without looking away. "Did you have a good time?"

"It was great, Mom, and I think they raised a lot of money."

"Wonderful. Literacy is the first step to success. Especially for young women. If you give me their information, I will look into donating as well."

"That would be awesome."

I meant it. Their pretenses for luring the board out were false, but the organization and the money raised were real. I hoped a dent was made in offering more resources to improve literacy worldwide.

"Good night."

Mom finally turned around so I could get the full effect of her smile. "Good night, my only one."

A familiar twinge ached in my chest.

I wish I could tell you that I met Jonathan. I want to talk to you about how amazing, sweet, kind, dickish, irritating, and annoying my brother is. There is so much I need to say, but we have never been a family who talks, and honesty isn't what you taught me to expect from you.

"Is everything okay, Zela?"

I shook myself. "Yes, I'm fine. Just tired. See you in the morning."

My bed welcomed me with warm downy arms. I let out a soft sigh of relief.

Nothing sounded better than a hot bath and a snuggle beneath these sheets. I was sore in all the right places and a few of the wrong ones. No regrets, but that truck bed was hard.

Thinking of us together, I pulled out my phone to shoot Landon a gooey and incredibly explicit text.

My cell buzzed with an alert. I opened it on dozens of messages—all from Jordan.

Oh no. She must have spoken to Lucia and it can't have been good.

I wiped the smile off my face and called Jordan. This was going to be a long night.

Chapter Six

"He's so great, Derek."

"Uh-huh."

"We like a lot of the same movies and music."

"Cool."

"He said I had integrity."

"Yup."

Derek was beside me on his bed, his face stuck between the pages as usual. I leaned over and smacked the book out of his hands. He looked at it on the floor, shaking his head.

"Sometimes, I don't know if you're my gift or my curse," he muttered.

"Definitely gift," I said cheekily.

It was the Sunday night before the start of school. I got in later than usual since I spent the rest of the weekend with Jordan, fulfilling my mission to cheer her up. I kept my good mood to myself until I entered the academy and knocked on Derek's door.

Derek went to grab his book and I tackled him in a hug. "Ah!"

"Thank you, thank you, thank you," I squealed. "Getting to have a real conversation with him meant a lot to me. Did you think he was serious when he said we should pick it up where we left off?"

"Yes." Derek was slightly muffled from being pushed in-to the sheets.

"How do you know?"

"Dad said I could invite you over anytime."

"Really? But I thought they don't like you having friends over?"

"They don't. You'll have security on your ass everywhere you go."

Derek got me around the waist and threw me off. I bounced on the mattress laughing.

He straightened up and settled on the pillows. "But I fig-ured you would see that as worth it," he finished.

"I do. Can I come over this weekend?"

"I'll ask, but they should be cool with it."

"Great." I motioned at his book. "I finished that one last week. What do you think so far?"

"I think you like this book because the main character is into math."

I laughed. "So what if I do?"

A knock interrupted his reply. Derek heaved himself off the bed.

"What do you want?" he asked in typical Derek charm.

"Is Zee in there?"

I twisted around. "Landon?"

A raven-haired head appeared under Derek's arm. "Zee is here, guys."

"Guys?"

Landon came inside and on his tail were Michael and Cole. He folded his arms.

"See? Whenever I can't find my girlfriend, I assume she's in Derek's room."

"So what if she is?" Derek asked. He jumped on the bed and landed ankles crossed and hands laced behind his head. "She's in my room all the time. She likes to sleep with me too."

I frowned. "Don't say it like that and wipe that smirk off your face. You're making it sound weird."

Cole scoffed. "It is weird that you can stand being around this asshole for more than two minutes."

"You stop too," I said to Cole. "Derek isn't an asshole. He's really sweet underneath."

"You hear that?" Derek asked with a smirk. "I'm sweet."

"Who gives a shit." Landon pierced me with a look. "I've been waiting for you to get here, babe. I believe my orders were to put the goofy smile back on your face."

Heat surged to my cheeks as Cole, Michael, and Derek looked at us, trying to puzzle that out.

I cleared my throat. "True. Very true. We should take care of that right now."

Landon swept over his hand. "After you."

I crawled up the bed and encircled Derek in a hug. He didn't lift his arms to return it. On the contrary, he picked up his phone and messed with it while I held him to my chest.

Goodness. I swear this guy has the soul of a wet cat. He only gives affection when he feels like it.

"We'll talk books in the morning," I promised, "and we'll figure out this weekend later."

"What's happening this weekend?" Michael spoke up.

"I'm going to Derek's place," I said as I gathered my stuff and climbed off the bed.

"Good." Michael hooked his arm around my neck and kissed my cheek. "Then you'll be in Evergreen. We can go out to dinner. Italian."

"I'd love that."

Michael's shirt rode up where he held me. I gave into the urge to slip under his shirt and caress the smooth, hard muscle hiding beneath.

"What about dessert?" I whispered.

"I'm sure we'll think of something."

Landon tugged me out of his arms, bringing our flirting to an abrupt end. The world spun as he swept me off my feet and threw me over his shoulder.

"Good night, guys." Landon punctuated his goodbye with a smack to my bottom.

I really need to talk to him about that.

Landon carried me to his room and tossed me on the bed. The look in his eyes held the promise of a long, sleepless night.

But we can talk later.

"YOU SHOULD READ SUE Grafton too."

"I'm not a straight mystery person," replied Derek. "I always end up guessing who it is."

I cut my chocolate chip muffin in half and gave it to him without prompting. Derek was back at our table. I was back to giving him half of my good stuff. We fell into our routine like nothing broke us apart.

"Does that mean you don't like Agatha Christie?"

"No, I like her, but she's written every kind of mystery story there can be. Once you've read all of her books, you've pretty much read them all."

I goggled at him. "That's not true. Read Sue Grafton," I ordered. "You'll like it. Have I steered you wrong yet?"

"Guys," Tanner said. "Please end this incredibly boring conversation and look up. Something's going on."

That's when I noticed the room had gone quiet. Derek and I broke out of our little world and found we had been graced with a visit.

"Good morning, students."

Principal Whittaker stood behind his seat at the head table while his entourage of teachers, coaches, two therapists, and a vice principal fanned out around him.

The man wasn't out of his office without a pack. My friends liked to toss around the rumor that Whittaker and Argyle were one mind because they crushed on each other as hard as they did policy.

I'd say that wasn't likely since she was a "Mrs." but I had learned to dread seeing them together. Whatever was coming would be backed up twice as hard and enforced even harder.

"As I'm sure you know," he began, "the board of education is considering adopting our program within the public school system. They will make their determination this year and to aid in the final decision, members of the board have asked to return and hold interviews among the students.

"I want to be clear." Whittaker's gaze swept over us—hard and unflinching. "There will not be a repeat of last year. The flyers plastered in the F Wing and the lies it leveled at the school were bordering on an expulsion-worthy offense. Unfortunately, we haven't found the person or people responsible, but do not think you've gotten away with what you've done or the path is clear to try again.

"If anything like that should take place during their time here, the whole school will be punished with a suspension of privileges for an entire month."

"What?!"

The first shout set off a torrent. Students shot to their feet, shouting over each other at once.

"But that's not fair!"

"If you'd put some cameras up, we could catch the bastard who has been harassing us and end this!" This came from Heath. "For All must have done it and they've done nothing but come after the Elites!"

"Yeah!" a group of As shouted.

"Settle down," Whittaker said.

"It's got to be some bitter-ass F! Why should we be punished because of them?!"

"Don't bring us into it!" Tanner shot back. "You fucking blame us when you splash piss on your golden toilet seats! We have better things to do!"

"That's enough!" bellowed Whittaker. "Sit down!"

Silence descended as quickly as it took the students to drop their asses in their seats.

Argyle grasped Whittaker's shoulder as she stood. "Believe us when we say we have no desire to resort to these actions," she said calmly. "Our hope is to have a smooth year and an end to the attacks and slander against the school. If this can't be achieved, we'll be forced to take stronger measures until this For All is found. Is that understood?"

"Yes, ma'am," a few people muttered.

"She said is that understood?" Whittaker repeated.

"Yes, Principal Whittaker!"

He inclined his head. "In regards to the interviews, they will begin next semester. Your vice principal and I will choose the students who will speak to the board. Are there any questions?"

Nico raised his hand.

"Yes, Mr. Kazan?"

"Are you going to choose students from all classes?"

He nodded. "Two students from each class. One from each campus. Juniors and seniors only. Any more questions?"

I lowered my head a fraction, peering down at my phone as I typed out a text.

Me: We have until next semester.

A faint buzz sounded to my right.

Adam: What do you want to do?

Whittaker and Argyle spent ten more minutes answering questions. Afterward, they sat down to eat with us. We dutifully ate our meals and remained quiet for the rest of breakfast. Until the door slammed shut behind Whittaker.

"Can you believe that?" Melody burst out.

She wasn't the only one. The cafeteria erupted into a riot of arguments, accusations, and unleashed frustration.

"He's going to make sure the only people who get near the board are in love with the battle system," Melody said.

Nico shook his head. "He'll have a hard time finding them in the F Class. If he really picks students from every class, one of the Cs, Ds, or Fs is bound to tell them how much it sucks being denied everything."

"I guess that's true," Hunter said. "I know I'm Elite, but that should mean I'm smart enough to see this isn't the right way to teach students. Keeping kids out of the library and SAT prep? At some point, it feels like they want to keep people down."

Tanner, Nico, Justin, and Owen nodded their heads.

"What can any of us do about it?" Cole asked. "Whittaker isn't the only one determined to make this expansion happen and it'll come down on all of us if we make trouble."

Six pairs of eyes flew to Melody. She straightened under our attention. "It will be difficult. Especially if Whittaker takes to Heath's idea and puts up cameras. Even worse, no one will thank us if we get the whole school punished."

"Does that mean Stand Up is sitting this one out?" I asked.

She pinned me with a look that snapped my mouth shut. "Of course not. Nothing has changed. I'll think of something that can't be traced to us. If nothing else, I'll find a way to speak to one of the board members and tell them the truth. Whittaker can't be on them every second of their visit."

We bobbed our heads.

"It won't just be you," I said. "If Whittaker picks one of us to represent the Elite Class, we'll tell them the truth." I met the eyes of Cole, Michael, Landon, and Derek. "Right, guys?"

I knew what I was asking them, and for some, it was a high price.

I lingered on Derek. "It'll be hard but... we have to do the right thing."

A smile curled his lips. "I'm nothing if not honest, Manning. You don't have to worry about me."

I wasn't sure what to make of that reply. *But I have a plan A if your version of the truth isn't mine.*

But that makes me think. I narrowed my eyes. *What is Derek's version of the truth? I don't think I've asked him if he wants the expansion. He's framed it as his father's orders, but why go along if this isn't what he wants?*

"Something you want to say, Manning?"

A knowing grin hung on his lips like he could hear my thoughts.

"Yes," I stated. "I have something to ask you and I will. We're going to talk."

He put fingers to his head in a mock salute. "Whatever you say."

"Thanks, guys." Melody's voice broke in. "It means a lot having all of you back me up."

"It's easy when we want the same things," Tanner said. "My little brother starts high school in three years. I'm not letting him put up with the bullshit I have."

I broke my strange eye lock with Derek and looked at Adam. I motioned with my head toward the door.

"We have to go," I said as Adam and I got to our feet. "I left something in Adam's room."

The two of us didn't speak until we got into the hallway.

Adam skipped the preamble. "Do we have enough time?"

"We do, but we might have to step it up." I bumped his shoulder. "I don't want you to take on more than you can handle, so tell me now if it's too much."

"It's not too much, but Coach is talking about stepping up practices as it gets closer to the swim meet. Can *you* handle being the Battle Doctor, your boyfriends, school, and your clubs?"

"I won't let it get as bad as I did last year. I have a system. It's working. The real trick is getting around the coaches. I'm sunk if they all ban me from helping."

"We'll think of another way if that happens."

Adam veered off course and bumped me back. I'm not sure when that became our thing but it was another in a million ways we were cute. I told him as much.

Chuckling, he replied, "We are cute, aren't we? No wonder your boyfriends think there's something up with us."

"We'd be a great couple," I mused. "And we'd make the most adorable Moon babies. With pudgy cheeks and curly hair and bright green eyes—"

"Please stop fantasizing about our babies."

I busted up and bumped into him again. This time I snuggled up to his arm and he pulled me close.

"But you have eyes for another Manning woman," I teased.

"Speaking of Jordan..."

My smile dimmed. I knew this was coming. I was surprised it took Adam this long.

"Yeah?"

"Is she okay? She canceled our date the other night and refused to say why. Did I... do something?"

We reached the staircase. I grabbed him out of the line of kids going up and stepped off to the side.

"You didn't do anything wrong. Jordan is going to talk to you herself, but you should get that out of your head right now. She really likes you and wanted nothing more than to be with you. Her messed-up ex saw to it that didn't happen."

"Her ex? You talking about Malcolm?" Anger stole the sweet, affable expression off of his face in a blink. "What did that fucker do now?"

I squeezed his hand. "Jordan will talk to you. You'll get it all out, forgive each other, and get back on course to planning the future where I get those curly-haired, green-eyed chubby babies in the family. Got it?"

Adam rolled his eyes, but I didn't miss the smile. "I got it."

We continued up to class. Adam's mind was most likely on Jordan. Mine quickly returned to my main problem. This expansion had to be stopped and I had little time to do it. Worse, I had no clue if my plan would work.

It has to work. It's all I've got.

"WHY DO YOU DO THIS?"

I pressed against Michael, enjoying the warmth on my back. He rubbed his stubbly cheek against mine. Slowly. Up and down. And it was having a magic effect deep in my lower belly. He must have heard I had a thing for facial hair and he wasn't using his power for good.

I sighed soft and contentedly. "What do you mean?"

He gestured at the boys grappling on the mat. "You take time out every day to help the lower classes with their battles. Do you feel like you owe them something now that you're Elite?"

His question was a sharp reminder that I was supposed to be watching, not cuddling. To be fair, I planned on doing this alone, but Michael caught up with me after tutoring and asked to join. I thought about saying no in the brief moments before he kissed me until my heart stopped. After that, no was no longer a part of my vocabulary.

I blinked out of my haze just as Daxton lunged at Marco.

"Dax!" I shouted. "You know grabbing clothes will lose you points. Don't do it now *or* during the battle."

Dax let him go immediately. "Sorry, Zeke. Won't happen again. But can you tell me what to do for the takedown one more time?"

"Bend your knees, lower your head, put your shoulder in his belly, and then grab both legs to take him down. Practice a few times before you do it."

"Okay."

The boys squared off and set to do as I ordered. I went back to Michael.

"I'm not helping them because I feel like I have to," I replied. "I do it because I want to. I had to fight for every little scrap as an F. My teachers and our coaches are great and I'm not saying they didn't teach us to the best of their ability, but we didn't get what we deserved because of the patch on our chest.

"If I can help people snag a little more time in the computer lab or a night at the dance with their girlfriend, then

I'm happy to spend an hour of my afternoon passing on some tips." I twisted around and kissed him. "I've learned most of it from you guys."

"I love that about you." Michael rubbed my nose with his. "You're always thinking of how you can help."

"Hmm. Did you just say love, Michael Young?"

His smile revealed the tiniest dimple in his cheek. "I believe that is what I said. Got a problem with that?"

"No problem here."

"Uhh. Guys?"

Our flirting came to an abrupt end. Daxton and Marco both stared at us.

"I'm ready to try the takedown," said Daxton. "Are you going to watch?"

I flapped a hand at him. "Do it. I'm watching."

I paid them my attention this time as Daxton smoothly went through the steps and dropped his friend to the mat.

"Nicely done," I called. "Do it one more time and then we'll try the single leg take—"

The gym door flew open.

The rest of my sentence was forgotten as Sully, Jose, Lars, Mason Prescott, and a few other A boys loped in. Bringing up the rear, was Zach and Rhys.

"This is why I asked," Michael said in my ear. "A lot of people don't like what you're doing, Zee. I walked up on them talking when I went out for my run. They were bitching about Bs and Cs losing to Ds and Fs because of you."

"What's this?" Mason asked. The mocking grin sharply reminded me of the basketball to the face that ended our battle. It was his parting shot to me as he walked out. Mason was an A and a highly unpleasant one.

"What's it look like?" I asked. "They're practicing, Mason."

"And let me guess..." He strode closer, holding out his hands. "You're giving them some *tips*."

"So what if I am? It's none of your business."

Rhys barked a laugh. "Damn, Young. Aren't you two cozy? I didn't know you swung that way."

I felt Michael's shrug. "Now you do."

"I don't give a shit where you put your dick," Mason snapped. "I do have a problem with you and Manning helping these Ds cheat."

I heaved a sigh. "Will you give it a rest? It's not cheating."

Zach pushed through the boys. "If it wasn't against the rules, Coach Fineman wouldn't have kicked you off the field. How about we tell Franklin what you're doing?"

"Go for it. He'll tell you what I'm telling you. It's not against the rules because it's not cheating."

"No?" Mason strolled over to Daxton and Marco. He appeared to be enjoying himself. "Why is he here? Why couldn't you practice on your own and face your battles like the rest of us do?"

Daxton bared his teeth. "You don't do it on your own. You practice together just like everyone else. Stop talking shit, A."

"That's right. *A*," Mason said. "I got into the A Class by working my ass off, and you think you can steal my privileges by having your misguided friend tell you what to do?"

"If one afternoon of practicing with Zeke is enough to *steal your privileges*," Daxton replied, flaunting his air quotes. "Then you didn't deserve them in the first place."

"What was that?"

Mason got in his face and Daxton shoved him hard. I was off and running as Mason came roaring back, fists raised.

"Stop!"

Mason and Daxton fell to the mat, limbs flying. Michael streaked past me and grabbed Mason. Rhys, Sullivan, Lars, and Jose were on him before he could get him off.

"What is wrong with you guys?!" I shrieked. I pounded on Lars's back. "Get off of—"

A hand snagged my collar and yanked. Gasping, I flew back and hit the floor.

"You started this!" Zach cried. He towered over me, fists balled for another strike. "You should have stayed in your fucking lane, F!"

I scrambled up. I ducked Zach's swipe and bolted across the room.

"Hey!" Heavy footfalls sounded behind me.

I fell against Coach Franklin's door.

"Coach! Coach!" I pounded on it. "Coach!"

I prayed he was in there. Daxton, Marco, Michael, and I were outnumbered by too many and I had been beaten by a few of these boys before. I wasn't eager for a repeat.

"What is going on out there?!"

I shot away just in time. His door flew open and Franklin stomped out—all two hundred pounds of steaming, muscle-bound, wrestling champion. Two of the A boys that came with Mason scrambled off the mat and bolted.

"If you run out that door, you'll have detention for two months! If you're tough enough to fight, you're tough enough to face the consequences!"

Franklin reached into the writhing pile and lifted Mason off one-handed. "That's enough!"

Franklin picked them apart until all the boys were red-faced and lined up in front of him—silent as a cemetery.

"Now," Coach began. "Who do I start with?"

Coach gave everyone two weeks of detention. Mason and Zach tried to defend themselves saying it was my fault for messing with the system but Coach would have none of it.

We trudged out of the gym. The boys shot daggers at me on their way to the dorm. I saw in their eyes this wasn't over.

"It's pretty clear they're choosing to blame me for getting them into trouble," I mumbled.

"Fuck them," Daxton spat. "We didn't do anything that they don't do. They're just coming for us because we're not afraid to challenge the upper classes anymore."

Daxton punched my shoulder. "Thanks for the help, man. I'm going to crush this battle."

He and Marco walked off while I hung back with Michael. I slipped my hand into his.

"I'm sorry you got mixed up in this."

Michael's shirt was torn and there was a small cut over his eyebrow. Otherwise, he didn't seem to be hurt.

"Don't be sorry. You didn't start that fight." He shook his head. "They're taking this way too far and I don't like it, Zee. What if they come back with more guys and there isn't a coach around?"

"I've never let Zach get in my way before and I'm not going to do it now. At some point, he needs to accept he doesn't get everything he wants."

Michael rested his chin on top of my head. "Sleep in my room tonight. Please."

"Are you worried they'll try to break into my room?" *A valid concern.*

"Maybe that and maybe I just want to be with you."

I smiled for the first time since our interruption. "Okay. I'd like that."

That night, I burrowed under the covers, inhaling Michael's scent. I heard a chuckle.

"You're not a cover hog, are you?"

"You'll find out."

The bed dipped and hands found me beneath the sheets. I rolled into Michael and pressed my lips to his chest.

A soft groan fell from him. "It will be hard enough being in this bed with you and keeping my hands to myself. Don't make it impossible."

"You can feel free not to keep your hands to yourself." I peeked out of the covers like a naughty gopher. "I certainly won't stop you."

"Well, they might wander a bit..."

Michael gently guided me back and climbed on top of me. Anticipation pulsed in my veins hotter than blood. My chest rose and fell with heavy breaths—exposed in a low-cut tank top. Michael bent and brushed his soft lips on my collarbone.

"Yes," I breathed. "Don't stop."

"Ah! Ahhhhhhh!"

Michael shot off me. Bloodcurdling screams ripped through the once-quiet floor. Michael tumbled out of bed and raced to the door. I leaped up and chased him.

No, wait! I'm not dressed as Zeke!

I skidded to a stop and slammed the door shut as someone streaked past. The shouts got louder in the hallway as I hurriedly shoved on my cap and wig and wrapped myself in his comforter. There was no time for my bindings.

"Michael?" I ran into the hall. "Michael, what's…"

I trailed off as I took in the sight that struck half a dozen pajama-clad boys frozen. Bright, dripping wet blood covered the wall between Sullivan's and Lars's rooms. A chilling message stained the stark white plaster.

"Her blood is on your hands."

Beneath the message was an upside-down A.

Michael reached out.

"Don't!" Sully rasped. His throat was hoarse from shouting.

"It's okay." Michael swiped a finger through the blood. "It's fake."

"Fake or not."

Our heads whipped around as Cameron stalked down the hall.

"We have to get Whittaker. Go, Young. You're the fastest."

Michael didn't argue. He came over to me and guided me to his room. "Go inside. Lock the door. I'll be right back."

He ran off before I could say anything. Not that I knew what to say. Who was For All talking about? What did that message mean? And why would he do something so horrible as to write it in fake blood?

I ducked in the doorway as Cameron shouted orders. He tried sending people back to their rooms but the noise brought more guys out. Forty boys packed into the hallway, expressions grim.

Derek spotted me across the hall and came over. "Get your stuff. You're staying in my room."

"But Michael—"

"He can take the couch if he wants, but you're sleeping with me, Zee. Don't argue. This isn't stolen tablets or stink bombs." A crinkle broke the smooth skin of his forehead. The last time he'd been this serious was that night on his patio. "For All has gone off the fucking rails and if he gets it into his head to do worse, these locks aren't hard to pick. Get your stuff."

I thought about arguing and then my gaze drifted over his shoulder to the dripping message. I got why the new For All did what he did last year. I didn't get this. Derek was right to be worried. An adversary you didn't understand was one you couldn't predict.

"Okay."

I ducked inside and dressed for real. When I came out, Derek was backed up by two others.

"—fine. Zee is staying with me."

"And me," Landon said. "I'm not leaving him alone until this guy is caught." Landon secured me to his side. "Heath made a good point about putting up cameras. Why hasn't Whittaker done it?"

"Probably can't afford them," said Derek. We passed by the message, all of us averting our eyes. "I heard Cameron's dad say once that the way things are set up funnels most of the school budget to the Elite and A Class—like almost all of it. Breakbattle doesn't charge tuition so they rely on donors and money from the state. It doesn't leave much left over for extras."

"I never thought of it like that," I admitted. "It does make sense."

Derek grabbed the doorknob just as Whittaker and Michael burst onto the scene. I'd never seen my principal out of his standard suit and tie before, but Whittaker in his night clothes turned out not to be much different. He marched down the hall in matching black silk pajamas and a thick robe. Despite his neat clothes, the rapid gait and hair sticking up in the back revealed he was frazzled.

Whittaker took one look at the message and the blood drained from his face.

"All of you, in your rooms now!"

We didn't need to be yelled at twice. The guys bundled me into the room, locked the door, and put Derek's chair in front of it for good measure. Landon stripped me out of my Zeke clothes and carried me to bed. He was gentle as he got in next to me and pulled the covers to my chin.

"Blankets are in the wardrobe," Derek said to Michael and Cole. "If you're staying."

"We're staying," said Cole.

Derek slipped beneath the sheets. My vision adjusted in the dark and fixed on the white of his eyes.

"What is going on?" I whispered.

"I don't know." A warm hand found me under the blanket. "But we'll figure it out. I won't let anything happen to you, Zela."

Slowly, I shook my head. "This isn't about me. I don't know what it's about but... For All isn't playing games anymore."

"Then we need to figure out who he is so we don't get caught in the middle."

I nodded. Solid plan, but would For All let it happen?

Her blood is on your hands.

What is going on in this school?

Chapter Seven

In the weeks that passed since For All's message, life slowly returned to normal. We woke the day after to discover the message had been left on all floors and the cafeteria. It only made us feel marginally better that the dark message wasn't meant solely for the Elites, but there was still tension in the days following.

Eventually, when we didn't hear another word from For All, we fell into a haze of homework, club activities, tutoring, sports practice, and sex.

Now that the proverbial cherry had been popped, Landon and I had no qualms about doing it whenever we could.

"We're going to be late to class." I buttoned my undershirt and then looked around for my blazer. Landon was fond of throwing my clothes all over the place.

"We have some time." Landon reclined against the headboard naked as the day he was born. The sheets were a crumpled mess at the end of the bed, leaving him on full display. "What are you doing after class?"

"I'm going to watch a battle. Mitch needed my help to win more study hours in the library. This time with math tutoring. I want to see how he does."

"After that?"

"I'll be studying in the library too," I said pointedly. "We have finals next week and all the places you're ticklish won't be on the test."

Grinning, he patted his lap. "They'll be on my test tonight. We'll be together after dinner, right?"

"I'm hanging out with Derek after dinner."

"Argh." He flung his head back. "Damn it, Zela."

I plopped on his lap and kissed his neck. "Right after that, I'll be sneaking into your bed. Okay?"

"Okay," he said, sounding mollified. "And I'm not letting you out until you pass my test."

"Deal."

I left his room and almost ran into Mr. Sondheim.

"Oops. Sorry, Mr. Sondheim."

He smiled wide. "No harm done, Mr. Manning. Have a good day of classes."

"Thank you, sir."

I waved goodbye to the latest addition to Breakbattle Academy and continued to the Elite Wing. Installing cameras throughout the entire place would take a lot of money and too much time. Whittaker promised nonetheless that it would happen as soon as it was possible, but in the meantime, the boys now had their own matron, Mr. Sondheim.

He was a super sweet guy who was always smiling and greeted me every time he saw me. He was also as tall as a tree trunk and just as thick. He roamed the halls from eleven at night to seven in the morning, ensuring we all stayed in our beds where we belonged.

"Morning, students," Mrs. Peterson said as we trailed in. "Finals are next week, so we're going to jump right into our review. Open your chemistry textbooks to chapter nine and go over the information. We're having a short quiz in twenty minutes."

A short quiz turned out to be a forty-five-minute test. We had a quick break that lasted the amount of time it took to pull out another textbook, and then we went over advanced literature.

The final bell brought blessed relief from review bootcamp. I tossed my things in my backpack and then bent to turn off my computer.

"What are you doing over the break?"

I turned my desk chair and peered at Cole upside down. "The break?"

"Yeah. Are you leaving town?"

"We might head up to New York, but it won't be for the whole break. Why?"

Cole rocked back and forth on his heels. He looked at my desktop, backpack, the floor, and then the ceiling—everywhere but at me.

"You should come over," he mumbled.

"To your place?"

"Where else?"

His snark was betrayed by his pink cheeks.

I bit back a smile. "You want to see me for Christmas?"

"I didn't say that," he snapped. "Doesn't matter when. You practically live at Moon's place, so while you're in Evergreen, you should come over. Play with Toby. Hang with Christina."

I closed the distance and pressed a gentle kiss to his flaming cheek. "If I go over your house, it won't be for your dog or your sister. I'd love to visit, Cole. I don't want to go the whole break without seeing you."

"Yeah. Well…" He roughly cleared his throat. "Cool."

Cole pulled back and strode off quickly like he thought I would chase him and get him to blush some more.

Tempting but I promised to watch Mitch's battle. I'll corner him later.

A voice in my ear broke me out of my thoughts.

"Ready to go?"

I threaded my arm around the crook of Adam's elbow. "Let's go."

We left the dorm building and crossed the lawn for the natatorium. I helped with the academic part, but I left improving Mitch's swim game to Adam. I kept my time in the swim building to a minimum and Adam was better at it anyway. I was happy to let him take over.

Coach Nelson was the only one inside when we came in. He saw us, pointed toward the bleachers, and then returned to his clipboard without a word.

"How do you think he'll do?"

"Mitch improved his swim time," replied Adam, "but he's going up against Carter Renault. He's on my team and he's good. It's going to come down to the academic test." He bumped my shoulder. "I hope you taught him well."

"He'll do fine. Mitch aced the last two practice tests I gave him."

The Mitch in question strode inside with two teachers and Carter. He waved happily when he spotted us.

"He looks really excited for a C that is about to go up against an A," Adam said out of the corner of his mouth.

"He's confident he can win. He told me all he needed was a little help from the Battle Doctor." I motioned between us. "Battle Doctors."

"Damn if that's not a cool title though."

We cracked up until a sharp whistle silenced us.

"Alright," Nelson began. "You know how this works, gentlemen. You'll swim to the other side of the pool. Whoever touches the pad first wins. Step up."

Mitch took his place and tossed us another thumbs-up.

"Ready?"

Fweet!

The boys launched off the platform and dove into the water. Carter pulled ahead almost immediately. Adam wasn't lying about him being good, but Mitch wasn't far behind. The persistent C sliced through the water, pushing hard to keep pace.

Carter smacked the touch board and burst out of the water milliseconds before Mitch. Mitch glanced at the scoreboard and whooped. The winner was clearly not him, but that didn't stop his celebration.

He hefted out of the pool and ran at us. "I did it!" he cried. "I know I did! I aced the math test and Carter only beat me by a few seconds! I won!"

Adam chuckled. "Calm down, man. Your prize is a few extra hours in the library."

"I beat an A! I—"

"—Whittaker right now!"

My smile faded as I looked past Mitch to the commotion on the other side of the pool. Carter stood before Nelson and the teachers, shouting and pointing at us.

"What's going on?" asked Adam.

Carter stomped over to us with Nelson right behind him. "I saw him! Mitch gave them a thumbs-up before the race. I bet they coached him for the battle."

Nelson looked from us to an irate Carter, his brows drawn together. "Adam, is that true?"

"Yes, Coach," Mitch spoke up. "Adam and Zeke helped me train. What's the problem?"

"What's the problem?" Carter snapped. "Adam is captain of my fucking team! He knows my strengths and weaknesses and he told *you* so you could win! How is that not cheating, Coach?!"

Adam lurched to his feet. "No, I didn't!"

"The fuck you—"

"That's enough!" Coach barked. "Carter, I will handle this!"

Carter shut his mouth but that didn't stop him from glaring at Mitch hard enough to make the boy step back.

"Adam," Nelson said in a calmer tone. "Did you train Mitch for this battle?"

"He asked me for help to improve his time. I gave him advice and didn't bring up Carter's name once. I'm not that kind of guy."

"I see." Nelson's gaze flicked to me. "And what was your part in this? Am I right in assuming Coach Fineman's lunchtime topic of students becoming coaches included you as well?"

"I tutored him in math, sir," I replied. "Mitch wanted more time in the library with finals coming up. I said I would help."

"See, Coach," Carter burst out. "I told you they've been helping kids cheat."

"I didn't cheat!" Mitch argued.

Nelson held up a hand. "Technically, tutoring and tips cannot be considered cheating, but"—he looked hard at Adam—"I will be very disappointed to discover you've used your position as captain to give others an advantage over your teammates."

"I haven't, sir," Adam said firmly. "I swear. I only gave him some advice on swimming faster."

"Yes? And how long and how often have you and Manning been doing this?"

"All year," Carter threw in. He leveled a finger at us. "Coach Fineman even told them to stop but they won't. They've been telling lowerclassmen to challenge us and then teaching them how to beat us."

"He's making it sound more sinister than it is," I protested. "Elites, As, and Bs practice together all the time."

"They practice with each other," Nelson corrected. "People they don't battle against so they have nothing to win or lose." He grasped Mitch's shoulder. "Mr. Klein, on the other hand, has a lot to win by having two Elite students as his personal trainer. Keeping things equal among the classes prevents the very situation that we are in now."

I swallowed hard. I knew this was a possibility but I wasn't expecting it to happen over a simple thumbs-up. It was too soon to shut us down. Way too soon.

"Does that mean we're in trouble, sir?" I asked.

"I'll let Principal Whittaker be the judge of that." He jerked his head at Carter and Mitch. "Get dressed. We're going to the office."

Mitch trudged off, smile nowhere to be found. Carter followed him looking triumphant.

Adam and I shared a look. I could practically hear the thought go through his mind, asking what we were going to do now.

The boys returned and Nelson led us out. None of us spoke on the trek to the administration building. My mind spun with arguments to convince Whittaker there was nothing wrong with Elite students helping other classes. Each one was unlikelier to work than the last. Whittaker wasn't one to be swayed when he made up his mind.

Whittaker's secretary, Dimas, looked up when we came inside.

"Can I help you?"

"We need to speak with the principal," said Nelson.

"You messed with the wrong one, F."

The hiss made my teeth clench. I didn't give Carter the satisfaction of acknowledging him.

"You're done helping them challenge us."

"We'll see," I said simply.

Nelson opened the door and motioned us inside. Whittaker did not rise from his desk when we came in, but why would he? This was his domain and he observed us from his high-backed leather chair like he knew it and we did too.

"Gentlemen, take a seat," he said. "What can I do for you?"

"It's come to my attention that Adam and Zeke have been coaching other students in preparation for battles," said Nelson. "What action should be taken, Principal?"

Whittaker looked from me, to Nelson, to me, to Nelson again. "Action?"

He nodded. "What they're doing isn't cheating and normally I'd applaud them taking their time out to help their fellow classmates, but it could be seen as giving certain students an edge not available to everyone."

I sighed. *This is it. Stopped before we truly started.*

"I don't see how, Coach Nelson."

I blinked. *What did he just say?*

"Every student is free to practice and study with who they wish. There are no rules that state students can't go to others to prepare for a battle. If anything, it's their only recourse since coaches and teachers can't give any more help at that point."

Whittaker turned to me. "As it happens, I'm aware of how Mr. Manning spends his time. He told me and Mrs. Jeong weeks ago and we were both impressed. He couldn't have known that moments before he arrived, Mrs. Jeong and I were discussing the possible downside of our system and that it encourages students to see those outside of their class as nothing more than opponents.

"She was then delighted when Mr. Manning shared with her all he was doing to help his lowerclassmen." I think he was making an effort to keep his expression neutral. It wasn't working. A tiny grin of victory tugged at his lips. "She said if the battle system results in more students like Mr. Manning, then it's worth adopting.

"Frankly, I can hardly punish Zeke or Adam after receiving such praise."

Silence filled the room as Nelson stood before his boss, expressionless.

"You're right, sir."

My eyes flared. *How is that happening? And when did Mrs. Jeong say all of this? I walked in here thinking I would be spending the night scrounging up a plan B.*

"What they are doing is kind and I would hate to see them punished for it," Nelson continued, "but I'd say there are still grounds for concerns. They may be Elite students, but it doesn't make them qualified to coach. They could give advice that results in a student making a wrong move and being injured. Not only that, but the accusation has been leveled that Mr. Moon is using his position to help others beat his teammates. True or not, I can't have disharmony on the team."

Whittaker inclined his head. "Your concerns are valid, Nelson. How about this?" He pointed at Adam. "You don't offer help on swimming to anyone outside of scheduled swim practices. You can practice other sports and subjects, but as captain, you can't have your own team thinking you're working against them."

"Yes, sir," Adam replied without argument.

"Good. As for them passing on bad tips, let's agree that practices between any students should be supervised. In truth, I've been considering proposing this after the brawl in the wrestling gym. We've trusted the students to use the fields and gyms on their own, but maybe that trust was misplaced. From now on, they can't practice alone."

Whittaker must have seen something on Nelson's face because he added, "Of course, the coaches have a lot on their plates and I do not expect you to take on more than you already do. I will find volunteers to handle this."

Nelson inclined his head. "Thank you, sir."

"I believe these measures will put your fears to rest."

Whittaker didn't wait for a reply. "Excellent. If that's all, I must get back to work, but commendations to you once again, Mr. Manning. You are a credit to this school."

Beaming, I shot up and shook his hand. "Thanks, sir. I do my best to give back what Breakbattle has given me."

I tried to turn down my grin in the face of Carter's poisonous glare. He knocked me aside stomping out the door and Mitch skipped after him, shooting me one more thumbs-up on the way.

"Wow," said Adam. "I was not expecting that."

"Tell me about it."

"Will his changes get in the way of your plan?"

"It won't make it easier, but it shouldn't stop us. We will be fine."

Adam ran out in front of me, jogging backward. "As always, it's a pleasure planning total and complete annihilation with you, Zee Manning. I can't wait to see it all unfold next semester."

I laughed. "Neither can I."

THWACK! THWACK! THWACK!

"JoJo? Did the beef come back to life and is now attacking you?"

Jordan turned on me, knife aloft. "What?"

"Why are you going at that thing so hard? Take it easy."

The two of us were in her kitchen while our moms argued in some other part of the house. Christmas Eve had visited the Manning women and we spent it the way we always did—together.

"Why should I take it easy, Zee?" Jordan demanded. "My ex is a sociopath. My best friend cheated with him. All of my other friends knew about it and have been looking at me with pity behind my back for months. And my boyfriend is never here!"

Jordan dropped the knife down on the steak with a vicious thwack that made me jump.

"Okay." I grabbed her elbows and pulled her away. "I think I'll take over that while you finish the salad."

She huffed. "I can't believe she would do that to me, Zela. Fuck Malcom. Lucia and I have been friends since sixth grade."

"I'm really sorry, Jordan. I wish there was something I could do."

I felt next to useless throughout this whole situation. It had only gotten worse in the weeks since Malcolm's confession. Lucia admitted what she did with a heavy dose of excuses saying it was Malcolm's fault for pursuing her relentlessly. Then it all came out that her other friends were in on the secret. The cherry on top was finding out the last day of the semester that Malcolm and Lucia were talking about getting together.

Jordan was going through hell at school and it didn't help that I could only see her on the weekends and Adam less than that. Adam asked her out every weekend, but sometimes Aunt Bev said no to her driving an hour away and Miss Val often claimed Adam for babysitting. She was fraying at the seams and I hated that she was going through it alone.

Arms encircled my waist. "You're already doing it, Zee." Jordan rested her cheek on my back. "You've listened to me bitch nonstop without complaining and you've brought me ice cream on demand. I'm sorry I've been such a Grinch. I just hate that I won't see Adam for Christmas."

"They're visiting Ezra's brother's family, and supposedly, it's going to be a huge family reunion thing. He couldn't get out of it or he would absolutely be here with you."

"I know," she said softly. "I just miss him. Sexual frustration might be adding to my grouchiness."

"Preach," I mumbled.

"You too? Michael still not giving it up."

"Nope." I sighed. "I respect that he wants to wait and I would never push him, but his reasons kill me. Whatever he needs me to do to prove my feelings for him are real, I'll happily do it."

"What feelings would those be?" Jordan thumped me with her forehead. "Do you love him?"

A goofy grin broke out on my lips. "More and more every day."

"Maybe he needs to hear that."

"Telling a guy I love him to get sex?" I teased. "How the tables have turned."

We giggled.

"Only tell him if your motives are pure, Zela Rae," she said. "What about you and Cole?"

"I'm going to see him the day after Christmas. Things are even more complicated. We had that great talk and he was really honest with me, but it's the same thing where I feel like I don't have any control in my relationship. He wants to wait until he's sure his friendship with Michael can handle them both dating me, but who knows when that will be? In the meantime, we're hooking up but we're not having sex." I sighed. "Either way, I'm happy I'll get to see him over break."

I finished chopping the beef and tossed it in the stockpot. The pot roast with cider gravy and sweet potatoes would taste heavenly when it was finished. Everything was going to be great for our Christmas celebration. The chocolate gingerbread cake. The spicy roasted carrots, roast chicken, and cranberry cheesecake. The Christmas tree Jordan and I stayed up late decorating—listening to Christmas music and belting out tunes while we danced around with ornaments.

Jordan tapped my back. "I'm good now, so let me do it. I'm a better cook than you anyway."

"You are not," I protested.

"Last year you dropped the cheesecake on the floor."

I sniffed. "That makes me clumsy, not a bad cook."

Jordan chuckled. "Fair enough, but I want to do it. Cooking is giving me an outlet for my stress. I'm about to smash the hell out of those potatoes."

"Stress?"

Mom and Aunt Bev entered the kitchen. "What stress, Jordan?"

Jordan hid her face as she took my place. "Nothing, Mom," she said. "Junior year is just intense with college and stuff."

"You don't need to be stressed, JoJo." Aunt Bev took hold of her chin and made her look up. She kissed her forehead. "There's no way you don't get into Somerset."

"Thanks, Mom."

"How's it going in here, girls?" asked Mom. "Need help with anything?"

"No, no, no." I took hold of Mom and guided her out of the kitchen. "This year, we're doing everything and our beautiful, smart, radiant mothers will relax on the couch drinking eggnog and watching Christmas movies."

"Okay. If you're sure." Mom sounded amused but partly pleased.

I was laying it on thick but I couldn't help it. Cole was not the only person I was visiting in Evergreen. I was also dropping by the Grayson Mansion.

I had been to Derek's house twice since the fundraiser. His father was a busy man despite him being between movies, so it wasn't like I got much face time with him. Nevertheless, he obeyed Naomi's orders to have meals together as a family and I would get my chance to talk to him then.

So far, I'd learned that he didn't have much of a sweet tooth except for a weakness for fried banana sandwiches. He loved Switzerland and not just because his parents lived there. He snuck into his first R-rated movie when he was eleven and that he taught himself to play basketball so he could do it with Derek.

I felt immense guilt for lying to Mom, but every second I spent with him and everything I learned made it worth it.

Or at least, that's what I'll keep telling myself.

I sat Mom down and kissed her cheek. "I love you, Mom."

She squeezed my hand. "I love you too, only one."

I spent Christmas Eve and Christmas Day trying to show her how much I loved her. Jordan and I pulled off dinner without a hitch and our moms praised us and said we had the job from now on. Afterward, we opened presents and I gave Mom a pair of pajamas covered in the titles of all the books she had written. She gasped when she pulled them out.

"How did you do this?" she asked.

"I found someone online who makes them. Do you like them?"

"Oh, Zela. They're wonderful."

After presents, we stayed up late watching a Christmas movie together and then went to bed. We woke on Christmas Day to more food, music, and movies. Christmases were hard for me, but that motivated us to celebrate harder. Mom and Aunt Bev tried not to fight. Jordan and I didn't stop moving for a second.

On December twenty-sixth, I felt the tiny thread of relief I always did that the holiday has passed, but also, I was happy at making another memory with my family. And if at some point I wished Derek, Jonathan, and Naomi were with us too, I didn't let it bring me down. One day that could be our future.

Cole's car pulled into the driveway. I darted away from the window and got my stuff.

"Bye, Mom," I shouted into the living room on the way out.

"Goodbye, Zela. Back by eleven."

"Yes, Mom."

Cole hopped out of the car and went around to open the back seat. Someone was already sitting next to him.

"Zeke!" Christina squealed. "How cute is your house? You have to give me a tour sometime."

"She forced her way in the car," Cole said under his breath. "She wanted to see your town and Christina has never taken no for an answer in her life. I'm very sorry about her."

I giggled. "It's okay. I like your sister, Chubs."

Cole snaked an arm around my waist and crushed me to his chest. "Call me that again and you're in trouble."

I made a soft noise in my throat. "I might like being in trouble."

His grin was wolfish. "You'd definitely like—"

"What's taking so long?" Christina stuck her arm out and pounded on the door. "Hurry up, Chubs."

We snuck a quick kiss and then piled in the car. Christina blasted her music the whole ride while Cole and I traded glances and smiles in the mirror. It was amazing how relaxed he was away from school.

Cole's parents were home. They invited us to hang out with them.

"How about a game of pool?" his dad asked. "We can knock out a few rounds in the game room."

"Can't, Dad." Cole backed away, tugging me. "There's something I have to show Zeke... in my room."

"Well, come spend time with your family afterward," his mom called.

"Okay."

We spun and bolted up the stairs. We were partway up before we noticed we picked up a third wheel. Toby bounded up the stairs, tail wagging furiously.

"Toby, no!"

He shot through us and knocked us aside like bowling pins. He was comfortable on Cole's bed when we made it to the room.

Cole ordered him out and then came for me before I could get my shirt over my head. We fooled around under his sheets, ignoring when Christina knocked on the door, and indulged a private moment, just the two of us.

Afterward, I curled up on his chest and enjoyed the feel of him swirling small circles on my bare back.

"How was your Christmas?" I asked after a while.

"Not bad. Christina got me a fender."

"What? A real one?"

"Oh, yeah. That's my sister."

I laughed. "She's really great."

"What is it about you that you're drawn to the evil?"

I ran my finger up and down his chest. "I'm drawn to you, so what does that say?"

"We've established that I'm an asshole."

"You're not," I whispered. "You're just... Cole."

We were quiet for a little while. I was so content under those covers with him, I let my eyes drift shut. We had never slept together. Right then, I wanted nothing more than to fall asleep and wake in his arms.

"You know I want to be with you, don't you, Zela?"

My eyes opened slowly. I held still—not breathing.

"You probably believe it should be easy. You're okay with it. Landon is okay with it. And Michael says he's okay with it. But it's not that simple."

"Why?" I whispered.

Cole moved to my hair. My eyes closed again as he played with it.

"Michael doesn't always say what he wants. I mean, he doesn't say what he *really* wants. He doesn't want to hurt the people he loves, so he gives in. Unfortunately, I'm his best friend, so when I went full dick and dropped Landon and Adam, he did too because he thought I'd drop him too. He didn't admit it, of course, and he still says he's not mad about what went down in middle school, but who wouldn't be?"

I nodded. "You think that because he wants us both, he's pretending he's okay with me dating you too."

"Yes," he stated clearly. "It's not easy getting the truth out of him when he thinks it's going to hurt me, but I have to before there can be an us."

His words squeezed my heart even while his hand teased ripples throughout my body.

"I understand."

He sighed. "I was supposed to stay away from you while I figured it out but you've made that impossible."

I cracked a smile. "You're blaming me? Who is the one who had to show me something in his room?"

"Did you like how subtle I was?"

Shaking my head, I chuckled. Cole called himself an asshole, but the guy could make me laugh.

"Do you really have to go?"

"Yes," I replied. "Derek is picking me up in thirty minutes."

"You said one day you would tell me what's up with you two."

"I will"—I swung my leg over and climbed on top of him—"but not today. We have thirty minutes left. How will we fill up our time?"

"I have a few ideas."

"BYE, MR. AND MRS. COLE. Bye, Christina."

"Bye!" someone shouted from the depths of the house.

Cole kissed me and I took off running down the front steps to Derek's idling car.

"What do you see in that guy?" Derek asked.

I made sure he saw my eyeroll before I buckled up. "You've asked that about Landon and Michael too."

"Because I want to know."

"Why?"

"They don't deserve you, Zela."

"Then who does?"

Derek met my gaze. He didn't say anything, but something in those enigmatic orbs made me look away. For some reason, I felt like I said the wrong thing.

"Landon is sweet," I said faintly. "He does things like surprise me with my favorite ice cream and tells me I'm beautiful even when I'm wearing a rumpled uniform and itchy wig. Michael looks up obscure math problems just so we can talk about them. He was there for me at my lowest and never once judged me or made me feel like there was something wrong with me. And Cole..."

I looked over at the boy still standing on the steps. "He's one of those people that doesn't know the right thing to say or do, but yet he puts a smile on my face without really trying." I drifted back to Derek. "And that's only a few things. I could go on all day."

"So all three of them," he said.

I nodded. "It'll take time, but yes. I know we'll work it out."

Derek turned away. "Okay."

There was a strange atmosphere in the car on the ride to his house. I sensed it. I thought of things to say to break it.

I kept my mouth shut. Warning bells rang in my mind. Things were good between us right now; I didn't want to mess with it.

We passed through the gates and two guards at the front door to get into his house. One of them peeled off and followed us upstairs to Derek's room.

Every time I walked inside, I marveled that he truly lived like this. I went to the center of the room and spun around. The bookshelves covering every square inch of the walls swirled in my vision. Books reached the ceiling. Books covered his bed. Books spilled out of his desk.

Not to say his room was messy. All of his books were stacked or shelved around his opulent room according to a system only he knew.

Derek snatched a book off his pillow and flopped onto his bed. He patted the spot next to him. "Grab a book. Mom will be by soon to call us down for lunch."

I claimed my spot and my book. "Thank you for doing this, Derek. You know I appreciate it, right?"

"Yeah."

"It hasn't been easy on you," I continued. "But you've supported me anyway. I couldn't ask for a better brother."

Derek smiled lopsidedly. "You could definitely ask for a better one."

I wasn't sure what to do with that. "I'm trying to have a moment with you, Grayson."

"I know what you're trying to do, Zela." His tone lost the joking lilt. "And I'm not going along. I won't say I'm the best big brother ever or call him *our* dad."

"Why?"

"You know why."

The warning bells went off again. *I should stop. Leave it alone.*

I didn't listen. "You said you would let this go."

"No, *you* said I would let this go. I promised I wouldn't dig into your mom's past anymore, and I haven't, but there's someone else, Zela. I'm not your brother."

Anger flared up fierce and corrosive. "Yes, you are!"

"No," he said calmly. "I'm not. I can feel it. And you feel it too. You just don't want it to be true."

"Don't tell me how I feel."

"Don't tell me not to feel."

I glared at him, chest tight with all the things I wanted to shout at him. He couldn't have romantic feelings for me. Why was he fighting this? His need to be right would crush him in the end. It would destroy him and us.

Someone knocked on the door. "Derek, darling."

We didn't break our eye lock.

"It's time for lunch, sweetie. Chef made your favorite."

Derek tossed the book at the end of the bed and slid off. He didn't look away from me the whole time. "Coming, Mom."

He strode to the door and left without waiting. My guard companion didn't. He escorted me to the small dining room and we sat to a tense lunch of stilted conversation, angry glares out of the corner of our eyes, odd looks from Naomi, and turkey bacon clubs.

"Is everything okay with you two?" she asked.

"We're fine, Mom." Derek pushed aside his half-eaten sandwich and picked at his salad.

"Doesn't look like it."

I sat up straight as Jonathan breezed into the dining room. He bent to kiss his wife and then gave us both a look.

"You got into a fight." He wasn't asking. "I know just the thing. Finish up lunch and we'll go outside."

"We can't play this one out, Dad."

"Won't know until you try."

Jonathan urged us to finish eating and then dragged us out. December brought a chill in the air, but the sun shone bright enough on the basketball court to make it bearable.

Jonathan tossed me the ball. "First to ten wins. You have until then to be angry about whatever you're angry about. Then you let it go."

Derek and I shared a look over the white lines. *Let go that he has feelings for me? Let go that he won't accept he's my brother?*

Jonathan retrieved the ball and tossed it in the air. Sailing above my head, Derek tipped it to his side. So began the strangest one-on-one match Derek and I ever had.

I didn't know what to do with myself. What was I trying to win? A few baskets wouldn't fix things. Derek seemed to know that because he had never been more off his game. He missed easy shots, threw the ball out of bounds, and didn't fight to steal it back.

I sank my fourth shot and dove for the ball at the same time Derek did. The next thing I knew, he crashed into me and we went down. The air punched out of my lungs as Derek fell on top of me.

"Zee? Zee, are you okay?!" He scrambled off and bent over me. Concern was etched into the lines of his face. "I'm sorry. I didn't mean to do that. I swear, I tripped."

"I-I'll be there," I forced out.

"What?" He picked up my head and pulled me closer.

"I'll be there... for you," I whispered in his ear. "When you're forced to accept the truth and it threatens to rip you apart. When pain leaks into every part of you and you can't breathe for it. I'll be there for you through everything like you were there for me. I'm not going anywhere. I promise."

Something flickered in his eyes. It was gone so fast it's possible I imagined it, but all that mattered was what he saw in mine. I wanted him to be my brother on my terms and that's not how it works with him. Derek would have to get there on his own.

"Let's drop it," he said. "Or Dad will make us play again."

"You alright, Zeke?" Jonathan called.

Derek helped me to my feet. "I'm fine. Why don't you play with us?"

"You boys good?"

We shared a look.

"We're good," we replied.

Chapter Eight

"Seems like things are getting worse."

Adam swiveled in my desk chair. Side to side. Round and round. He spoke more *at me* than to me.

"She's been texting me all morning. Lucia and Malcolm walked into class hanging off of each other's lips and her friends are taking Lucia's side."

My shirt crumpled in my fist. "I know. She told me the same. They said Jordan has already moved on to someone else, so she should let it go. They're tired of the *drama*. I hate that she is over there facing those assholes alone."

"Why didn't your aunt let her transfer to Breakbattle?"

"Because she wanted Jordan to go to school with her wonderful friends. Isn't that ironic?"

Adam's head fell back against the chair. "I wish there was something I could do."

"You can." I gave up on unpacking and perched on the edge of my mattress. "Get her out of Chesterfield this weekend. She'll feel insanely better just spending time with you."

He cracked a smile. "I can do that."

I reached for him and Adam took my hand.

"What are you going to do?" he asked.

"My mission is the same. Stop the expansion and Cameron."

"I'm with you." Adam suddenly pulled a face. "Speaking of Cameron, have you noticed…?"

"That he has been off lately," I finished.

He nodded. "Can't complain. Cameron's been quiet lately. Him and Santiago, Heath, and the rest of them. They're seniors now. Maybe they realized there are more important things than the war they started with you."

"Maybe," I agreed. "It doesn't change that he's still working to make the expansion happen. Derek told me there have been more dinners and golf games since the fundraiser."

"What if what we're doing isn't enough?"

"It has to be."

Adam heaved himself out of the chair. "Then tomorrow we're back at it. First day of the new semester, the Battle Doctor is in."

I laughed. "I kinda like that."

My best friend dropped a kiss on my head and then left for his dorm. I reached for the phone immediately after he was gone. I needed to check on Jordan.

The next day, I walked up to the lunch line and picked up a tray. I turned and bounced off a hard body.

"You got Whittaker to back you up."

I took a deep breath and held it. Zach being pissed was inevitable, but I was long past tired of this guy getting in my face.

"What do you mean?" I stepped back, putting distance between me and Zach, Rhys, and Sully. "He's the principal. He doesn't back students up. He makes the rules. Whittaker says there's nothing wrong with us helping the other students."

Rhys snapped, "He said that because his head is so far up the board's ass, he wears them like a hat. If he wasn't trying to impress them, he would have sided with us."

I smiled mirthlessly. "But he didn't."

"Is there a problem here, guys?"

Suddenly, I went from staring down Zach to my nose in Maddox's back.

"This has nothing to do with you, F!"

Maddox laughed. "You know, I'm really getting tired of you calling me an F like it's an insult. *You're* in the same class, dick."

"You and I will never be in the same fucking class," hissed Zach.

"Whatever, man. Just back off Zeke. We're not letting you fuck with him."

A nasty laugh slipped into my ears and made me cringe. "We?"

"Yes. We," said another voice.

I poked my head around Maddox.

At Zach's back was Mitch, Daxton, Marco, Tanner, Nico, and a bunch of other guys I helped train for battles. I don't know how they assembled so fast, but Zach's smirk vanished in a flash.

"What the hell do you think you're going to do?" Sully asked.

Maddox shrugged. "The same thing we've been doing. Coming for your precious privileges. Matter of fact, I heard there's a 'welcome back' movie night for the Bs, As, and Elites. I think we'd like to crash that. What do you say, boys?"

"Oh, yeah."

"For sure."

"Movie night sounds fun."

Zach's face flushed an alarming shade of purple. "Manning and Moon aren't helping you cheat anymore!"

Maddox stepped up to him. "Stop them. Go ahead," he taunted. "Do something about it, Fields."

The boys glanced around the pack penning them in. They weren't the only ones. The entire cafeteria had fallen silent.

"Fuck this!" Zach shoved through the boys and stormed off. Rhys and Sully were right behind him.

"We got your back, Zeke." Maddox and the boys proved it by escorting me through the lunch line and then to my table.

Amazing, I thought as I watched them walk off. *The lowerclassmen are fighting back.*

AFTER CLASSES, I RAN up to my dorm to shower and change. I was thrown right in it. A lot of the guys made good on their threat to challenge for spots at the movie night which meant they needed the Battle Doctor now.

A C named Peirce was meeting me and the new volunteer assistant coach in the basketball gym. It was pretty smart of Whittaker to offer university students credit and job experience in exchange for volunteering at one of the best schools in the country. The guy just had to be there to make sure I wasn't giving advice that could result in a snapped neck, but Assistant Coach Wilson seemed decent and if he joined in and helped even better. I wanted my lowerclassmen to win.

I jogged down the empty hallway, mind spinning with basketball moves and drills.

"Fuck you!"

I stopped. *Where did that come from?*

"—over it."

My eyes fixed on Cameron's door just as a hard thump shook the wood. I took off running.

"Cameron?! Cameron, are you okay?!" I rattled the doorknob. "Cameron! Who's in there with you?!"

"I'm fine!" a voice that could only be Cameron's shouted back. "Go away!"

"Open the door, Cameron."

"I said leave!"

I didn't listen. I pushed harder on the door, twisting the knob and trying to get in. I heard nothing else from Cameron during my struggle, and eventually, I gave up. I wasn't getting in and he wasn't opening the door.

My mind was on Cameron all through basketball practice. *What is going on with him?*

THE FIRST MONTH OF school passed quickly, but not quietly. Adam, Cole, Landon, Michael, Derek, and I had our hands full offering battle tutoring. The boys were happy to let me do my thing until the resentment brewing among the upperclassmen began to reach a boiling point.

People passed me in my own hallway and spat that I was a traitor. Rhys, Zack, and Sully tried to corner me again coming out of the basketball gym. Derek heard the commotion and raced out. A swift punch to Zach's jaw shut him up temporarily, but I can't say it solved the problem. Even so, from then on the boys signed up to help to show their support of me.

"What you're doing is amazing," Melody said.

The two of us were out in the hall, a few feet from the dining room. We agreed to meet up before dinner to talk.

"I wish I could start up your battle tutoring on the other campus, but I'm known as the girl against the system. People won't buy that I'm trying to help girls work within it."

"Little do they know..."

Melody smirked. "You are truly fearsome, Zeke Manning."

It was wrong to toot your own horn, but I couldn't help returning her grin. "What? All I did was turn the school against each other and get Whittaker to support the ruin of his own plans. Easy."

She shook her head. "I couldn't believe it when Adam told me what you were doing. Building on what you did last year and training the lowerclassmen because you knew it riled the Bs, As, and Elites up. Eventually they'd stop sitting back and taking it. Someone would get in the wrong person's face and it would be class against class. Junior against junior."

"I don't want anyone to get hurt," I stated. "No physical fights. But yes, the hope was given enough time I could fray the peace between classes so that when the board came back, it would be impossible to cover up the harm the battle system does. It was pure luck that I got an invitation to the fundraisers and a chance to get Mrs. Jeong on board with the battle tutoring. I had all these speeches written up to convince Whittaker to let me keep going and she handled it for me."

Melody gazed at me with a whole new respect. "I've underestimated you and your support for the cause. Sometimes I think people believe in what Stand Up is trying to do, but the closer we get to graduation, the more they convince themselves it can be someone else's fight."

"Not me. This is my fight."

"Mine too. That's why I want you to see this." Melody reached in her bag and pulled out her tablet. She tapped the screen a few times and then showed me. My eyes widened.

"Do you think this will get the board's attention?"

"Oh, yeah," I breathed. "That will do it."

A line of text caught my eye and I paused. I went back and read it again. A fragment of memory broke loose and drifted through my mind.

"Let's go in." Melody shoved the tablet in her bag. "I'm hungry."

I lost the thought as I walked behind her into the cafeteria.

Landon waved me over to the table.

"I have your dinner." He motioned to the tray next to him. "And your VIP seat." Landon patted his lap.

"Thank you very—"

"No! I'm fucking sick of this!"

I froze with my butt hovering over Landon. Across the room, a boy with a C on his chest faced off with a table of Bs—or that's what it looked like. All of the B boys were on their feet.

The C didn't appear concerned. "Are you refusing the battle? That's ten points off your grade."

"I'm not losing ten points and I'm not going along with this bullshit! I used to never get in battles but because of you fuckers targeting us, I had seven last semester. I'm not doing it anymore! I'm going to Miss Val. This is bullying."

"That's not even one battle a week," Tanner shot back. "Zeke had way more than that freshman year and he didn't bitch."

"So what? This is revenge for two-year-old shit?"

Tanner got to his feet. "No, this is us playing the game like everyone else. The only thing that is pissing you off is for once we're winning."

Slowly, I lowered myself onto Landon's lap as the argument played out. I wouldn't intervene. This is what I wanted.

"We're not doing anything wrong," Tanner went on, "and Zeke always says he's not going to help anyone trying to battle the same student over and over. So, Miss Val won't back you up." He jerked his head at the C who started it all. "Jamie challenged you. Are you going to accept or not?"

"No," the boy ground out.

"Fine," Jamie spoke up. "Lose ten points." He pointed down the table. "You. Omari Rodrigo, I challenge you to a battle in—"

"Challenge this, Cunt Class!"

Omari Rodrigo hefted his tray and sent it flying.

I leaped out of my seat. My gaping surprise matched Jamie's expression as the glob of mashed potatoes dripped down his face onto his jacket.

"Guys!" I yelled. It was time to intervene. "Cool it!"

Jamie dove for the table and snatched up a plate. He flung the heavy, ceramic object at Omari's head. The boy ducked at the last second and it smashed on the table behind him, causing the girls to scatter screaming.

"Stop!"

My cry was swallowed by a furious roar. Omari knocked his friend aside snatching up another plate, but he wasn't the only one. Weeks and months of bubbling animosity exploded at once.

Food, plates, trays, and even silverware flew across the cafeteria. Omari and Jamie ran at each other and went down on a bed of mashed potatoes and roast chicken. I ran to pull them apart and was jerked to a stop by a tight grip on my arm.

"We need to get out of here!" Derek bellowed.

"Wha— Ah!"

Derek tossed his blazer over my head and dragged me out.

"Derek!"

Our shoes squeaked on the polished hardwood as loud in my ears as the screams and shouts from my classmates. We escaped into the hall and I threw off the jacket.

"Derek, I have to do something!"

The rest of my friends were right behind us. Landon intercepted me when I tried to go back in.

"No, Zeke! They're losing their fucking minds in there and they blame *you* for starting it all. Zach has tried to get you when you were alone before. I'm not letting someone come for you in the chaos."

Melody clutched her chest, breathing hard. A dark red stain eerily similar to blood stained her shirt. "No one is going back in there."

"Someone could get hurt," I protested. "They're throwing forks!"

"The dining room workers are inside," Hunter said. "They must have called for help by now. There's nothing we can do but be far away when Whittaker hands down punishments."

I wanted to argue but I didn't like my chances of getting through Derek, Michael, Cole, Adam, Landon, and all of my friends. I let them drag me away. We rounded the corner just as Whittaker and Argyle came tearing down the hall.

A THICK SILENCE BLANKETED the auditorium. No one moved. No one coughed. No one even breathed too loudly. We all just sat as Whittaker's glare swept over us. I'd never seen him so mad. Those caught in the cafeteria the night before said he shouted so loud, he terrified them back into their seats.

"Last night's display," he began after a solid ten minutes had passed, "was a disgrace. In all my years as an educator, never have I seen students behave in such a fashion."

His voice was a low rasp. It was a disquieting effect to his unnaturally calm speech.

"Next week, the board of education is coming to meet the bright, proud pupils who embody the spirit of this school and reflect excellence every day. As I stand here before you, I don't see those students.

"You have shamed Breakbattle. You have shamed your parents and your teachers. And most importantly, you have shamed yourself." Whittaker shook his head. "I can't stand the sight of you."

With that parting shot hanging in the air, he walked off the stage.

No one moved for a minute, and then a soft noise drew our attention. Miss Val approached the podium.

"Good morning, students. Principal Whittaker is understandably upset at what transpired last night, so I will tell you what this means going forward. Thankfully, no one was seriously hurt and most students walked away with nothing more than a few scrapes.

"Nevertheless, it could have been much worse. Beginning immediately, the entire school will lose their privileges."

That didn't elicit the shouts of rage I was expecting. It seemed everyone knew this would happen.

"No more weekend activities. Televisions and computers will be removed from those who have them. Tablets will be turned in. The structure of library times and things of that nature will be suspended. No one has designated slots or a right to be anywhere other than their classroom or their dorm unless their teacher chooses to grant you access.

"This brings me to my next point. Battles are temporarily suspended."

This brought a murmur of surprise. Adam and I shared shocked looks. Never in a million years did we think we'd get this outcome.

"It appears tension came to a head over 'battle tutoring' and the decision to not put a stop to it. Rest assured, we will look into it and if this is what we want to allow moving forward. Targeting will never be allowed, and no matter what happens, we will ensure the system remains fair for all classes."

Miss Val cleared her throat. "There will be no questions. That is all. You're dismissed."

THE WEEK BEFORE THE long-awaited school board visit was the quietest in Breakbattle history. The administration was serious about the loss of privileges. My room was stripped of the television and computer. The computers were also taken out of our classrooms. To do anything or go anywhere, I needed written permission from Mrs. Peterson. The irony of it all was this was the first time all the students in Breakbattle were treated equally.

Monday morning, I sat with Melody at our table. We both pushed our food around on our Styrofoam plates. There was a question between us begging to be voiced. I decided to be first.

"The board comes today," I said. "Are you going to go through with it?"

Melody didn't look up from her plate. "I have to. What happened last week changes nothing."

"I've never seen Whittaker so angry. If he traces it back to you, you'll be expelled."

Her hand stilled for a beat. "He won't trace it back to me," she finally said. She speared a piece of potato and brought it to her mouth.

"Melody—"

"I'm eating, Zeke. We can talk later."

After it's too late.

I let it go. Melody wasn't one to let people sway her after she's made up her mind.

Partway through breakfast, Argyle entered the cafeteria.

"Morning, students." She took her place before the head table. "As you know, the board has arrived. You all will continue your day as normal except for twelve students who I will ask to stay behind. The board will call you one by one to be interviewed, and with any luck, we'll get through these quickly and without incident."

She took a piece of paper out of the pocket of her pantsuit and rattled off the list.

"—Cassie Nim and finally, Zeke Manning."

I started. What did she just say? Me?

"That is all," Argyle finished. "Have a productive day."

I traded looks with my friends as the final bell sounded. Melody gave me a stiff nod on her way out, telling me louder than words what she expected me to do.

The room emptied out and I sat back in my chair. Nerves crept in. I never thought I'd be one of the students chosen. I had a thousand things I wanted to say about this system, but would my influence be enough in the face of Dominick Dupre and even Jonathan Grayson.

I have some time. I'll write down what I want to say and—

"Zeke Manning?"

I froze, bent over my backpack.

"Zeke Manning, will you come with me? Your interview begins now."

Stiffly, I straightened and rose from the seat. A thin woman in glasses I had never seen before held out her hand as I approached.

"Hello, Zeke. My name is Miss Black. I'm Mrs. Jeong's assistant. Follow me, I'll give you a quick rundown on the way."

She set off and I hurried to keep pace with her.

"The interview should be no longer than thirty minutes. They will ask you questions about your time here. As well as what you like about the Breakbattle system and what you think can be improved. Afterward, you are free to go to class."

"Okay. Sounds simple."

My phone vibrated in the depths of my pocket. I took it out and saw what I knew would be there. A message from an unknown number.

As Miss Black chattered on, I opened the text and clicked the link.

I stopped dead.

"What?" I whispered. "What the hell is this?"

This wasn't the website Melody displayed proudly the week before. That was a simple, clean site titled "The Harm Caused By Breakbattle" with a list of reasons why Breakbattle wasn't good for students. Clicking on each point took you to a separate page that backed it up with research, dates, and incidents at the school. Her decision to send the website to every student, parent, and teacher would be the final tip to the scale that forced people to see what truly went on at Breakbattle. But that was not the website I was looking at.

A bloodred background made the black text stand out even sharper. The title was the same, and there was a list, but this one didn't speak of impaired adolescence or disharmony. There were only three things on this list.

- **The hatred among classes is so strong, they beat on each other rather than work together.**
- **They relentlessly push their classmates to the breaking point in pursuit of worthless privileges.**
- **They kill.**

"Mr. Manning?"

I read the last bullet point once, twice, three times. The memory jarred loose once more.

"Mr. Manning? Is everything alright?"

"Becca Taylor," I whispered. "That's what this is all about. That is what For All is punishing us for.

"Becca Taylor."

"Mr. Manning?"

"I'm coming."

Lifting my chin, I put my phone away and continued to the library. Miss Black ushered me on and I walked inside to three familiar faces. The board sat side by side at the table like a panel of judges. Completing the atmosphere was a lone leather seat sitting in the middle of the room.

"Ah, Zeke." Mrs. Jeong beamed. "Great to see you again. I've been looking forward to speaking with you most of all. Please sit and we'll begin."

I did so.

They shuffled some papers around, whispering among themselves and passing things back and forth.

"Alright," Jeong began. "First, tell us about a time—"

I held up a hand. "I'm sorry, Mrs. Jeong. I don't mean to interrupt, but I was hoping you'd let me say something first. If you do, I believe it will answer all of your questions."

"By all means."

"Thank you."

Lowering my head, I let out a slow breath. When I looked up again, I knew what to say.

"Breakbattle Academy is the first school I've ever attended. Over the past few years, I've grown in ways I never expected I would. I've made friends. I've found love. I've learned the meaning of revenge and forgiveness. I have pushed myself past what I thought possible to achieve the highest goals."

A smile spread over their faces as I spoke.

"I would be lying if I said Breakbattle didn't make me who I am today. I would also be lying if I said I didn't like that person."

Adam's smile flitted through my head. Landon's laugh. Michael's scent. Cole's arms. Derek.

I felt them all.

"I'm stronger, tougher, smarter, and kinder than I knew I could be," I said. "If I had the chance to go back and make another choice, I would choose Breakbattle again. This is where I was meant to be."

Mrs. Jeong clapped enthusiastically. The other members joined her, nodding their heads.

"Well said, Zeke."

"Thank you, ma'am," I replied. "I thought a lot about what I wanted to say, but none of it would have been complete if I didn't tell you how Breakbattle has helped me. It's the only way you'd understand how serious I am when I say... you cannot approve this expansion."

Their smiles melted away. The three of them exchanged looks.

"Excuse me?" asked Jeong.

"This school fosters a level of competition that is unhealthy. No, it's dangerous. It's dangerous for students to push themselves so hard they become sleep-deprived to the point of hallucinations. It's dangerous to teach young people to look at the world around them and only see what they can take.

"It's dangerous to allow all of that to fester unchecked until a group of students believe the only way to move up is to target a girl so mercilessly, she makes the heart-crushing decision to kill herself."

I met their gaze in turn. "Becca Taylor and her story haunt Breakbattle to this day. We have *not* learned enough from what happened to her and we don't have the systems in place to stop this from happening again. You may think you can adopt a version of the battle system that is better than this one, but I'm asking you, why would you want to?

"Why would you want students to be defined by their test scores or our athletic ability? Aren't we more than that? Before I came here, I had never taken a standardized test or played an organized sport outside of messing around with friends. I failed the orientation test and crapped out in half the sport trials, but here I am, with an E on my chest.

"You can't measure a student's potential in one week. You can't even measure it in four years. Like me, we're spending these years trying to figure out who we are, but these letters want to do it for us. For some, it says they can achieve anything. For the rest, it tells them they've lost before they ever really tried. Life is going to give students like me plenty of reasons to close our hearts to those around us. You can decide right here today to not give us another one."

I gazed at Mrs. Jeong steadily. "Because believe me when I say, if you approve the expansion, it will be the biggest mistake you've ever made."

She stared at me, face stricken. A sallow pallor drained the color from her skin. For a long time, no one spoke.

I got to my feet. "I'm guessing you don't have any more questions for me?"

Jeong's throat bobbed with a hard swallow. "No, Mr. Manning. You may go."

I walked out and softly closed the door behind me. Head held high, I went to class.

Chapter Nine

"When do you think we'll find out their decision?" asked Cole.

My friends, the boys, and I gathered in front of the main gates. We made it to Friday with no word about the board's final decision and no relief from our school-wide punishment. No one had reason to stay on campus, so we packed up and trekked outside to wait for our families or drivers to pick us up.

"I don't think they do these things quickly," Michael offered. "They're talking about revamping every school in the state. It could be months before they decide."

A hand gripped my wrist. "Zee?"

"Yes, Derek?"

He led me a bit away from the group.

"Do you want to come over this weekend? Dad's forcing me to watch all these old detective movies and he says you're to blame. It's only right you suffer with me." Despite his words, he was smiling.

It tugged one to my lips. "You won't be doing any suffering this weekend, Grayson. You will love those movies and I totally want to come. I'll tell my mom I'm going to Adam's."

"Sweet." He backed away, looking happier than I usually got to see. "See you tomorrow."

Mom picked me up soon after he left. We talked a little about my week before I brought up Adam's.

"Just for the day," I asked. "We're going to watch old movies and binge on popcorn."

"You cannot go to this boy's house every weekend, Zela."

"I know. I promise I'll spend the next few weekends at home."

She hummed. "Okay. Just for the day."

"Thanks, Mom." I leaned over and hugged her the best I could.

When we got home, I ran upstairs and stripped out of my Zeke clothes. I pulled up Jordan when I was me again.

Me: I told my mom I'm going to Adam's house tomorrow. Will he be there to back up the lie or are you going out?

She replied within minutes of the message.

Jordan: We're going out. He's taking me to all of my favorite places and buying all my favorite foods to cheer me up. Why? Are you going to see Jonathan?

Me: Yes. If she asks, I'll tell her I meant Miss Val when I said we. It'll be fine.

You guys have fun tomorrow and forget about Chesterfield and their funhouse of villains. Lucia is the stupidest chick alive for choosing that walking STD over you and you deserve way better than them.

Jordan: This is helping. Keep the insults coming.

Laughing, I called her up so we could trash them properly. Jordan sounded a lot better when we hung up.

The next day, Derek pulled into my driveway himself. I peeked him from the window as I rushed around getting ready. From where I was, I had no problem seeing his still damp strands of hair curling around his temple. Derek leaned against his sports car looking comfortable in a form-fitting blue sweater and a pair of black jeans. I could practically sense everyone on our block pressing their noses to the window to catch a glimpse of the movie star's son.

Derek leaned off the passenger door and held it open for me. "Ready? Where's your mom?"

"In her office. She's not coming out until lunch if you thought you were going to meet her."

He chuckled. "I'll meet her one day. Doesn't have to be now. Let's go. Chef is making your favorite."

"What does it mean that your chef knows my favorite meal and makes it for me whenever I come over?"

Derek slammed my door shut and then leaned over, coming in so close I could count his eyelashes. "It means you're one of us now."

"Is it like joining a cult?" I teased. Although underneath, overwhelming happiness bloomed inside of me. I waited so long to hear Derek say that.

"The Graysons are worse. I hope you know what you're in for."

We kept up a steady string of joking and teasing throughout the ride to his house. We stopped before the gates and the guard let us go without making me step out to search me for listening devices or plastic bags for Naomi's locks of hair.

"Dad said he'd be ready by the time we got here."

We passed his grand staircase and entered the doors just off the dining room. Jonathan glanced up from his phone.

Their living room was just as grand as the rest of the mansion and the other Evergreen homes I've been in, but where the Graysons differed was the massive projector screen hanging over their mantle. The only way to watch movies according to Jonathan.

"Hey, boys. Come in. Get comfortable." He winked at me. "It's time I did something about my son's appalling lack of taste in movies."

"I saw that wink," said Derek. He threw himself on the sectional and threaded his hands behind his head. "I told you guys about talking to Zeke about me behind my back."

"Ah, but we think you're bluffing about emancipation. Mom is busting out the baby pictures later."

"Those I want to see," I said.

"I hid them a long time ago." Derek tapped his nose. "Always one step ahead."

Jonathan looked at his phone again. "Sorry, guys. The studio is calling. Give me ten minutes."

Derek and I talked movies while we waited for him to come back.

"You'll like them," I said. "The movies are dark and gritty. Just your type."

"It's the overdramatic acting that makes them unbearable. I'm the son of a pro. I can't stand watching actors fling themselves all over the screen because they got a paper cut."

I chuckled. "I'll give you that one, but I know you'll like it anyway."

"How do you know that?"

"Because I know you."

He lifted a brow. "Still convinced you have me all figured out?"

"I do, Derek Grayson. Whether your brooding, tortured, loner-soul persona wants to admit it or not."

Derek held up his hands. "Whatever you say."

I glanced at the clock. "It's been thirty-five minutes. Where's Jonathan?"

"He probably got held up on the call. It happens. Let's start the movie anyway. It's not like he hasn't seen it."

My phone went off.

"Okay," I said as I took it out. "Start with anything Humphrey Bogart."

I hit accept.

"Hey, JoJo. How's it going with—"

"Zela?!"

I jumped.

"Zela, are you there?! You have to go! Now!"

"What? What are you talking about?"

"Zee, I'm so s-sorry." Jordan's voice cracked on a sob. "She knows. Your mom knows about Jonathan."

My throat seized. I couldn't breathe. Couldn't move. Couldn't hear for the roaring in my ears.

What did she just say?

"—on her way right now. Get out of there."

"How?" I whispered.

"It was Mom," she cried. "She looked through my phone while I was in the shower. She said it was because I've been angry and distant and wouldn't talk to her. She read all the texts about Jonathan and called Aunt Dronika."

"But— but Mom wouldn't—"

"She's on her way there right now and I'm grounded for forever. Longer than forever when she finds out I stole my phone back to call you. I don't know how long it's been since Mom told her. She might be closer than you think."

Panic surged to my heart. I bolted off the couch. "Derek, we have to go!"

"Zela?"

"We have to go... right..." I trailed off, slowing to a stop.

Jonathan Grayson stood in the entrance. The look he gave me as he stepped into the room made my blood run cold.

"Who are you?"

"Dad? Are you okay?"

Jonathan did not acknowledge his son. He didn't seem to have heard him at all.

"Who are you?" he asked through gritted teeth. "Why is Brenda Manning outside of my gate demanding to be let in to get her daughter?"

"Dad—"

"Quiet, Derek."

"But, Dad—"

"Quiet!" he roared.

I flinched and tears sprang to my eyes. He was so mad. Why was he so mad?

"I-I'm her daughter," I rasped. With hands that shook, I removed my wig and cap. "My name is Zela."

Jonathan reared back. "How is that possible? I looked into you. Your mother's name is Andronika."

"She changed it."

His lips twisted. "Of course she did. Was that a part of your plot?"

I blinked at him through tear-heavy lashes. "Plot?"

"You wormed your way into my son's life. Into my life! Is that why you're disguised?!"

"It's not like that!"

He stalked up to me, eyes blazing. "It didn't work eighteen years ago and it won't work now! You stay away from my family!"

"Dad, stop!" Suddenly, Derek was between us. He shielded me as I burst into sobs. "What is wrong with you?! Just listen to her!"

"Listen to— Dear God. Did you know about this?"

"Zela told me everything a long time ago. Whatever you think is happening, you're wrong."

"I'm wrong? So she didn't trick her way into my home to claim I'm her father?" His voice was hard. "Am I wrong about that, son?"

"You are my father." I gripped Derek and guided him out of the way. I faced Jonathan head on even while tears dripped down my face. "I've been looking for you my whole life and all I wanted was to get to know you... and maybe I hoped, if you got to know me... you'd want me."

His face could have been chipped from stone. "I'm afraid that won't work. I am not your father, Zela. Whatever you came for, you won't get it from me."

I balled shaking fists. "You can't lie to me," I said with more strength than I felt. "I won't be lied to anymore. I found my birth certificate. It's your name written down."

Jonathan's eyes flashed. "Your mother shouldn't have done that."

"Why not? Why shouldn't she write down the name of my father?" My voice rose. "Why shouldn't she write the name of the man who abandoned her?! Left her alone with a baby and ran back to his pregnant wife!" I screamed. "Why shouldn't she have done that?!"

"I'm not your father!"

"Dad, stop shouting at her!" Derek hooked me and crushed me to his chest. "You can't pretend you don't know her mother. Just— Just tell us the truth."

"I can't believe this."

Through the circle of his arms, the first crack in Jonathan appeared. He looked at Derek like he was a stranger.

"My own son. How can you think I would abandon my child?"

"Because you did," I sobbed.

"You're not my daugh—!" Jonathan let out a groan. He doubled over, breathing hard as he tried to get himself under control. "Look, it's clear you're suffering under incorrect information. I understand that your mother led you to believe that I am your dad, but it's not true."

"She didn't lead me to believe it. She never told me a thing about you." I pulled away from Derek. "Not even your name. I found you on my own."

"Then... that's even worse."

"What do you mean?" Derek asked.

Jonathan didn't take his eyes off of me as he said, "You've chased after the wrong man."

"I don't believe you."

"How do you know her mother?" Derek demanded. "Why are you so angry if she's just making things up?"

"Stop it, Derek," Jonathan said.

We replied at the same time.

"Tell me, Dad!"

"Why are you lying!?"

"Both of you, you don't understand—"

I cried, "You're my father—"

"I'm not—"

"I don't want money," I plowed on. "I didn't want any of this! I just wanted to know you."

"Zela—" Jonathan began.

"You slept with her, didn't you?" Derek's grip on me tightened. "You really did it. The fuck, Dad! You cheated on Mom!"

"It's not like that!" he cried. "Just listen—"

"You had an affair with some coed and then left her alone with a baby!" Derek flung. "How could you—"

"I can't have kids!"

The bellow echoed through the room—silencing my sobs. Jonathan fell back against the door, clutching his head.

"I can't have children." It ripped from his throat. "I'm sterile, Derek."

Derek went slack. I slipped out of his hold and slumped on the couch.

"What?"

"I didn't know," he whispered. "Not until after your mom and I were married. We tried and we tried for two years but she never got pregnant. We went to a doctor. We went to *three* doctors and they told us the same thing. The problem was me."

"But, Dad..."

"It destroyed us," he croaked. "Naomi always wanted kids and she wouldn't let go of her dream of being a mom. She was willing to do whatever it took from sperm donors to adoption but I said no. All the waiting and hoping only to hear I could never give her what she wanted tore me apart. I couldn't go through it anymore.

"Your mom wouldn't accept that. Our marriage strained to the breaking point. She made it clear she would never give up... even if it meant losing me in the process. We stopped talking. Became strangers in our own house. Eventually, Naomi started coming home later and later—giving the excuse filming ran late."

"Dad, no," Derek pleaded. "Stop."

"I knew what she was doing. I was so angry and betrayed that I had an affair of my own."

"With my mom," I whispered.

Jonathan lifted his head and met my eyes. He nodded.

"In my heart, we were over. We would get a divorce and Naomi would move on to a man who could fill her home with children.

"But then, she found out she was pregnant. She read the test and realized in that instant she didn't want a future where we weren't a family. She came back to me and asked if I could forgive her and love this baby. I said I would... and I do." Jonathan moved toward Derek. He gripped the back of his neck. "I love you. You're my son. You have been since the day I found out about you and you always will be."

His eyes slid to me. "But you're not my daughter, Zela. I ended things with your mom but she begged me to stay because she was pregnant. I rejected her and haven't spoken to her since. I was with your mom when you were conceived, but the only thing that's certain is she was with someone else too."

Jonathan brushed my damp cheek. "I wish you were my miracle. If you had been, there was nothing that would have stopped me from being a part of your life. But I'm not your father, Zela, and honestly, I believed all these years that your mother went to the man who is."

I didn't speak. I couldn't. His words were going in but they didn't move me.

"Zela?!"

My head snapped up.

"Zela?! Where are— Get your hands off me! Where is my daughter?!"

Jonathan released Derek. "It's best that you leave, Zela. We have a lot we need to talk about as a family." He opened the door. "Ben, let her go. Your daughter is in—"

Derek seized my hand. I cried out as he yanked me up and raced out of the door.

"Zela!" Mom ran to me.

Derek pulled me away and her arms closed on air. I stumbled after him, uncomprehending as Jonathan and Mom shouted at us.

We made it outside. Derek ran to his car, lifted me up, and dropped me in the passenger seat. I was too dazed to fight him.

The car peeled out of the drive in a shower of gravel. The last thing I saw in the rearview mirror was Mom chasing after the car. Then we turned onto the road and sped away.

I MADE IT AN HOUR INTO the car ride before I broke down. My tears came slow at first—building until stomach-clenching sobs wracked my body.

Derek leaned over me and pulled the lever to lower my seat. He rested his cool palm against my aching head. "It's going to be okay, Zee."

How could he say that? The only thing I knew for sure was that it wouldn't be okay.

I cried and cried until the car came to a stop.

"We're here."

"What?" My mouth tasted of cotton. I made out Derek's blurry shape through swollen eyes as he came around the car and picked me up.

"Dad bought this place to crash whenever he's caught out late at the studio. No one will bother us here."

Derek carried me up the wraparound porch of a tiny, cabin-style house. He set me on the deck chair. I did nothing but sniffle and stare as he dug around the porch planter. He came away with a key and let himself inside.

"Won't they know to check here?" I asked in a small voice.

"No." Derek lifted me again. "It's the obvious choice for me to come here, so Dad will assume I'm not here."

Derek carried me over the threshold into a space that was warmer and cozier than I was expecting. Thick, soft rugs covered most of the floor, but what I could see was a warm brown that matched the leather couches. Derek placed me on one and then disappeared. When he came back, he was carrying a blanket.

"Here." He draped it over my body and tucked the blanket in. "Just relax for a little bit. When you're ready for food, I can get anything you want delivered."

"Why are you doing this?" I whispered. "Why did you bring me here?"

"You were freaking. The last thing you needed was a fight with your mom. We'll take a break and talk to them when we're ready."

My lips curled. "You must be happy. You kept saying I wasn't your sister. Looks like you were right."

Derek looked hard at me. "Yes, Zela. That's what I'm feeling right now. Happy."

I winced. It hit me what I had said.

"No," I whispered. "I'm sorry, Derek. Your dad— I don't know what's wrong with me." Wetness leaked down my cheeks. "I didn't mean to say that. I just— I don't know what to do."

"Hey. Shh." A soothing hand stroked my hair. "It's going to be okay."

Derek crouched on the floor. He pressed his forehead to mine. "I'm here for you, Zela. When... you're forced to accept the truth and it threatens to rip you apart. When pain leaks into every part of you and you can't breathe for it."

I stopped crying as Derek recited the words I said to him that day on the basketball court.

"I'll be there for you through everything like you were there for me. I'm not going anywhere."

He pressed a soft kiss to my forehead. "I promise."

Tilting back, I offered him a wobbly smile. "Thank you."

"You're going to get past this soon, and when you do, I'll help you find your real father if that's what you want."

A minute ago, I wouldn't have been able to hear that, but now, Derek's promise reached inside of me and beat back the pain—just a bit.

I kissed his cheek. "I don't know where I'd be without you," I whispered. I kissed him again. "I've turned your life upside down and you're still here. Why?" And then again.

"You know why, Zela." His nose bumped mine as we gazed at each other. "Don't make me say it again. I can't. Not if you won't say it back."

I slipped my hand out of the blanket. My touch was featherlight on his forehead, tracing the lines and furrows of his perfect skin. My heart pounded in my chest. The warning bell that should be ringing had fallen silent.

Derek's eyes fluttered shut as I traced his lips.

"Say it," I said softly. "Please."

"I love you, Zela."

The pain retreated further still.

"I love you too, Derek. I—"

Derek surged forward. Our lips clashed together in a wild kiss that set my nerves alight with electricity. I clung to him as he lifted me off the couch and carried me where I didn't know.

Nothing existed outside of him. The way it has always been and would always be. He was mine. My obsession.

My Derek.

WE SPENT THE REST OF the weekend in our hideaway. Eating, talking, watching movies, and just being together away from the world. The only thing we didn't do was have sex. It was too soon for so many reasons. Even so, my swollen lips carried his kisses.

Sunday morning, we drove away from the little house for the real world. Our parents would be waiting for us at home to reinforce that everything we thought we knew was a lie. So we drove to Breakbattle.

"I won't be able to hide here for long," I said. The gates of the academy loomed in front of us. "My mom will pull me out of school."

"Are you ready to talk to her?"

I shook my head. "I've been lying to her for years. This won't be— Derek, look."

The car jerked to a stop. Taking up most of the parking lot, was an ambulance and three police cars.

"Oh my goodness," I said. "What's happened?"

"Maybe they caught For All."

Derek reversed and found a parking spot on the street. Together, we got out and approached the school. We passed through silent hallways to the cafeteria. There weren't many people inside. Most of the school left for the weekend. Of those that remained, they sat around with grim faces that caused my hair to stand on end.

"Hold on," I said to Derek. "I'm going to ask someone what's going on."

I walked over to a familiar face and sat across from her. "Shannon? Shannon?"

Zach's girlfriend started. She squinted at me like she was trying to figure out where I came from.

"What happened?" I asked.

She sniffed. "You might as well know. Everyone will soon enough." She expelled a shuddering breath. "One of the Elite boys was killed. They found his body this morning."

I rocked back. "What? Who?"

It can't be one of my guys! It can't be! They all left campus. Please, tell me it's no one I love.

"Who was it, Shannon?"

She jerked her chin over my shoulder. "The cops are right there. Ask them."

I twisted around. Sure enough, two uniformed officers entered the cafeteria, looking around.

"Excuse me." I raced up to them. "Excuse me, I'm one of the Elite students. Can you tell me who was hurt, please?"

"What's your name?" one of them asked.

"It's Zeke Manning."

"You're Zeke Manning?"

"Yes. Can you tell me who—"

"Zeke Manning." A rough hand seized me and spun me around. I cried out as my arms were twisted behind my back. "You're under arrest for the murder of Cameron Dupre. You have the right to remain—"

"What the fuck are you doing?!"

Derek rushed at them and one of the officers stepped out to meet him. I didn't see them clash. I didn't see anything. The world faded.

Faintly in the distance, I heard Christmas music.

The Elites

Final Year, Final Battle

I thought my biggest problem was being kicked off campus, but I'd rather trade my blazer for a skirt than an orange jumpsuit.

There's a killer on campus and they think it's me. I have my boys on my side, but this might be one fight we can't win.

Someone is determined to bring us down, but with enemies on all sides, the suspects are endless and I'm running out of time.

I'm not the only one who came to Breakbattle with a plan.

A legacy of deception, sabotage, and death will no longer be ignored, but this time the innocent may pay the price.

Keep In Touch

Join Ruby's mailing list for news, teasers, and more:
https://www.subscribepage.com/rubyvincentpage
Join Ruby's Facebook Reader Group:
https://bit.ly/3bNuCOq

ABOUT THE AUTHOR

Ruby Vincent is a published author with many novels under her belt but now she's taking a fun foray into contemporary romance. She loves saucy heroines, bold alpha males, and weaving a tale where both get their happy ever after.